PRAISE FOR VIVIAN AREND

"If you've never read a Vivian Arend book you are missing out on one of the best contemporary authors writing today."
~ *Book Reading Gals*

"Brilliant, raw, imaginative, irresistible!!"
~ *Avon Romance*

"This story will keep you reading from the first page to the last one. There is never a dull moment..."
~ *Landy Jimenez*

"Arend became a favorite author of mine because not only does she write about sexy cowboys, she gives us families who love and take care of each other."
~ *SmexyBooks*

"I started with Six Pack Ranch and have followed through to Heart Falls. Hands down the best series I've read.
~ *Anonymous Kindle Reviewer*

"Heart Falls and all the characters woven together make for great reading and relaxing.
~ *Rita Cornell, Goodreads*

"A wonderful introduction to these three brothers, and a great way to spend some time with recent favorites."
~ *Dargood, BookBub Reviewer*

ALSO BY VIVIAN AREND

The Stones of Heart Falls

A Rancher's Heart

A Rancher's Song

A Rancher's Bride

A Rancher's Love

A Rancher's Vow

The Colemans of Heart Falls

The Cowgirl's Forever Love

The Cowgirl's Secret Love

The Cowgirl's Chosen Love

The Skyes of Heart Falls

A Cowboy's Bride

A Cowboy's Trust

A Cowboy's Claim

Other Heart Falls Series:

Holidays in Heart Falls

Heart Falls Vignette & Novella Collection

A full list of Vivian's print titles is available on her website:
www.vivianarend.com

A COWBOY'S CLAIM

THE SKYES OF HEART FALLS
BOOK 3

VIVIAN AREND

This is a work of fiction. Names, characters, places, and incidents either are the product of the author's imagination or are used fictitiously, and any resemblance to any persons, living or dead, business establishments, events, or locales is entirely coincidental.

NO AI TRAINING: Without in any way limiting the author's [and publisher's] exclusive rights under copyright, any use of this publication to "train" generative artificial intelligence (AI) technologies to generate text is expressly prohibited. The author reserves all rights to license uses of this work for generative AI training and development of machine learning language models.

A Cowboy's Claim
Copyright © 2025 by Arend Publishing Inc.
Digital ISBN: 978-1-998508-38-9
Print ISBN: 978-1-998508-48-8
Edited by Angie Ramey
Cover Design © Damonza
Proofed by Linda Levy

All rights reserved. No part of this book may be used or reproduced in any manner whatsoever without written permission except in the case of brief quotations.

1

———

The knock came sharp and fast, loud enough to rattle the glass on the clinic's front door.

Sydney rolled her eyes. The sign on the outside of the Heart Falls Health Clinic door clearly read *Closed*. Typical Monday chaos. Probably someone wanting stitches or a refill without an appointment—

When the second knock came—harder, more impatient—she huffed and marched to the door, yanking it open with all the grace of a sleep-deprived ER nurse.

"What—?" She froze.

"Lovely to see you, too." Her grandfather strode inside as if he owned the place.

Which, in a manner of speaking, he kind of did.

"Grandpa. I didn't know you were coming."

"Last-minute decision," he said, already sweeping his gaze around the lobby. "Had a layover in Calgary and figured I'd stop in to check on things."

Sydney stepped back and folded her arms, watching him with wary affection.

He was taller than her—though that wasn't hard, considering she barely reached five foot four. His auburn hair had faded to silver at the temples, but his eyes, like hers, were a striking silvery blue, sharp as ever. The way he held himself—straight spine, chin lifted slightly—was a familiar echo of her own posture.

Nathaniel Jones had always been the family force of nature. The brains. The legacy. The financier of her clinic and the author of the invisible rulebook Sydney had lived under for the past thirteen years—whether she'd wanted to or not.

Grandpa Nate's brows winged skyward. "Did you forget what I look like?"

"I video chat with Grandma nearly every week," she said, dry as toast. "But you're never in the frame, so forgive me for checking to see if you're still as handsome as ever."

He frowned. "Please. You're usually the only one of my five grandchildren who I can count on not being a bootlicker."

"I wasn't complimenting you, sir. I was calculating what percentage of your genes I inherited. Because damn, I'm going to be *gorgeous* when I'm old."

That earned her a rare guffaw, and when he stepped forward to pull her into a hug, his grip was tight and real.

"You truly are the best of the bunch."

"The most like you, you mean."

"The apple didn't fall far from the tree," he agreed.

They stood in the quiet for a moment before he cleared his throat and scanned the space again.

"I remember this place is small. Won't take long for you to show me around."

"You reviewed the blueprints and financed the reno three years ago, and you've visited twice a year since. I'd think you remember more than the square footage."

Still, she led him through the clinic. Two exam rooms. A

staff area. Lab, receiving, waiting room. The only recent updates were a couple of new chairs and a narrow sterilization enclave Petra had helped her design last winter.

In the second exam room, Grandpa Nate lingered long enough for her to wonder if he was trying to make her squirm. Not that she had a thing to worry about—she kept her nose clean when it came to anything involving the clinic.

Sydney kept her expression bland and her spine straight. It was just his annoying way.

Finally, he looped back to the front and settled into the comfiest chair in the waiting area as if he planned to stay.

"Your clinic's only open three and a half days a week," he said, gaze level. "Even so, your salary is meager."

"This is a financial check, then?" Sydney asked. She kept her tone level, knowing full well she owed her ability to run the clinic at all to his backing.

"Call it curiosity," he said. "My assistant, Jeremy—you remember him—tells me that with less than full-time hours, your expenditures remain high. Explain."

"I run the clinic days with support staff. The other days, I do relief shifts at the hospital in Diamond Valley or I make house calls. It's what this community needs."

"I've always agreed that your talents are best used outside of a lab." He tapped the arm of his chair. "But I also expect you to keep growing. A practice in the city, eventually. Something scalable. Prestigious."

Here we go again.

"I like working with people," Sydney said with deliberate coolness, "in a place that needs me. Being in Heart Falls is not a stepping stone. It's my job."

He watched her for a long moment. "And no distractions, I trust?"

There it was. The line drawn in invisible ink.

Her grandfather was rich enough to be odd, she supposed, and until now, his generosity had always worked in her favour. The money he threw her way allowed her to run the clinic how she wanted and the only rule was she had to keep her career first and foremost.

No entanglements. No serious relationships.

Nothing that might pull her off course. Which had been a fine thing when she was twenty-three.

Now at twenty-nine?

"I haven't forgotten," she said quietly.

"Good." He stood and adjusted his coat. "You're too valuable to get sidetracked. I didn't invest in you so some man could mess up your path."

It might already be too late. She offered a polite smile. "You'd be the first to know if I lost my focus."

Satisfied—or at least pretending to be—he stood and adjusted his jacket. "I won't keep you. Just wanted to see you."

"Good to see you, too." Sydney tucked her hands in the pockets of her scrubs top. If he went by rote, he'd give her a few final bits of advice, then be out the door in under two minutes. Which Sydney was immensely grateful for this visit.

She wasn't sure how good her poker face was.

He had a hand on the doorknob when he turned back. "One more thing. I know of a doctor who needs a change of scenery. Fully qualified. She'll be a good fit here. Jeremy's handling the paperwork. She starts Tuesday."

Sydney blinked. "You're adding another doctor?"

"And doubling your salary. It's overdue." He didn't wait for her reaction. "You can put more into investments if you'd like. Jeremy can deal with that if you want, but I didn't set you up here to suffer for your work. You have an outstanding mind, and you deserve the chance to shine in your career. If right now you feel house visits should be your priority instead of working the clinic, that's your choice. But progress means not sitting back and letting life happen. Take control. Be in charge."

Frustration flared. He did this every single time. Told her to be a take-charge and decisive person, and then he waltzed in and took over. Even though the financial freedom he'd given her was a gift beyond measure, the reins were getting tight. "Grandpa, I'm happy with—"

"No, this isn't a conversation, it's a reminder," he returned. "You're a brilliant, talented woman who I'll support to the fullest so that your light never gets dimmed. You deserve the best," Grandpa Nate said, resting a hand on her shoulder, speaking now like a wise, gentle guide. "That's why I suggest you shouldn't get distracted by emotional entanglements. They'll dim your light faster than anything."

Sydney nodded, because that was the expected response. Inside, though, something twisted.

Maybe involvement wasn't a distraction. Maybe it was *connection*.

But she wasn't ready to argue. Not yet. But the rules? They were already bending.

Grandpa Nate hugged her tightly, and within the two minutes she'd predicted, he was gone.

She shut the door behind him and leaned on it for a long moment, breathing deeply. As she had with increasing frequency over the years, Sydney wondered if her grandfather truly knew what brilliance looked like.

Her grandfather's words echoed in her ears, but she shoved them aside with effort. It was Monday. There were surfaces to sterilize and lies to tell her best friends.

She was slowly shuffling around the clinic when Petra burst in, holding a box of supplies and wearing a wicked grin.

"Did you tie Declan to the bed?" her best-friend-number-one demanded.

Sydney blinked as the question triggered a flood of vivid mental pictures—all of which involved the delicious cowboy, Declan Skye. Broad shoulders. Firm pecs. Powder-grey eyes that reminded her of storms over the mountains. A mouth that should've come with a warning label.

The man she'd left in bed just over an hour ago, looking very well used and very well satisfied. Which, to be fair, had been the goal.

But the fact that she and Declan had been setting fire to his sheets for nearly a year was still a secret. Not even Petra and Tansy, her two closest friends, had pieced it together yet—though Sydney was starting to wonder how much longer that would last.

Guilt over having lied so blatantly to her grandfather was such a faint wisp, Sydney almost felt guilty for the lack of it.

"He's so damn stubborn," Petra continued breezily, pushing into the first exam room and dropping a box of medical supplies on the counter. "Trust me, we all agree that tying him down is probably the only way to get him to rest after that knock to the head."

Oh. Right. The head injury.

Sydney's face heated. Of course, Petra was talking about Declan's head injury, not the, uh, *other* things Sydney might've been up to with him this morning.

They were having fun. Great, no-strings fun. Declan had been clear from the start that he wasn't looking for anything long term because he was still grieving his first wife. And Sydney? She had the rules. She had a clinic to run—and a career that only existed thanks to that one very specific condition.

No entanglements?

Grandpa Nate did not need to know how flexible that line had become.

Sydney leaned back on the counter and cleared her throat. "Declan is stubborn, I'll give you that. But he knows better than to push it when his doctor"—she tapped her chest—"and both his brothers are on his case."

"Jinx is the worst," Petra said with pride. "You'd think she was the boss of us all. Yesterday at her birthday dinner she rearranged the entire table to reduce Declan's movement and Tansy's stress on the leg cast."

"Good for her," Sydney said, returning to wiping down the countertops. "Better to find your voice with the people who love you before you have to use it on the ones who don't."

Petra stilled. "You okay?"

"Fine," Sydney lied automatically.

Petra raised one brow. "You've got that Sphinx face again. What happened?"

"Nothing," Sydney said then sighed. "Grandpa Nate showed up. Surprise inspection."

"Oof. And?"

Sydney lifted her shoulders briefly. "It went about how you'd expect. Got a raise. Got a new doctor coming onboard here at the clinic. Got another reminder that *all* relationships are distractions, and I need to be careful. So, you know, I might have to fire you as a bestie."

"*Pffft.*" Petra blew a raspberry.

Petra knew all about Grandpa Nate's obsession with Sydney being the best—but not about the strings tied to the clinic's funding.

When Sydney didn't tease back, her friend paused, examining her face closer. "And how do you really feel about that?"

Sydney offered a faint smile, and this time she answered honestly. "Distracted."

~

DECLAN STEPPED into the ranch house and was nearly trampled by Jinx, her golden retriever guard dog, Dixie, in hot pursuit.

"Hi, Declan. Bye, Declan," Jinx called over her shoulder, already halfway down the porch.

"Did you get the license plate of the truck that hit you?" Aiden teased from the kitchen, where he was filling a large pot with water.

Declan blinked then closed the door behind him. "Where's she racing off to in such a hurry?"

"Check the calendar, bro. You signed off for her to attend horse camp the next two weeks with Sasha Stone. They're picking her up in a bit. Logan's going along as a wrangler."

Declan paused mid-step toward the fridge. "He's barely back to riding."

"Short periods of time," Aiden agreed. "But he's strong enough to help saddle and skilled enough to help instruct the campers who need guidance around the arena. Kevin suggested it would be good for him to have something specific to help out with in the community, and I agreed."

"Huh. Okay." Two weeks without the girl around was going to feel odd.

Declan settled at the dining room table. The massive wooden surface was large enough to seat sixteen without crowding, and it had become the heart of the High Water home. Not just for him and his brothers, but for everyone who found shelter, even temporarily, at the ranch.

And that list was growing. Constantly changing as people

who needed a little time away from their past mistakes and some help to get back on their feet arrived and then left. Most of the men stayed for under a week although a few had needed close to a month to put their affairs in order.

Logan had arrived nearly five months ago, beat up and super cagey about his past. While he hadn't shared much yet, he'd slowly and steadily proved his worth, and he now seemed nearly as firm a member as the young woman who'd raced out the door moments earlier.

Logan dodged sharing the same way Declan had dodged feeling anything real for months after his wife had died. Watching the kid, Declan wondered how long someone could carry secrets before they buckled.

Jinx had arrived nearly a year ago, and was now known in the community as Declan's ward. Getting to watch the seventeen-year-old lose her fearfulness so her real personality shone through made every bit of work it had taken to get to this point worth it.

The only full-time staff at Heart Falls was their live-in psychologist, Kevin Robb. He seemed to have his own ghosts to deal with, but mostly, he kept all of them at the ranch subtly focused on finding a smoother path forward.

The most recent permanent arrival was Jeffrey, Jake and Tansy's five-year-old son, and having a kid around was still a huge adjustment—

The sound of Aiden clearing his throat brought Declan's attention back from his musings.

"You've been pretty distracted lately, so I wanted to make sure you remembered we have a new ranch hand arriving any minute." Aiden kept his gaze fixed on Declan.

"I knew that." Declan fought for the details. "A Rick. Or a Ryan?"

"Russ." Silence fell for a moment before Aiden cleared his

throat again. "If you want me to take lead on this one, I'm willing. You don't have to always be the one—"

"I'm fine. But you're right; I've been distracted. It's not fair to any of you," Declan announced firmly.

Daydreaming was one thing, and his mind was tangled with all of the things he'd been pondering lately, especially since he'd gotten injured.

Fucking around enough that he couldn't do his job was inexcusable, though. If he couldn't hold the ranch together, what business did he have trying to build something with a woman like Sydney? "I'll get him settled, and we'll prep the stalls for the seniors coming in tomorrow."

"Seniors?"

"A woman in the foothills is moving into town. She's placing the rest of her livestock, but the two oldest horses are being retired."

Aiden grinned. "We're becoming a retreat for horses in their golden years."

"I have a soft spot."

"No argument here," Aiden said then nodded toward the table. "I did get a lead on a new dining table. Community hall over-ordered. Malachi asked if we wanted one."

Declan frowned. He'd been tracing the tabletop under his fingers unconsciously as he spoke. The surface was marred with teeny nicks and scratches from wayward cutlery and overly enthusiastic moments during family game nights. "What would we need a new table for? This one seats sixteen. There's no room for anything bigger."

Aiden shrugged. "It's big enough, but it's a little beat up."

Somehow, the offer felt wrong. "This one is still sturdy, and now it's got some character. Being a little bumped and bruised is sometimes what gives a thing its value," Declan pointed out.

His brother paused then nodded slowly. "Good way to

think of it. I'll let Malachi know thanks anyway, but we don't need the new one."

A knock sounded, and Declan headed to the door.

The man on the porch wore a dirty backpack and an even dirtier baseball cap. He peered past Declan into the house before meeting his eyes. "This High Water?"

"It is."

The man glanced over the porch toward the barns and building that held the guest housing. "Heard you might need help for a few days."

"We do. I'm Declan. Come with me."

"Food first," the man snapped, then winced. "Sorry. Haven't eaten in a bit."

Which sometimes happened, so Declan ignored the momentary rudeness. "Supper's in a couple of hours, but there's a basket of food in your room. Most people tend to need something to tide them over when they arrive. We're used to it." He put his hat on and stepped off the porch, trusting that Russ would follow.

Over the next hour, Declan didn't get much more out of the man than he hoped to be gone in under a week. Russ nodded at the rules, but his eyes never stopped scanning exits. He looked exhausted but on edge, the way someone looks after weeks of dodging trouble.

Declan gave the man a pass. Escaping a situation where you had to constantly watch your back—it wasn't a thing to turn off in an instant. Hell, living on fumes and fear made a person jumpy as well. Declan knew that from personal experience.

"Clean clothes are in your room. Supper's at six. Family style. You'll be number ten at the table tonight."

Alarm lit Russ's expression. "Seriously?"

"Unless there's a good reason for you to avoid showing your

face, it's how we do things. If it's too much, I'll make other arrangements."

Russell mulled it over. "No, I'll manage. Just didn't expect so many people."

"Only two ranch hands besides you," Declan said. "The rest is family and staff. My brothers, their partners, two kids, and our counselor."

Russell stiffened. "Don't need therapy. Don't want a shrink up in my business."

"Good to know. Then you can just have a nice quiet meal and listen to everyone else talk."

The man nodded then shuffled off, head swaying from side to side as he kept watch on his surroundings.

Declan stood his ground and pondered until Russ vanished into his room. What effect did having that kind of burden on a man's back cause? To be so fearful for his life that he couldn't walk across the yard with his head held high?

Declan slipped into his apartment and grabbed a quick shower himself before heading up to the house.

He was one step from the porch when Sydney's truck rolled down the lane.

And just like that, his thoughts scattered like startled birds.

He'd been turning their situation over in his mind for weeks. The sex had started as spontaneous and secret. Now it was...*more*.

Or at least he wanted it to be.

He'd been about to suggest they should take their relationship out into the open when he'd gotten clobbered on the head. It hadn't seemed the time to change things up. Not with all the other big adjustments in the High Water household plus adding a five-year-old.

But the twisting in his gut at the simple sight of her made it clear something needed to happen.

You set the rules. You can change them.

It sounded like Sadie's voice, no matter how many years had passed. Clear as ever. Calling him out on his own bullshit.

It still hurt, thinking about her being gone. But his subconscious, or his id, or whatever the hell they called the part of the brain that wouldn't let a person blow smoke up their own ass, was calling the shots right now.

It was time.

He'd been grieving for Sadie, and nothing had interrupted that pain but the plans for High Water. Then he'd still been grieving but ready for sex, and Sydney had jumped in with both feet.

He didn't think he'd ever fully be done grieving for Sadie, but superficial sex, even spectacular superficial sex, wasn't enough anymore.

Which meant he had some figuring out to do. Sydney was everything Declan had ever wanted in a woman. He liked them smart, he liked them sexy, and he liked them stubborn.

But the affair with Sydney had a strict fun-and-fucking-only mandate. Now that he was ready for more, he'd have to convince her she wanted him too.

The petite redhead dropped from her massive truck, bouncing up like usual. She slammed the door shut and marched forward, all fiery flash and determined motion. "Hey, you. Petra invited me to crash your dinner party yet again, and I couldn't resist."

"Tansy isn't cooking; Aiden is," he warned her.

Sydney laughed. "I know, but even your brother's cooking skills are better than mine. I'll take my chances. I do need to eat."

He had to be feverish, or simply too mentally tangled up to be thinking straight. Because what he should have done was open the front door and follow her in. Take his time and develop a game plan of some sort.

But if he didn't say something now, when? Life didn't come with guarantees—and the look in Sydney's eyes this morning said she'd noticed the shift too.

So he met her on the bottom step and caught her fingers in his to keep her from blowing past. "We could go out. Just us. Not secret. Not by accident. A real date."

2

———

*H*oly hell.

Sydney blinked. Declan was actually standing there, his hand wrapped around hers, eyes brimming with something dangerous—

Hope? Hunger?

All that popped to mind was, "*What?*"

As far as responses went, it was the worst. It didn't even buy her time to get her head screwed on straight.

Declan cleared his throat then tilted his head toward his truck. "I'd like to take you to dinner. We can go somewhere casual—and there's no problem with us not being at the table. The guys will demolish every ounce of pasta Aiden cooked without any trouble."

Dinner with Declan. A date, official-like.

Temptation wrapped in a six-foot-three package.

If her grandpa hadn't picked today to drop in, she might've landed at the restaurant before it even sank in what a terrible idea it was. Terrible, but wonderful. She wanted so, so badly to take hold of his hand as well and tramp down the stairs toward...something new.

Instead, she stiffened her spine. "That's not our arrangement," she said softly.

He met her gaze evenly. "Sometimes arrangements change."

This was going from bad to worse, because while his suggestion came out of the blue, it wasn't something she hadn't daydreamed about. Especially with her best friends hooking up and falling in love.

She was brilliant, yes—but not a romantic at heart. That soft part of her, the part that longed for fairy tales and slow dancing in the kitchen, had been hidden deep. Buried like forbidden treasure.

Sydney took the coward's way out. "We need to go in for dinner."

She stole her hand back and pushed past him into the house.

Shoes kicked off under the coat rack, she all but sprinted forward until she landed beside Tansy.

The blonde woman had her casted leg propped up on a chair and Jake's son in her lap. "Hey, Sydney. Petra said you might come."

"Free dinner? Wouldn't miss it for the world." Sydney settled into what was normally Jinx's seat, leaning in to wiggle her fingers at Jeffrey. "Hello, kiddo. Have a good day?"

He nodded, dark brown eyes wide in his pale face as he clung tightly to Tansy. "We went to the bookstore. Grandpa Mal said I was a hoot."

Amusement escaped, even as her stomach tightened when Declan slipped into the house and settled at the other end of the dinner table. "Well, Grandpa Mal knows his hoots very well, so I'd take that as a compliment."

"I assume that's some kind of poke at me," Tansy offered with a wink. "But yes, my dad is the king of hoot-spotters."

Jeffrey looked pleased, but didn't give up his grip on Tansy until Jake sat to the left of Sydney. Then Jeffrey switched allegiances in a shot and settled in on his new father's lap as if he'd known Jake his entire life.

Tansy took a deep breath and shifted her foot to the floor. "Love that kiddo, but it's nice to be able to move around a bit more. Also to chat with you without watching my language as hard. Glad you could come tonight."

Sydney's reply was drowned out as Petra arrived with a tray piled high with warm garlic knots, the scent of butter and rosemary trailing behind her like a ribbon. Aiden followed with steaming bowls of pasta, meatballs, and sauce. A Caesar salad and endless supply of lemonade were added, and the entire meal was finished off with baked apple crumble and ice cream.

Through it all, Sydney chatted with Tansy and Petra. Or more like she let them chatter a million miles an hour while she nodded a lot.

She was somehow linked into Declan three chairs down the table from her. She couldn't see him directly, didn't talk to him.

But she was utterly aware of his presence all the same.

Late in the meal, Tansy leaned a shoulder into hers. "You okay?"

"Yeah." Sydney lied with quick ease then smiled at her friend. "Long day."

"Stay and relax by the fire?"

"Head home and crash," Sydney countered. "I love you guys, but tonight I need to escape."

"Love you too." Petra patted her hand. "Escape as needed. If you change your mind, or need an intervention, we can travel to your place."

"I promise I'll call."

Avoiding eye contact with any of the men still seated at the table, Sydney carried her dishes to the counter then tried for a smooth getaway.

It didn't work. The second she stepped onto the porch she spotted him. Declan leaned against the side of her truck, staring at his feet as he tapped one toe gently.

"Fuck," she muttered, motionless on the stairs.

He snorted, still staring at the ground.

"How did you hear that?" she demanded, making her way to his side.

"I was expecting it," he admitted. "I've been thinking it all night."

Yeah. She could believe that.

She should've walked past him. Instead, she stopped and stared up into his deep blue eyes. God, the depths she saw in there. The strength, and the compassion. Beyond temptation. "You threw me for a loop."

"Threw myself, to be honest. Timing wasn't very smart," he said quietly.

This was lining up to be the worst moment ever, Sydney decided. The only way to make it more painful would be to draw it out and hurt a good man for longer than necessary. "I'm flattered, but the answer is no."

Because trying to explain without telling the truth—that she couldn't, and that on top of it, she had too many phobias to even consider being with someone full-time...

No is a complete sentence. It felt like a cruel one at a moment like this, but it was a full arentence.

She wondered if he would flinch or look sad.

He simply nodded sagely. "Okay. I won't argue with you. But just so that I know the lay of the land, is this a *no* forever because you've zero interest in ever getting involved with a man like me on a permanent basis, or is it—"

"What kind of bullshit is that?" Sydney snapped, seeing red on his behalf. "What do you mean *a man like you?*"

Declan made a face. "You don't have to sugarcoat it, Syd. I know I'm not the sharpest tool in the shed. I can understand if that bothers you."

For fuck's sake. "The only sign you've given that you're not playing with a full deck is trying to make an idea that fucked up sound logical," she growled. "I'm not turning you down because I think you're not smart enough. Dammit, man, you can fix anything, build anything, and you're the type who can get wild animals to walk up to you and eat out of your hand. There's no way I could do any of that in a million years. Who cares if my brain and your brain operate on different wavelengths? There's nobody out there that you need to be thinking is too smart for you or too *anything* for you. So stop that bullshit. I never want to hear it again."

Declan sat quietly for a moment. "Question still stands. Is this a no forever? Or is there a chance down the road you might be inclined to change your mind?"

Sweet baby Jesus. She was really starting to understand the phrase about being between a rock and a hard place.

If she had free rein over her decisions, she might be tempted, with a whole lot of rules involved to keep a relationship within acceptable parameters, but being with him —with anyone—wasn't something she was free to do.

Not if she wanted to keep running the clinic.

Not if she wanted to avoid a life that was the exact opposite of everything she'd worked for.

"You are one hell of a man, Declan Skye. I wouldn't have gotten involved with you in the first place if you weren't. I'm just not looking for a relationship. Period." She squeezed his fingers even as she cursed inside. "I don't know *when* I will be, if ever, and it would be a travesty for you to wait around for me.

If you want to find somebody to be with, I think you should make that happen."

It physically hurt to say the words.

Sydney forced herself to keep a neutral expression. Something edging toward optimism, but not gleeful. She could fake the expression on her face but couldn't do anything about the hollow pit in her belly.

She could perhaps keep a good man from wasting his life.

Declan thought for another moment. "Slightly different topic. Did you want to stop seeing me completely? Now that I changed things up, are you calling us off?"

This answer was easy and instant because the idea of having to give him up a second before she needed to might be the straw that broke her. "If you're talking about sex, as long as you're not involved with anyone else, I'm okay keeping our status quo intact. I will not see you once you have another woman in your life."

"Thank God," he muttered.

A snicker-snort escaped her.

Declan offered a sheepish smile. "Excuse me for being crude, but I really like fucking you."

"Trust me, the feeling is mutual. But while we have a very healthy relationship within our parameters, if you're really looking for more, you should find someone who can give you more. I want that for you."

He shrugged. "I'll think about it." His expression turned darker. Needier. "Okay if I come over?"

Hell yes. "Give me an hour and I'll be ready for you," she promised.

During the trip home alone in her truck, Sydney stared at the passing countryside and debated one more time if she was making the right choice.

She saw no other answer. The clinic couldn't run without

the financial support of her grandfather. The support would be cut off if she got involved with Declan.

Frankly, that was the least of her worries. Getting involved with Declan, seriously involved, might make her gut tense with anticipation, but the mental images swiftly morphed into terror goosebumps and stomach wrenching nausea.

Physician, heal thyself.

Great idea, but it wasn't that easy. Her fears were still too raw and too real. Until she got over them, she couldn't be with *anyone* long term.

Not even a gentle giant with pale grey eyes that seemed to peer right into her soul.

LATE THAT NIGHT when Declan let himself into his apartment under the High Water artists' studio, his body was loose and spent. But beneath the surface, his soul pulled tight with a need he couldn't name.

He moved around the unit quietly, putting things away more out of rote habit than with deliberate thought. The place was cool, the fan on the heater/air conditioner running with a soft hum. In the shower, cold water sprayed down and enveloped him, goosebumps rising even as he washed traces of Sydney off his skin.

Crawling under his cold sheets to lay staring up at the ceiling, it didn't take more than a minute for clarity to arrive.

The scent of her lingered even after the quick rinse. But it wasn't just her touch he couldn't shake—it was the way she looked at him, as if she saw everything.

Enough moping. He had other things that he needed to concentrate on for the good of his family and the good of High Water.

As always, when he thought about the ranch, Jeff's old saying came to mind. *Pay it forward.* The reason High Water existed.

Declan had needed a major distraction after Sadie died. And Jake needed something to focus on after becoming completely disillusioned with his job with the RCMP going sideways.

But if he wasn't here in Heart Falls with his brothers, Declan like to think that he'd still be doing something like this with Sadie. Giving to those who needed some help. Offering a second chance to people who had taken a wrong turn.

It wasn't exactly what Jeff had done. Declan and his brothers hadn't been doing anything wrong when their mom died. They'd been three little lost boys, and Jeff had been there, a solid place for them to stand as they dealt with loss and sorrow.

A shot of pain cracked through Declan's chest.

He gasped, pressing a hand to his heart

Not often, but sometimes—grief still hit brutally hard. The pain of losing someone who was your whole damned world.

When he lost his mom, there were moments when he couldn't breathe. He'd gone deep inside himself, and his stepfather was the one who'd let him grieve yet kept him from sliding into the darkness.

Losing Sadie—

Another shot of pain.

I still miss you, babe, he thought. *You left way too soon.*

At moments like this he swore the cool caress of her fingers over his cheek was real. Reassuring him. Chastising him.

Remember, I said you weren't to spend the rest of your life mourning me.

No, he was smart enough to have realized that, despite the

grief he bore because Sadie's life had been cut off far too short, she wouldn't have wanted him to crawl into a grave as well.

In fact, she would've really liked Sydney, he decided. They were alike in some ways—

Which made sense. He had a type. It wasn't on the physical side because there they were polar opposites. But when it came to what mattered, both Sadie and Sydney had a way of looking straight at him and letting him know in no uncertain terms they wouldn't put up with his bullshit.

Which meant right now, he had a very fine line to walk. Because while he had listened to what Sydney said, her words and the look in her eyes hadn't lined up.

He was smart enough to know what that meant, and she should have known better than to try and hide it.

He'd accepted her scold for cutting himself down. She was right—he had a way with animals, and with people. Sometimes he could sense a second before it happened when a horse was about to bolt or a dog fight was about to break out. He often knew when someone was uncomfortable in a room full of people or when they were plotting mischief.

Sasha and Jinx didn't like that he saw right through their plans at times.

Well, Jinx *pretended* to not like it when he casually mentioned he forbid them doing something they shouldn't, but she was secretly pleased to have adults who cared about her in the right ways.

So yeah, as he lay there feeling dejected and rejected, he also knew something was up. Sydney might've said no, but he'd like to think he wasn't just some creeper reading more into her body language than was there. And the way she'd clung to him during sex—

He needed to keep his eyes open and his wits about him.

He wasn't holding his breath, but damn it, if she gave him even a hint there was a crack in that wall—he'd be there.

Hell, he would be there for her no matter what. If nothing ever developed, at least he'd have continued to follow the mandate that the best man in the world had taught him.

Not because he could get something out of her, but because as Jeff always said, it was the right thing to do.

A sense of mental ease and satisfaction slid in. Strange, considering the things that had been shut down that day, but somehow Declan felt as if he was in the right place at the right time. He'd take it even though it was a bunch of touchy-feely shit.

The upside of having an emotional bender come to a satisfactory conclusion? Declan slept like a log, and when five a.m. hit, he was ready to take on the day.

He grabbed a quick breakfast out of the fridge and a cup of coffee and made his way up the stairs and onto the porch outside the artists' studio. The view over the rolling foothills as the land slowly shifted upward into the jagged silhouette of the Rocky Mountains never got old. Sunlight painted the tips of the rugged peaks a pale yellow gold, the tree line far below the rich green of full summer.

Declan sipped his coffee and counted his blessings.

He also got to silently observe when Brian, the ranch hand who'd arrived four days earlier, crossed to the barn and vanished inside.

Which was fine until a few minutes later, Russ also strolled across to the barn, checked both ways, and slipped inside.

That sensation in Declan's gut clicked on full. The one that said he needed to be aware.

Brian had assigned chores. Russ did not.

Declan abandoned his coffee cup and plate, moving

quickly but without running. He slipped into the barn as quietly as the man ahead of him had.

He probably could've been as noisy as he wanted because raised voices echoed off the walls.

"That's all I've got. I can't get you more. There's nothing else I can do."

"Bullshit. You've got access. You've got contacts. Use them—"

"I'm out of that, and so are you. That's why we're here."

"Broke with no prospects? Fuck that."

The voices cut out as a fight began. Grunting, the smack of fist on flesh, wood creaking, and gasps of pain. Declan's gut clenched.

Not just fear—*certainty*. Trouble had come through their doors.

He rushed around the corner and spotted Russ with Brian in a headlock as the man clawed desperately at the forearm wrapped around his throat.

"You'll get me what I want," Russ snarled.

Words weren't necessary, surprise was. Declan barreled into Russ, fingers on his right hand held in a tight beak-like shape as he aimed hard and low into the man's gut.

With his left hand, he pushed at Russ's face, and the arm trapping Brian in place loosened enough the man dropped out of the hold and scrambled away.

A second later Russ was on the ground, arms pinned behind his back as Declan sat on top of him to keep him down. "Seems as if we have a problem."

Brian stepped forward. "I'm sorry. I should've come to you, but last night he told me if I didn't meet him, he'd hurt the kid. I didn't know what to do."

"Bullshit," Russ snapped, writhing under Declan. "He's lying. He knows my name, and he was trying to—"

"I saw enough to know which one of you is lying," Declan said quietly, increasing the pressure on the arm twisted behind Russ's back.

Russ stilled instantly.

Yeah, that position hurt like a motherfucker, and Declan knew it from training with Jake. "Brian, you okay?"

The man stretched his neck from side to side then nodded. "Yeah."

Keeping a firm grip on Russ, Declan slipped his phone from his back pocket, thumbed it open and hit the emergency call for Jake. He kept most of his attention on the man on the ground, just to be safe.

"Yeah?" Jake muttered sleepily.

"We need a Bluejay, stat."

Sleep vanished and Jake's response came sharp and clear. "Shit. Coming. Where are you?"

"Barn."

"Safe?"

"Yeah. Two minutes," Declan offered, thanking every one of the stars in the heavens that between Jake and Aiden, they'd prepared for a moment like this. They had codes, not many, but specific for certain circumstances.

Red Robin—a fight with blood involved.

Black Bird—a dangerous situation to be dealt with stealthily.

Bluejay—anything that would need to involve Jake's contacts with the police force to help get a troublemaker as far away from High Water as possible.

Less than two minutes later, and he had to have dressed while running, Jake arrived. Aiden showed up a minute later, and between them, they got Russ restrained and situated in Jake's locked truck, fury on his face.

Jake stepped to the side, phone to his ear as he spoke rapidly to one of his contacts.

Aiden laid a hand on Brian's arm. "You're not in trouble, but can you tell us more? Anything will help."

The man stared at the ground then sighed. "I thought I recognized him, but it seemed impossible. All the way up until he shoved his way into my face. Said he knew who I was, and if I didn't do what he said, the kid was toast."

The white hot anger that flared got pushed aside for now. "Who is he?"

Brian hesitated and spoke softly. "He's an enforcer for Trident. One of the ones who does the dirty work when deals fall through."

Shit. That was way above the level of dangerous persons they'd intended to help at High Water.

Aiden cleared his throat. "You want someone to look you over? Sydney, the redhead who was here last night, is a doctor, and she's discreet."

"I'm good," Brian insisted. A shiver took him from top to bottom. "If it's okay with you guys, I'm going to fast track my departure. I feel the need to keep moving for a bit."

"We understand, although you should know Russ is leaving within the next few minutes," Aiden said. "We'll be dropping him off with someone who will get him into a controlled location a long way from here."

"We're the ones who need to apologize." Declan took a deep breath. "This is supposed to be a safe place."

"Sometimes bad shit happens." Brian tilted his head toward the house. "Think there's food and coffee yet? I'm still more comfortable to load up and then be off, but food before I go would be appreciated."

"Tansy was up," Jake offered, obviously listening in on the

conversation. He held a hand over his phone as he waited on hold. "Go on inside."

Declan waited until Brian was out of earshot before he turned to Aiden. "Russ's name came in through the usual channels, yes?"

"Yeah, nothing out of the ordinary." A frown folded between his brows. "We'll need to start double-checking them."

Guilt slid in. Declan had been so distracted the previous day. Had there been some sign *he'd* missed while showing the man around?

A solid squeeze landed on his shoulder. Aiden leaned in close, meeting his eyes. "Don't beat yourself up over this. You couldn't have known, and you did everything by the book when it was time to react."

"I guess."

Still, the knot of tension in his gut wasn't going away for a long time. High Water was supposed to be a refuge.

For himself as well, he realized. The fact danger could slip in that quickly rubbed something inside him the wrong way, an ache wearing away at his soul.

Maybe doing the right thing wasn't always the safe thing. He didn't know if he liked that truth. Not when the people he loved could pay the price.

3

———

Sydney decided she should've gone back to the office instead of trying to sleep. Sex with Declan should've left her boneless and floating on endorphins. Instead, she tossed and turned for hours until getting up and scrubbing her kitchen until it was surgery room clean.

As a person in the medical community, she knew some of the fears she had were irrational, but that didn't make them any easier to get over.

In spite of a very strong coffee, she was still feeling a little blurry at the first visit of the day.

Nora Yemen's little cabin sat at the end of a gravel lane, a good twenty minute drive from Heart Falls. The woman was in her late seventies and doing fairly well on her own, but in the three years that Sydney had been casually coming out to provide healthcare, she'd spotted the changes.

It was easier to deal with the issues of aging by planning ahead. Convincing people of that fact was an uphill battle.

She picked up the basket of fruit from the passenger seat,

dropped out of the truck, and headed for the door with her chin held high. A visit like this was why she did what she did.

The Skye brothers weren't the only ones who were trying to make a difference in peoples' worlds.

The door opened before she could knock.

Nora offered a small smile then shuffled backward, gesturing her in. "Saw you coming up the drive so I added a little water to the teapot. Do you have time to stay?"

"Of course. I brought you something as well. Just some fresh fruit that made more sense to buy in bulk, and there's no way I'll eat it all before it goes bad." Sydney lay the basket on the counter then settled in at the neat-as-a-pin table as ordered.

Nora rolled her eyes for a moment, but she didn't turn the gift down. Just went to work, making up a plate of cookies and cups of tea. Which gave Sydney time to observe her motions and conclude the woman was still safe in her own home, but the time was coming when that wouldn't be true.

Like most of their visits, this one began without a lot of words. Sydney nibbled on a cookie, sipped tea, and breathed in the quiet. Nora watched Sydney like a hawk.

"I've been thinking about what you said," Nora finally informed her. "About how the wise plan ahead to enjoy all the seasons of life."

"I said something that poetic?" Sydney shook her head. "I'm sorry, you must be confusing me with someone from daytime TV."

Nora laughed. "Okay, fine. You didn't say it that way, but that's how I started to think about it. You're right. It's always smarter to make a move when it's your choice than when it's forced on you. I called the senior lodge in town, and they'll have room for me sometime in the next month or two."

Sydney deliberately let her jaw fall open. "Get out."

This time Nora glared. "Young lady, sarcasm does not become you."

"No, this isn't sarcasm. This is outright shock that someone is taking my good advice and, in fact, speeding ahead faster than average." Sydney raised her glass to the woman. "But then, I always knew you were above average."

Pleased, her cheeks flushing slightly, Nora waved her fingers. "My children were equally shocked when I called them this morning to let them know the news. But that's the good thing about having always been a stubborn old woman. I'm doing what I want regardless of what they think."

Good to know that the family was in the loop. Support at a time like this was invaluable. "It's a big transition. If you need help along the way, let me know."

"We'll take it as it comes," Nora assured her.

The next hour was spent in a companionable conversation as Nora brought out a deck of cards. Sydney drank tea, played the game, and thought how sometimes things did work out the way she'd hoped they would.

She helped put the fruit away in the fridge and took the basket back, accepting Nora's firm handshake before heading out the door.

Outside the house, Sydney paused. Two vehicles screeched to a stop beside her truck, plumes of dust swirling into the air. Unfamiliar faces peered out the windows, scowls firmly in place. Doors slammed, and two women and a man in their late forties rushed toward the cabin.

They didn't look like any religious proselytizing drop-ins that Sydney had ever seen. She stood her ground and waited with a smile in place.

At her back, the door creaked open. "Are you still there, Dr. Jeremiah?"

"Doctor? *This* is the woman who demanded that you

move?" The shorter of the two women, heavyset with a tangle of brown and grey curls, marched up to Sydney and glared in disgust. "How dare you interfere in things that are none of your business?"

Sydney straightened to her full height even as she took a step back to make sure she had ample room to duck if necessary. "And you are?"

"This is our mother," the other woman declared. She shook her head, and her brown bob swayed, her thin fingers clutching the strap of her oversized purse. "What are you doing here?" She glanced over her shoulder at the slender man behind them. "Adam, she's trespassing. Can we get her arrested?"

"She's not trespassing, Cara," Nora said firmly. "She's my guest, so you can all stop your—"

"Mother, get back in the house. Cara, Cindy. Go inside with her." Adam stepped around his sister, shoving her toward the front door so he could loom menacingly over Sydney. "I'll deal with this."

"There's nothing to deal with," Nora insisted, pushing off her daughters' grasp. "I'm sorry, Sydney. I had no idea they'd be like this."

Sydney held her hands in the air as if showing she was unarmed. She slowly eased closer to Nora, just in case. She'd seen abuse masked as family concern before. The tone. The expressions. "I'm not sure what brought on all the aggression, but I need to tell you that right now, with the way you're behaving, I'm not comfortable leaving you alone with your mother."

"How dare you?" Cindy snarled.

Cara tugged on Nora's arm. "Mom. Get into the house and away from this scammer right now."

Gravel sprayed in the driveway, but other than hoping it

wasn't another child coming to join in the fray, Sydney didn't have a second to look.

Instead, she slipped her body between Nora and her daughter, facing the older woman straight on. "This is your decision. Do you want me to leave you with them? Do you feel safe?"

"Is this the kind of nonsense you have been feeding her? Our mother, not feel safe around us? How ridiculous." Adam roared loudly enough the metallic ring of a truck door slamming shut was a faint sound.

What she did hear was a gasp of pain as Cara tightened her grip on her mother's arm and tugged.

"No," Nora insisted, jerking away.

Sydney moved. She wrapped her fingers around Cara's wrist and squeezed.

Cara shrieked, her fingers flew opened, and Sydney pulled Nora free.

The older woman shuffled for a second, wavering on her feet, and Sydney fought to catch her.

Beside them, Cara flailed her arms as she stepped backward.

Shouting, shoving. Boots on gravel. It all mixed together as Sydney focused on making sure Nora landed safely.

"Let her go." Adam's deep voice drilled into Sydney's ears.

Pain exploded behind her eyes as her head jerked back, her braid yanked like a rope. White noise roared in her ears. Sydney twisted, raising her hands to defend herself, and another sharper flash of pain bloomed in her left eye. A second later, her butt hit the porch and she kept going, rolling toward safety.

"Don't even think about moving."

Sydney stopped in mid-roll. She was hands and knees on

the middle of the wide staircase and utterly in shock at the familiar voice.

She looked up. "Declan?"

Relief shot through her at the sight of him with stormclouds in his eyes and a face made of granite. He held Adam immobile, twisting the man's arm behind his back.

Fear widened Adam's eyes, and his sisters finally stood motionless.

No, check that. Cara had frozen in place, but Cindy had her phone out and held in front of her like a shield. Recording a video, Sydney assumed.

Screw them all. Now that she had Declan to watch her back, Sydney hurried to Nora, who sat on the porch with her arms wrapped around herself. "You okay? Did you get hurt?"

"I'm fine. Maybe some bruises." She glared at her son. "I'm outraged at your behaviour. What on earth were you thinking?"

"She's trying to commit elder fraud," Adam insisted.

"I'm recording everything," Cindy said. "Cara, call the police."

"Don't bother the police," Nora snapped, getting to her feet with Sydney's help. "Oh, wait. Unless you want us to call the police for you, Dr. Jeremiah. If you'd like to press charges after my son and daughters deliberately assaulted you."

"What?" Cara demanded.

The other two shouted over each other.

"She's tricking you, Mom."

"Wait until I get my hands on you—"

The threat from Adam died off instantly as Declan growled his disapproval.

How had this gotten so tangled?

After making sure that Nora was solid on her own two feet, Sydney stepped back slowly. "We don't need the police, but we should get to the bottom of this. I'm willing to stay and talk if you can all be reasonable."

"You talk about reasonable when I'm being restrained by a thug. Let me go, you monster," Adam demanded, wiggling against Declan's hold.

"I'm working really hard to stay polite," Declan said softly. "The only reason you and I aren't taking this somewhere else to have a detailed conversation on our own is because Dr. Jeremiah just offered to speak with you. So it's your choice. Stand down and step away so we can discuss this like rational adults, or *I'll* call the police."

"You're the one threatening our brother." Cindy raised her phone higher. "I have proof."

Declan stared at her. "Go ahead. Post it on social media. See how long you last before they rip you to shreds, Karen."

The woman looked confused for a moment, but when Adam relaxed his stance and Declan let him go, she finally put down the phone.

Sydney had no objection when Declan casually walked to her side and stood there looking all big and intimidating. Her face throbbed where she'd been hit, and her hands were still slightly shaky, but her words came out steady and calm. "Then let's have a discussion."

EVEN THOUGH THE shouting didn't start up again, things didn't improve much. Declan somehow kept his cool until the accusations were done, because Nora then made a few choice comments and kicked her children out.

Sydney looked Nora over one last time and promised to check in again soon, then she and Declan went to their separate vehicles.

When Sydney pulled off the road a mile down the hill into a small clearing, Declan didn't hesitate before following.

She didn't wave him down—but she wouldn't have stopped if she wanted to be alone.

Declan's anger remained, his jaw and shoulders tight with it, but he had to acknowledge Sydney was a fucking force of nature. He hadn't seen a quarter of what had just happened coming before it played out.

Sydney waited for him, silently perched on the dropped tailgate of her truck. Feet kicking slowly, she stared over the land to the distant mountain range.

Gravel crunched underfoot as he made his way over to join her. He jumped up to sit at her side and settled in. "Well, that was a thing."

"Fucking wet behind the ears, pretending to be adults, selfish idiots."

He snorted. "Tell me what you really think, Syd."

She snapped her head toward him. "And they had the gall to accuse *me* of elder abuse when the whole reason those pseudo-adult wannabes rushed their butts out to the house for the first time in fucking forever is because they don't want Nora to move to a seniors home. They think she'll end up spending their inheritance. Goddamn bottom-feeding leeches."

"That's kind of an insult to the bottom feeders of the world," he pointed out. He pulled a hanky from his pocket and cupped her face in his hand. "Hold still."

He pressed the clean cloth to the corner of her eye, and she hissed. "Shit, that hurts. Swelling's started in the orbital rim. My vision is clear, so I can skip the ER, but I'll need ice."

"You're supposed to duck faster," Declan murmured, softly cleaning the dirt from her face,

"Usually I would. Nora was there, though. Having a frail bystander in the mix really messes with thinking *me first*."

"Put on your own oxygen mask before helping others," Declan deadpanned.

Sydney pushed his hand away, ire in her eyes. "The next time I'm on a fucking plane and someone takes a swing at me, I'll remember that."

He leaned in, slipped his palm to the back of her head, and held her firmly in place. Then he curled himself around her, brushing his lips over hers in a first ghostly touch. He did it again, this time with a brief nip to her lower lip, easing his tongue over the little hurt. He kissed her slowly and softly until the tension eased out of her shoulders, and she leaned toward him, a sigh brushing past his cheek.

He kissed her one more time just because he wanted to, then he pulled back and gently leaned their foreheads together. "That was quite the visit. I'm glad you finally explained the truth to the kids, although calling people that old *kids* sounds wrong."

"Crybaby, pain-in-the-ass brainless twats takes too long to say," Sydney muttered against his lips. "The part that frustrates me is, so what? It's her money, and it's her cabin. She's lived there for over fifty years of her life, and if she's ready to move somewhere else, and she wants to spend every penny that she's scrimped and saved over the years, she should fucking do it."

"It would take a long time to spend the money that she'll get out of the sale of the land and cabin. She'd have to live to a hundred and twenty to run out of money."

"If she did run out of money," Sydney pointed out, "it's not as if the facility will kick her out. Government paid room and board in a seniors' lodge is pretty sweet. Which is something we could've told the kids at any time if they would've fucking *asked*. I hate it when people don't ask."

Declan gently massaged the back of her neck. "How are you feeling? Other than the pissed off and infuriated part?"

Sydney closed her eyes and leaned into his touch. "Better once you got there," she admitted quietly. She stilled before she cracked one eye open and examined him with suspicion. "Declan? Why *were* you there?"

"It never came up in our discussions, but Nora had phoned me to say she has animals that need to be rehomed before she moves."

The wariness in Sydney's eyes faded. "Sorry for suspecting you were stalking me there for a minute. I'm still in a fighting mood."

"It's okay. I totally plan on stalking you in the future," Declan promised.

She laughed, curling against him.

It would've been nice to leave it at that, but he did have a tendency toward too much honesty. "I'm not kidding. The stalking part."

"Have at 'er," Sydney said. "Petra's probably got us all GPS tagged like wildlife, especially since what happened with Tansy and the trip to Crazytown with Jake's ex."

True. Which was something that gave Declan a terrible, wonderful idea. Something to be dealt with when he didn't have Sydney right there with him within arm's reach.

He picked her up, twisting her until her knees rested on either side of his hips, her torso tight to his. He lifted her chin and stared into her eyes. "You're going to have a shiner," he warned.

"Feels like it." Sydney stroked her knuckles over the five o'clock shadow on his chin and cheeks. "Do you have anywhere to be right now? Since I noticed you don't have any horses in the back of your truck."

"I'm gonna go back and get them later, but as for my agenda? Right here and right now, I'm all yours."

What he'd like to have done was toss a blanket into the back of her truck, strip them both down, and make her see stars.

What he did instead was something he'd been longing to do, but it never seemed as if he could. Not when they very clearly established their sexual interactions as bedroom romps that led to screaming orgasms.

He kissed her.

It was a bid to distract her mind from the chaos and anger. Get her shoulders to ease and the tension in her body to loosen its grip.

Okay, he wasn't a perfect gentleman. He undid the buttons on her shirt and slipped her bra open, so that as they kissed, he got to drift his hands all over her soft skin. Got to cup and play with the full handfuls of her breasts.

He nibbled on the spot under her ear that made her squirm.

She shifted, gyrating over him. She rubbed their groins together to try and take the edge off, and he let her use him until her fingernails dug into his shoulders. Until she gasped into his mouth, the movements of her hips unsteady and out of rhythm. He clasped his hands on her hips and dragged her up, increasing the pressure, increasing the tempo.

Sydney sighed. *"Declan."*

Her body quivered, and her head landed on his shoulder. She squeezed her thighs tight then let go.

There wasn't an ounce of stress left in her. She wasn't watching, she wasn't in control. She gave it all up and let him be there for her. It was probably the most intimate moment they'd ever had, in spite of mostly wearing all their clothes.

The quiet enveloped them for a moment before she shifted over him. She lifted her head and offered a satisfied smile. Her fingers drifted in a gentle stroke over his shoulder. "Did you want to meet tonight?"

Every fucking night. Every fucking minute.

Instead, he shook his head, kissing her tenderly one final time. "Promised my brothers I'd spend the evening with them. If I'm meeting with you later, I'll be so distracted they'll win a shit ton of my money."

"We can't have that," she teased. "Thanks for the listening ear and the timely intimidating presence. Thanks for being awesome."

He stared at her face for a moment. He wanted to be the man to put this expression on her face all the time. "You make it easy."

Sydney gave him a final shining grin, and they both headed to their vehicles.

When they hit the main road, Sydney turned toward town, and Declan turned toward High Water, eager to get to the next part of his day. He had a specific agenda in mind that involved a tracking program, his phone, and a lesson with their resident hacker, Petra.

He had, after all, asked Sydney's permission. Now he needed Petra's tech skills to pull off the most considerate kind of stalking.

4

———

With Declan spending the evening with his brothers, Sydney realized it might be the perfect opportunity to steal some time with her girls.

> Sydney: Hey, ladies. What are the chances I can entice you to join me for the evening? Bring Jeffrey if you'd like, Tansy."

It didn't take long before she got responses.

> Petra: Perfect idea. We'll bring a salad if you can whip up your artichoke dip and nachos.

> Tansy: What she said. Excited to come over, but without the Jeffster. My parents have been begging for a chance to spoil him with some dedicated grandma and grandpa time. After the way he was cozying up to my dad at the bookstore the other day, I think he's ready.

> Sydney: Then I'll see you all when you get here.

Didn't take much work to prepare. The little house that she rented on the edge of town was a two bedroom. The location was convenient to both the clinic in town and the highway to access the rest of her reluctant patients. The place wasn't much to look at, but it had a big enough living space that Sydney had squeezed in three couches—more than enough for a full-on sprawl session with friends.

She took a few minutes to apply an extra layer of makeup. It wouldn't stop her friends from seeing the damage that had happened, but as long as it wasn't right there, staring them in the face, she might get a few less obsessive complaints.

She stepped back, eyeing her work. The bruising was masked, but the puffiness gave her away. So much for flying under the radar.

She was going to hear an earful over this one if Declan hadn't already informed them of the mishap.

With the dip in the oven to heat, Sydney made herself a drink and stepped onto the front porch, staring toward the mountains and the sun that was still high in the sky this time of year.

Such a pretty place. She was glad that she'd come to Heart Falls, but she had to admit the regrets over what couldn't be were growing.

Still, she had a lot of good things in her life, and that's what she wanted to focus on. She tilted her head back against the cushion behind her and let the sunshine heat her face.

Which meant thirty minutes later when Petra pulled into the yard, Sydney was a relaxed puddle. Partly because she'd been daydreaming about kissing Declan and his sweet touch in the aftermath of the chaotic visit.

"Lounging without us?" Tansy teased as she manoeuvered her crutches up the porch. "That bench is prime real estate."

Sydney gestured to the cushion beside her. "Saved you a spot."

"Don't mind if I do." A twist and a hop later, the crutches were under the base of the bench and Tansy stretched her cast toward the railing and let out her own sigh. "Not moving from this place until you tell me there's food on the table."

Petra stood, arms full of bags, eyeing them with amusement. "You're such a lazy butt, which I love. I don't love that it took you breaking your leg to get you to slow down, but taking care of yourself looks good on you."

"I agree," Sydney said. She popped to her feet and joined Petra. "Let's haul that inside and we can all grab drinks and enjoy the sunshine."

"Nothing alcoholic for me," Tansy reminded them. "I'm mostly off the pain meds, but I don't want to chance it in case I do have to pop a couple tonight."

"Not a problem."

Inside the house, Petra put the salad in the fridge and pulled out the giant pitcher of fruit punch Sydney had made for the evening. "Nice. This one isn't spiked, is it?"

"No." Sydney grabbed two more glasses, and within minutes, they were all on the porch, drinks in hand and sun beaming down on them.

The lovely type of quiet that usually only occurs among good friends slipped in then. All of them shifting from the business of the day to this time of connection with people they loved and who loved them.

Five minutes later when Petra spoke, her tone was carefully moderated and smooth. "Gonna tell us about the black eye?"

So much for Sydney's makeup job. "Declan didn't already fill you in?"

Petra twisted her head to the side, still sprawled in relaxation. "He said something about you getting into a dust-up but that you'd let us know the details. He also asked me to teach him how to use the Finder app because he assumed I would have everyone in our family tagged like well-loved deer."

"Because you do," Tansy said bluntly. "And thank God for that. Only I'm going with *tagged like rare ghost bears* because that's a little more exotic than a deer. Plus, people don't usually shoot them."

Sydney hid her amusement and focused on Petra's more important comment. "Declan wants to be able to track me?"

Petra shook her head. "Declan wants to track *all* of us. I'm kind of surprised it took him until now to ask, considering how much of an overprotective teddy bear he is."

Huh. The big guy had straight-up told her what he planned to do, so it's not as if Sydney could really complain. The jerk.

Sydney raised her glass, the sun lighting it up like stained glass. "I did a house visit today and the children of my patient decided I was trying to scam them out of the future money they might get. Looking at how healthy Nora is and the shape the three of them were in, I bet she outlives them by a good ten years."

Tansy swore. "They really accused you of being a con artist? Do they even know you?"

"Of course not. Worse, they don't know their mother. I hate to think they might try to barrel over her future decisions, but she seemed to have it under control before we left. Declan gave her the name of a good lawyer."

"Well, good for you for making a difference in another person's world. Just duck faster next time, okay?" Petra raised her glass.

Sydney topped up her own glass from the pitcher then did the same.

They were inside at the table, digging into the cheesy goodness that was Sydney's one claim to culinary fame when

Tansy laid both hands on the table. "Time for a serious question, and as always, tell me to butt out if you want." She met Sydney's gaze straight on. "You're not drinking."

Sydney lifted her full punch glass in the air. "Of course I am."

Her friend waved her hand. "Don't try the innocent act. Tonight isn't the first night I've noticed. It's absolutely your choice whether you dump alcohol in your system or not, but to be blunt, you used to drink a lot."

Petra made a face. "We all used to drink a lot."

It wasn't as if Sydney were keeping it secret. "We *were* drinking a lot," she agreed. "I'll admit the day I got up and went to work at the clinic and felt like shit until the end of the day was a bit of a wake-up call. I know better than most the effect alcohol has on the body, and while there are times I enjoy the buzz and the mental relaxation, I think it had become a crutch. A way to take off the edge when I didn't want to feel...anything. That's not who I want to be."

Tansy laid a hand on her arm and squeezed. "Whether you choose to drink or not, we'll support you. But this is a thing that it would be nice to know so we're not pushing your boundaries if you have a moment of temptation."

"I'm still drinking," Sydney said. "But only on the nights I don't plan to work the next day, and then no more than a couple. No more tying one on for the hell of it."

"Good to know." Petra raised her glass in the air. "In the interest of true confessions, I had kind of come to the same conclusion. In fact..."

She shifted in her seat, the mischievous glint in her eyes all too familiar. She rose from the table and went to the bag resting on the counter and pulled out two wrapped objects.

Tansy clasped her hands together and muttered in a low, reverent tone. "The infamous moment has arrived."

Petra shoved the tissue-wrapped object at her. "I love you. Now shut up."

"I'll treasure it forever," Tansy said, hand pressed to her heart. "Or until it's burnt down to its final nub, and then I'll recycle the glass container like a good little Canadian."

Which meant Sydney was laughing as she ripped the paper from her gift.

The vanilla-scented candle had a shiny gold label on the glass with the words *The Badass in Me Honours the Badass in You.* "Aww, I love it."

"Ha! Mine is nearly perfect." Tansy held her candle toward Sydney so she could read *Thanks for Being My Rock. If This Was the 80s, I'd Make You a Mix Tape.*

"Nearly perfect?" Petra demanded.

Tansy flashed a wide Cheshire Cat grin. "Now you need to make me a mix tape."

"Oh God." Petra took a deep breath. "I'm making changes, too. Declan is Jinx's official guardian, but she's gotten attached to me and Aiden. So we're considering making it official and adopting her."

Holy shit. Sydney's heart pounded at the idea. "Really?"

"We still have to ask her, but we're pretty sure she'll say yes." Petra wore a slightly guilty expression. "It's not as if the system will have anything to do with approving this."

"Since you plan to hack the system and make the paperwork magically appear?" Tansy asked.

"*Hacked* is such a harsh word," Petra complained before meeting their eyes in turn. "So, since you're the people I trust the most in the world, tell me honestly. Do you think being adopted is the best thing for Jinx? Or do we leave things the way they are?"

Sydney shook her head. "You don't keep doing a thing just to do a thing."

"Agreed." Tansy smiled wide. "Sometimes arrangements change."

The echo of Declan's words from the previous night caught Sydney off guard.

Petra's eyes held so much hope, and that was the important thing to focus on. "So you both would give your blessing to that arrangement?" she asked quietly.

"Absolutely." Tansy and Sydney's responses were instant and perfectly synchronized.

The three of them abandoned the table, and hugs were shared all around. Sydney soaked in the joy etched into Petra's face, all because she'd been brave enough to chase what she wanted.

At the end of the evening, when the girls were gone and Sydney was crawling into bed alone, one lingering thought kept sneaking through the euphoria of the night...

Too bad I'm not as brave.

Not yet anyway.

Two DAYS after dealing with Russ, Declan went to pick up the horses from Nora Yemen.

He examined the woman carefully as she helped load the beasts into the horse trailer. "Everything okay?" he asked. "Your children get on board with your plans?"

"Yes," she answered decisively. "I gave them what for and told them to support me, or if all they were worried about was money, they could receive their inheritance right now."

He tilted his head toward the other car in the yard. "Looks as if someone is here."

Nora smiled. "It didn't take long before they all rang, apologizing profusely for the big misunderstanding. They're good people at heart. They just get their brains tangled around things that aren't important."

"People have a way of doing that at times. Even the best of us," he agreed.

"Well, sometimes all it takes is a little time and thinking it through. I'm sure that helped. Plus, I told them their inheritance currently comes to about a thousand bucks each."

Declan chuckled. "I'm glad they came to their senses. Spending time with you is a privilege. You're special, Mrs. Yemen."

"You're not so bad yourself," she returned with a wink before patting the nearest horse on the butt affectionately. "Thanks for taking care of Salt and Pepper. It makes me happy to think they'll live out their days with some comfort."

"I'll do my best to make that happen," he promised.

Which meant when Jake and Aiden caught up with him, Declan was in the barn, currying the new residents. It was a peaceful activity he enjoyed, the steady repetition and the calming presence of the animal under his care leveling his mood.

"Good news," Jake announced, easing back against the stall wall.

Aiden stood beside Declan and stroked a hand along the horse's withers. "Hello there, sir. You are one fine looking animal."

"Pepper's been well cared for," Declan said. "What's the news?"

"Our misbehaving ranch hand from the other day has been relocated to a secure halfway house in Manitoba," Jake informed him. "It's not putting him back into the prison system, but it will keep him out of our hair for the immediate future. Hopefully if he's kept moving in the right direction for long enough, he'll decide it's far more worthwhile to keep on the straight and narrow."

"Good." Declan considered for a moment. "I'm guilty of thinking everyone who comes through these doors is eager to make a change."

"For ninety-nine out of a hundred, that'll be true," Aiden suggested. "The problem comes when they have enough bad habits from whatever trouble they were in. They don't see a different way forward. I think that's what Russ's issue was."

"And he was deep enough into dangerous territory to have formed some very bad habits." Declan shook his head slowly. That was the part that was worrying him. "I know there's no way we can permanently keep High Water off the radar—we're relying on the goodwill of everyone who comes through the door. If they don't keep their mouths shut, we could have more issues as we go forward, not less."

The three of them fell silent.

"Do we stop what we're doing?" Jake asked. "I'm not saying that on a whim." Anger heated his eyes. "Russ threatened my son. And now every time Jeffrey scurries off alone—and it's going to take time to teach him to stop running wild—I'm terrified someone might be waiting to snatch him. I don't want to live like this."

"We get where you're coming from," Aiden offered slowly. "We all have people in our lives now who mean everything. The idea of Petra being hurt makes me wake up in a cold sweat. And then there's Jinx—that girl doesn't need any more bullshit in her world."

Declan's thoughts instantly went to Sydney. She was as much a part of High Water as everyone else, even though she didn't live there.

"Let's really consider the question," Declan said slowly.

"Do we stop what we're doing? Find a way to slow down? Make the limits of who comes in a lot more stringent? Jeff gave us the means to open a place where we can help people. But helping people shouldn't mean putting our family in the crosshairs."

Aiden folded his arms over his chest. "Those are all the right questions, but I don't think this is a decision we should make in the barn or in a hurry."

"I don't think it's a decision we should make without including Tansy and Petra." Jake raised a brow. "Because I would very much like to not worry about what's going into my food for the next, say, five years."

"Good point," Aiden muttered. "They are the vengeful type, aren't they?"

"That's why you're all so perfect together," Declan deadpanned. "Let's put this on the agenda for a serious discussion. Because we set up High Water. We can make her whatever she needs to be."

His brothers wandered off, and Declan got back to the task at hand, hesitating when something crashed a few stalls over from him.

He paced slowly around the corner, wondering if one of the barn cats had knocked gear off a hook. He was still partially hidden behind the bracing wall when he spotted Logan moving quickly down the passage that led away from the office.

Huh. He hadn't realized that camp was over so soon. "Logan?"

The kid shot nearly three feet off the ground, twisting midair as if he hadn't seen or expected Declan to be there. "Oh, hi."

"You all back already?"

Logan shook his head. "I needed to grab some things. I wasn't very good at packing."

Declan nodded, but a thread of unease tugged at him.

Something about Logan's story didn't quite ring true. His extra gear would be in his room or in the tack room.

Declan didn't push, though. There were times the kid tightened up so much he seemed semi-terrified. It wasn't a reaction Declan enjoyed bringing out in others.

Perhaps with enough time at High Water, Logan would find his confidence.

"You heading back to camp right away?"

The kid's head dipped rapidly. "Oh, Jinx wanted a different halter. I should grab that."

Declan gestured toward the tack room, easing back to give the young man room. "How is Jinx?"

"She's awesome." Logan stumbled for a moment, his face beet red when he met Declan's gaze again. "I mean, she's doing well. Not as good with the horses as Sasha, but she's having fun. I *think* she's having fun."

God save him from the embarrassment of twenty-year-olds. "Good to hear. I'm gonna get back to my chores. Say hello to Jinx for me."

"Will do." Logan darted into the tack room as if eager to vanish from sight.

Strange kid. Still a mystery. But maybe that's why High Water mattered—because people like Logan needed a place to figure things out. A place to recover from whatever it was that happened in his past.

Declan finished his chores and was halfway back to his rooms when he realized he hadn't heard Logan leave. The kid had moved like a ghost, taking off without Declan being aware.

For some reason, the realization didn't sit well.

5

———

Tuesday morning at eight a.m., Sydney let herself into the clinic, prepared for anything.

"Hello, boss. Looks as if this week won't feature as much chaos and mayhem as usual," Edison Whorlen teased.

Sydney paced past the clinic's registered nurse, headed for the staff room. "Did everybody who had an appointment suddenly cancel?"

"No, but the new physician is here."

It wasn't that she'd forgotten about Lexie's arrival. Sydney expected the woman to ride shotgun for a week before taking over, which didn't make for less work.

"I did warn you she was on her way." Sydney stepped into the staff room toward the earnest blue-eyed woman in her early forties. "And by warn, I mean, hallelujah and thank God." She held out a hand. "Sydney Jeremiah. My grandfather spoke highly of you."

The woman shook her hand firmly. Her dark brown hair was pulled back into a ponytail high on her head, and the glint in her eyes said she was comfortable, even in this new setting.

"Lexie Jacobson. I'm glad to hear that. I'm excited to join the practice. The experience and the hours are much appreciated."

"It's small-town doctoring," Edison warned. "We get everything from farm accidents to helicopter parents worried about the sniffles to actual emergencies."

Lexie looked pleased. "Even better." She waited until Sydney had hung up her coat and grabbed her clinic lab jacket. "Edison has shown me around. The clinic is small, but it looks as if you have everything we need."

"For anything that requires more than nickel-and-dime surgery, we have access privileges at Diamond Valley Hospital just over an hour up the road. We'll have to make sure your credentials are added to the slate so you won't have to jump through any hoops when you're in a hurry." Sydney poured herself a cup of coffee then indicated for Lexie to take a seat at the table. "If you don't mind, I'd like to ask a few questions. Just to make sure I know your history, anything you excel at, or any areas where you're not comfortable. Edison, if you could listen in and take notes, please. Then you can be sure to brief Lexie before any patient visit in case I'm not here."

"Of course." Edison grabbed a notepad and settled to Sydney's side. "Our receptionist, Jenny, arrives just after nine. She drops her kids at school before coming in, which is why we open at nine thirty."

"We are looking for a second receptionist," Sydney admitted, "but there aren't a lot of available applicants."

"I understand. I was working at Toronto General, but I did my internship in a small community in rural Ontario."

Interesting. "My brother works at TGH."

Lexie studied the contents of her coffee cup. "I've met him. He's very talented."

Edison snickered. "Please. You're talking about the

Jeremiah family. There isn't one of them who isn't talented to the nth degree."

"Hush," Sydney mock ordered. "You start bowing to me again like I'm a deity, and I'll put you in quarantine the next time you have a date lined up with Kevin."

"Meany," Edison complained before glancing at Lexie. "Sydney delights in tormenting me regarding my blooming romance with a wonderful gentleman from one of the local ranches."

"Blooming romances are a good thing." Lexie smiled at him before turning her attention back to Sydney. "There seems to be a lot of romantically minded people in this town. My new landlady informed me there's speed dating at the local pub tonight, and she said if I was interested, she could get me an introduction to the organizer."

"Speed dating?" Sydney arched her brow. "Are you interested?"

Lexie shook her head firmly. "Right now I'd like to find out more about the clinic and what your priorities are. Your grandpa mentioned briefly that you do outreach in the community and that's where you truly shine. If it's true, I'm more than willing to focus on keeping the office moving smoothly."

Which was good news.

While Sydney hadn't liked the way her grandfather had simply up and hired someone new for the clinic, the longer she spoke with Lexie, the more she realized what a relief it would be to have extra help.

It wasn't simply the time Sydney spent out of the office. The community of Heart Falls was growing, and a rising population meant a higher percentage of accidents, illnesses, and straight-up need for healthcare.

By the time Jenny arrived to organize her desk and set up

for the first patients, Sydney felt good about Lexie being a part of the team.

Before they opened the doors, Sydney tugged Lexie aside. "Do you want to sit in with me as a physician, or would you prefer to be the physician with me as your shadow?"

"Let's jump in with both feet," Lexie said. "I'm comfortable, but it would be a good idea for you to stick around for the first few visits until the town knows I'm here and the patients aren't wild with curiosity."

"Word-of-mouth will get around pretty quickly, so we'll have you on your own in no time," Sydney promised.

True to her word, Lexie was more than competent. She was one of those doctors who was excellent at sensing when she needed to be a little bit of a kidder, and when she needed to be absolutely serious. Before noon, Sydney was introducing the patients to Lexie then leaving the room and letting her get on with the job.

It meant Sydney had time to catch up on backlogged paperwork and prescription refills.

Edison danced in out of the exam rooms as needed like usual, pausing during a break to lean in over Sydney's shoulders as she entered the complicated coding into the Provincial data bank.

"I have no idea why your grandfather thought that woman needed any kind of practice." Edison spoke quietly but with great enthusiasm. "I think we should admit we won the lottery and tell Lexie that she's a full-time Heart Falls resident. No take-backs."

"I had the same feeling," Sydney admitted. Once again it appeared her grandfather couldn't do anything the easy way. What on earth was he up to?

Although she wouldn't devote too much energy to worrying about it when the results were so strongly tilted in her favor.

By the time the day was done, Sydney had done the equivalent of three days' work, gotten compliments from some of the patients, and Lexie wore a bright, beaming smile.

The less positive sign of a great workday meant Sydney's brain had time to refocus on the problems on the personal side of her life.

Declan wanted to date her.

She'd been around the man for a full year, enjoying his thoroughness in bed. She'd also appreciated the dreams he'd shared regarding High Water and his worries at times for his brothers. He didn't up and spill all the beans like a tipped-over paint can, but he said enough that she very clearly knew what to expect.

Declan wasn't about to give up on the idea, not yet. So if she wanted to have some relief from the temptation hanging in front of her, she'd have to take matters into her own hands and do something about his single status.

Phoning him was a smarter idea than texting. No time to consider his answers.

He picked up on the second ring, which was slightly shocking. "Hey, Syd. Everything okay?"

"Everything's great. Just wanted to know if you had any plans for tonight."

He hesitated. "Not really."

"Because I was thinking about you and how you said you were ready to get back into the dating scene. They've organized speed dating at Rough Cut tonight. I thought it'd be a great opportunity for you to test the water."

Dead silence on the other end of the line.

"Declan?"

"Sorry. Got distracted there for a minute. One of our new guests has obviously never been anywhere outside of a city before. He's carrying a saddle on his head."

Now Sydney was the one distracted, trying to picture it. "Wouldn't that hurt?"

"Probably. I'd better go rescue him, but sure. I'll join you tonight at the speed dating. Do you want me to pick you up so we can go and register at the same time? That's probably the best for me. I know you're done at the clinic by five, so what time does the dating start?"

"But I wasn't going to—"

"It's probably something that I'd like you to go along for. Haven't done anything like this for a long time, and it would be good to see a friendly face in the room."

Goddamnit. The man was either the most brilliant liar or he simply didn't know what kind of knots he was tying her up in. "Sure, that makes sense. It starts at seven, so you can swing by and pick me up at six thirty."

"See you then."

As the phone clicked off, Sydney ended up staring into space, wondering what the hell had just happened.

After pulling in outside Sydney's small house on the edge of town, Declan wiped his palms on his thighs and cursed himself for creating a nightmare of a situation.

He hadn't felt nervous. Not until he'd lied to Sydney and said he was. Now all he could think about was how much of a fool he was about to make of himself, and wouldn't that just endear her to him.

Still, there was no getting around it. He was here and he had made this bed. Now he had to lie in it.

The sight of her stepping onto the porch wearing one of those old pinup model dresses in a sunshiny yellow and white made up for a ton of the nerves he'd developed since putting this in motion.

She was short, but somehow her legs looked a mile long in that frilly sundress, vanishing at mid-thigh. The neckline dipped down over the curve of her breasts and her shoulders were bare, the faintest hint of tan turning her skin a light brown.

She'd put her hair up in a half bun with little bits of it hanging on either side of her face, and he could've stared at her for hours.

He met her at the bottom of the stairs, holding out a hand. "You clean up nice, but we already knew that."

She laughed, and the sound brushed over him like a spring breeze. Fresh and clean and enticing. "You are a charmer."

"Bullshit. What I am is worried I'm gonna be so tongue-tied I'll have the women at this event running from my table screaming."

He tucked her fingers into the crook of his arm and led her toward his truck. Her fingers wiggled for a second, then she held on.

Her? Right there by his side?

Perfect.

She squeezed his arm lightly. "I spoke with the coordinator of the event. Madison, who is married to the pub owner, Ryan. I'm sure you've met him."

"Asian Canadian about five foot seven? He's a hard worker," Declan said.

"From you, that's a compliment of the highest level." She levered on his hand to climb into the truck. He appreciated the flash of bare thigh as she settled into the seat, somehow not staring. "Anyway, Maddy said they're doing this as a *modified* speed dating event. I'll tell you more in a minute."

He got them on the road. Then when she didn't start up again, he patted her on the thigh. "Modified speed dating?"

"Oh. So it turns out that dating apps are out, and speed dating and the like are making a comeback. People actually want to meet the person to know for sure that they're not getting scammed, sent crude requests, or about to be ghosted."

"Makes sense." If he had any real desire to get back into the dating world, he would never have used an app. Meeting people at a bar even seemed wrong. "Still think it was better when you found someone you had things in common with and got friendly before the dating urge hit."

Sydney eased back in her seat and twisted toward him. "Me too, but the world doesn't make that easy right now." She seemed thoughtful before lowering her voice. "How did you meet Sadie?"

Had he never told Sydney? Huh.

Then again, discussing his personal life in the past hadn't really been a part of what they did together.

"She worked at the town hall as the receptionist. She also coordinated the weekly summer Farmers' Market and Fall Fair. I was working as foreman at a local ranch, and volunteered to be the animal coordinator at the fair. We saw a lot of each other that September, and kept seeing each other after that."

"That's sweet," Sydney said. She paused then laid a hand on his. "Is it okay to talk about her?"

"Of course." Although, considering he rarely mentioned Sadie in public, it was easy to see where Sydney might've gotten the idea that the conversation was off-limits. He flipped his hand over and caught her fingers in his, squeezing lightly. "Sadie was a good woman who died too young. I'll always miss her," he admitted. "When I think about her these days, I tend to mostly focus on the good times."

The bad days were when he had nightmares where he wasn't able to save her.

"It's a rare thing to find a love like that. I'm glad you got to experience it, even though I hate that she left so young." Sydney stole her hand back. "I've lost friends young, and if screaming at the universe could change things, my throat would be raw right now. Those are the moments when I pull on my analytical side of the brain and turn off my heart so it doesn't hurt as much."

They sat in silence. "Sober thoughts as we head toward something that's supposed to be fun."

"Yeah. Sorry." She glanced over as he found a parking spot along the edge of Main Street. "Declan? Why are we doing this?" she asked, clearly confused. "I mean, I know I suggested it, but it doesn't really feel like your thing."

He didn't answer. Instead he made his way around the truck to open her door. He paused before helping her down, meeting her gaze straight on for a moment. "Humour me. I've got the feeling I'm supposed to go in there, but there's no way in hell I'm going by myself. So, what do you say?"

Sydney shrugged. "If you're sure. Let's go see what the kids are doing for kicks these days."

Declan pressed his lips together to keep from snickering. He was amused though. Almost forty years old and about to head into a speed dating event.

I hope you're getting some entertainment factor out of this, Sadie.

Inside the pub, music played quietly enough for once he could actually speak without shouting. Madison Zhao bounced up to them, and he dipped his chin politely in greeting.

Her brows winged upward. "Sydney. And *Declan*. Welcome, and I'll do my best to not let any intrusive questions escape my lips."

"Appreciate that," Sydney said with amusement. "Consider us scientists on a research trip. We will, of course, follow your rules to the letter. But both of us are just here to put out some feelers."

Thank God Sydney spoke for both of them because he didn't know what he would have said.

"Absolutely." Madison nodded firmly, her expression dead serious for a moment. "Since the dawn of arranged dating interactions, the best of them have always been clearly about entertainment, consent, and feeling at ease."

"The ease part," Declan said. "That's the thing I'm worried about."

Madison snickered. "I hear you. Which is why I've been doing a lot of research to come up with different activities rather than some of the traditional ones where one group sits at a table and one group switches every five minutes. It's never going to be completely smooth, but I'm glad you're here to give it a try. And if it the end of the night, you had a couple of good conversations and nothing else happens, that's fine as well."

She turned to the table behind her for something. Declan took advantage of the opportunity to examine their surroundings a little more thoroughly.

There were more than a dozen people in the room, including a group of women out on the floor doing some line dance moves. He recognized a few of the men from the community, and shockingly, he wasn't the oldest there. The youngest participant looked a little too young to be in the bar in the first place.

Sydney bumped his shoulder lightly with her own. "You okay?"

"Sure." For now he was, except the men in the room had noticed Sydney, and there were far too many admiring glances and outright stares in her direction.

Dammit, he'd messed up. He'd thought if she came along, he'd be able to charm her a little and make her reconsider his offer. Instead, he was going to have to watch a dozen men fall under her spell. And it wasn't as if he could deck someone for looking—right?

Which meant when Madison handed him a set of cards, he wasn't really paying attention. Instead, he was shifting through a dozen game plans of how to keep the sharks from circling Sydney all night.

"At the end of your time talking together, I'll change up the music so you will know it's time to move on. Say a quick goodbye and continue your journey around the room." Maddy finished her instructions. "Then if that person is someone you'd like to get to know better, take their name card and put it in your right pocket. Or fold it in half, or something so you know which cards to give to me at the end of the night."

"And no one receives the contact information for the other person unless both parties are interested, correct?" Sydney clarified.

"That's how it works," Madison agreed.

Good. Declan would have exactly one card to hand over.

"If you don't have any other questions, you should both grab a drink from the bar. It's included in your fee. FYI, we have a two drink limit for the night so no one gets out of hand."

Declan grabbed a beer and the orange juice and soda Sydney asked for, handing it to her where she waited at the side of the room. "Ready for this?"

She raised a brow. "Are you?"

"I guess." God help them both.

Maddy spoke up and did a quick recap, then the music started and Sydney shrugged. "Time to go socialize."

"Wait." Declan pulled out his cards and shuffled through them quickly. "May as well start by talking to each other."

She laughed. "Good idea. Let me see." She focused on her cards as he found exactly the one he was looking for.

"You go first," he offered.

Sydney held the card up in the air as if to prove the question was not her idea. "If you were an animal, which one would it be?"

Even six months ago, he might not have known the answer to this, but since asking random strange questions was one of Jinx's favorite pastimes, Declan was ready. "A barn cat."

Sydney blinked. "Really? I could've sworn you would've said horse."

"Horses are my favorite animal, but if I was going to *be* one, barn cats have it figured out. They're well fed, they get as much affection as they want, and as much alone time as they need. They're warm in the winter and cool in the summer and absolutely rule the roost."

Sydney's smile brightened her entire face. "And here you were worried you'd be tongue-tied. That was sweet and interesting. I've never thought of it like that, but you're right." She flashed him a quick thumbs-up. "What's your question for me? Time is ticking."

He raised his card as well. "Where's the one place you're the most comfortable and feel the most at home?"

"Oh. That's harder than you'd think." She got a far off look in her eyes. "To me, they're almost two different things. I'm extremely comfortable figuring what's wrong with a person's body and problem-solving how to fix them. There's a kind of Zen sensation I get when I'm doing that. But that's not where I'm the most at home."

Interesting that her thoughts went first of all to *comfortable* as it related to work. "Put the work aside," he suggested.

A hint of anger lit her eyes. "We're not getting onto that

topic again. I remember you lecturing me about working too hard, but it's something I really like doing, so don't—"

"Wasn't meant to be a lecture. Just wondering. If you didn't have any work to do, and you had no one that you wanted to go and visit just to make sure they weren't falling apart at the seams, where would you go to feel as if you didn't need to move. Didn't need to impress anyone?"

Sydney stared at him, an entire kaleidoscope of emotions swirling in her silvery eyes. "Well, shit."

It wasn't the clue he'd been hoping for, but it was somehow better. He touched her fingers gently. "Guess you just figured out a good question to research a little more."

"I guess I did."

The music changed in the background, and Madison spoke over the speakers to gently remind everyone to stroll around the room and find someone new to chat with.

Declan took a swig of his beer then twisted to place the empty bottle on the table behind him. When he turned back, Sydney was gone and three women stood in front of him, cards extended eagerly, including one girl who didn't look anywhere near legal age.

Fuck. Tonight was a bad idea coming back to kick his ass.

Declan awkwardly adjusted his hat before grabbing the nearest card that was not held by the girl.

Instinct had him glancing around the room for Sydney.

She stood five paces away from him backed against the wall. A cowboy with a handlebar mustache had his forearm to the wall above her head so he loomed over her. The stranger's gaze was firmly fixed on her breasts.

And that was a hell no. Time to change the program.

6

When people said eventually karma would catch up and pay her back for every bad deed she'd done, Sydney had always imagined it was a somewhere-down-the-road kind of deal.

But no. She was currently in one of the seven levels of hell as Mr. Mustache attempted to charm her with a story about how he had a big, fat...*wallet.*

Oh, he posed it as being the question on the card he wanted to hand her, but considering he attempted to tuck said card into her cleavage before she slapped his hand away, the man's self-preservation instincts were running dangerously low.

Across the room, Madison caught sight of the situation and hurried toward them.

Before the organizer made it even halfway, a clear masculine voice sounded in Sydney's ear.

"Hey, Syd. Got a question for you." Declan rumbled up beside Sydney, thrusting out a hand to Mr. Mustache. "Hey there, bro. Hate to interrupt, but my friend here needs to get in on this. You know how it is, looking out for your pals and all. Syd, there's a nice lady over there I want to introduce you to."

Declan's arm slipped around her back and guided her well away from her supposed current chatting partner.

When Declan stopped, Sydney was eye to eye with a woman in her late thirties who blinked in surprise.

"Oh. Hello," the woman offered.

"Lisbeth, this is my friend Sydney. I know it's completely sideways, but the card you gave me asking about my favorite food made me think of Sydney. She's good friends with one of the restaurant owners here in town."

Lisbeth still look shocked, but she politely faced Sydney. "You are?"

Sydney had the presence of mind to clue in, although she wasn't sure if Declan had come to her rescue or if she was coming to his. "Yes. Are you new in town? Have you heard of Buns and Roses?"

"I saw it, but I wasn't sure what it's all about."

"You'll love it. Casual, but super tasty."

Declan stayed silent as Sydney and Lisbeth chatted, a muscular wall of protection as he stood guard beside them and nodded when appropriate.

Across the room, Slimy Mustache Dude glared daggers but wisely chose to head to the bar to grab his second drink instead of coming over to make a fuss.

When the music changed up again, Sydney rolled with the punches and took the out while it was available. She caught Declan by the arm. "Change of plans. You ready to leave?"

"Fifteen minutes ago," he muttered, striding after her toward the door.

Maddy spotted them but simply shrugged. Sydney made a mental note to stop in and have a talk with the young woman in the week to come.

They hadn't meant to mess up the social event. Sydney would find a way to make up for their faux pas.

Barely out the door, Declan's arm slipped around her waist and attached her to his side. "You have somewhere in mind?"

"Out of there," she admitted. "Want to go for a drive?"

Because she was far too wired up to go home and try to sleep.

He helped her into his truck. Silence enveloped them, peaceful and content. Never awkward, never making her feel as if she had to work hard to fill space with noise.

Instead, she stared into the sky as the few clouds drifted slowly, the edges beginning to be painted with the promise of sunset. Speed dating had been hugely awkward. She was grateful that Declan had been there, and not just to rescue her ass.

Unbidden, an idea popped to mind. Down the road, when she could consider dating, she'd want it to be with someone like him.

The tentatively hopeful thought was immediately followed by a rush of terror shooting ice up her spine.

Okay. That was clear enough.

She leaned her forehead against the window and mindlessly watched fence posts flick by like dominoes waiting to fall.

The truck came to a stop, and she struggled out of her hypnotic state. "Where are we?"

"Somewhere we can enjoy the smart portions of this evening and not have to deal with the bullshit."

Next thing she knew, Declan had opened her door and was offering a hand. He guided her to the dropped tailgate, and she didn't protest as he lifted her up into the back of the truck.

Laughter escaped. "Declan Skye, you sly devil. When did you do this?"

She certainly hadn't noticed on the ride into town. The truck bed had a thick camping mattress on the base and pillows strategically placed to create a backrest.

He seemed pleased to have surprised her. "You came straight to the truck and hopped in. It's been there all night."

Sydney kicked off her shoes and wiggled into a comfortable position. She patted the spot beside her. "Time to explain your cryptic comment. What are the smart things we'll keep enjoying?"

"I don't have to explain what kind of bullshit we don't need to put up with?"

Yeah, no. "What's this?" she asked as she took the whatever it was he handed her. Turned out it was one of the cards that Madison had given them. "You still want to do the cards?"

He left his boots by the tailgate and settled his bulk beside her, moving a few pillows into better positions. "The entire evening wasn't a terrible idea. I just think there were some people there that were up past their bedtime or needed to check their manners."

"Thank you for not giving any etiquette lessons, no matter how much they deserved it." Sydney turned her attention to the card in front of her, pulling the ones out of her pocket as well. "Very well, let's have some meet-and-greet practice."

"Fuck that. Let's just get to know each other better."

He sounded as if he'd had enough, and she didn't blame him.

Out of all the Skye brothers, Declan was the one who kept the most to himself. Walking into a setting with all those strangers must've been pretty overwhelming. "Sounds good to me. First question from me. Out of all the official holidays, which one do you like the most, and which one would you toss out the window?"

"I like Thanksgiving." Instant response, firm and solid.

"Not so much because of the historic reasons, but it's gotten to be more meaningful the older I've gotten. It's important to be grateful and give thanks for the things we have while we have them. We never know how long we have with people, so the reminder to actually say we love them—it's a lesson I really learned."

God. She could relate to that. Both the fact that people could be gone in an instant and appreciating them while they were there. "I intensely dislike Valentine's Day," Sydney informed him. "Sharing we care about friends is important, but not because there's a capitalistic, Hallmark-created holiday. I wish it would vanish."

Declan look thoughtful. "Sadie loved all holidays. but she thought like you that it wasn't about what you could buy. She took a great deal of delight in making things. She wasn't good at all of it, but the gifts were always put together with love."

He'd mentioned Sadie more than he had in the entire year she'd known him. "People like that are special. I adore how Petra is constantly looking for the perfect candle. Or how Tansy knows each of our favorite treats, and they magically appear on the days we're feeling shitty."

"I get a kick out of how Tansy gets revenge when you do something to piss her off." Declan brushed his thumb over the back of Sydney's knuckles, and she suddenly realized they were holding hands. "Jake said something about the proper way to make lasagna, and to this day she deliberately mucks it up. It's still tasty as hell, and I could eat a pound of it by myself, but it was something stupid about the layers of cottage cheese instead of ricotta or hell if I know what. She puts the dish on the table and watches him gobble it down, and then she grins because she made it wrong and he loves it."

"Tansy is a bright star in our universe," Sydney said seriously.

Declan eased back on the pillows, his fingers stroking up her arm and over her shoulder to pull her shoulder strap back into place. "I've never seen that dress before. It's pretty."

His fingers traveled up farther. Stroking her neck, across her cheek. He traced his thumb over her lips, gaze fixed firmly on her, following every touch, every caress.

When he slid his hand to the back of her head and tilted her face upward to him, she followed his lead. She leaned into his kiss, curled herself up against him. Rested one hand on his chest where the beat of his heart thumped against her palm.

The kiss deepened, and Sydney gave in. She offered herself up to his control, to the tease of his tongue against hers. When he pulled her across his body, she let her thighs fall open so he rested intimately between her legs.

Kisses teased down her neck, followed by the straps of her dress being pushed aside. Declan nipped along her collarbone, down to the front of her bra to the exposed hollow between her breasts.

"Tell me you want me," Declan whispered urgently.

"Yes. I need you."

He pushed off her bra straps, exposed her breasts, and then his mouth was on her. Nipping, teasing, sucking until she squirmed. She drove her fingers into his hair and tugged him from one side to the other whenever the ache became unbearable.

A series of curses escaped her lips as he slid under her, tossing the layers of her skirt aside and hauling her forward until his mouth landed on her pantie-covered sex.

"Declan." She moaned as he jerked aside the gusset and swiped his tongue between her folds, landing unerringly on her clit. With both his hands clasped on her ass, she couldn't move. Not that she wanted to, trapped in place by pleasure and the promise of a mind-blowing orgasm.

Cool air swirled over her naked torso, and she cupped her breasts, pinching her own nipples as Declan did his best to drive her wild. He speared his tongue deep, then slid a hand under the layers of her skirt to rub her clit with raw determination.

Release hovered, but the need to give to this incredible man made her push herself off him enough to twirl and undo the button on his jeans.

"I was having fun," Declan complained.

"You're about to have more fun," she countered.

It was the work of a minute to get him to shove his jeans and briefs far enough down to release his cock. It snapped upright, eager and ready.

Sydney pulled a condom from her pocket and rolled it on him, grinning as Declan's curses became more creative than coherent.

"You better plan on hopping on my cock right here and now, or I'll flip you over and fuck you boneless."

"Promises, promises," Sydney gasped as she straddled him. She notched the head of his cock between her folds and slowly sank down, pleasure rippling up her spine.

The tingles that had begun when he kissed her leveled up again. Sydney undulated over him in a slow, even rhythm, his fingers digging into her butt cheeks as he allowed her to be in charge. But the heated light in his eyes and the tension building in his body said she wouldn't get to play for much longer.

Fabric bunched around her waist, untidy and unkempt, but from the pleased look in his eyes, he was into it.

She reached between her legs to rub her clit, and Declan picked up the pace. The grip on her hips elevated her far enough that he could thrust his cock deep and hard on each rock, shooting the air from her lungs in the best possible way. She wanted it all, wanted it hard and dirty.

Declan flashed his barely there smile, his eyes burning intently—

"You like this," he said quietly. "Naked from the waist up here in the outdoors. Those pretty tits bouncing for me. My cock fucking into you so you feel it everywhere. You taking what I give you so sweetly. You need this, need me to show you how to let go."

"Yes," Sydney whispered. "So close."

"Let me have it." Declan slowed his thrusts but held her so immobile that it seemed every drive went deeper than the one before. "Give it to me. Squeeze my cock so hard it feels like you'll never let go."

She broke. The rush of pleasure didn't come in a wave, but an absolute cascade that hit her hard enough she lost control of her muscles and collapsed on top of him. He held them locked together, and with every continuing pulse of her sex around him, she felt it so deeply it triggered another set of aftershocks.

It was pleasure, yes, but also connection, and she glowed inside at being known well enough by this man that he could play her body like a Stratovarius.

A minute later? An hour? Sydney wasn't sure when it was, but Declan rolled her back onto the cushions and delicately draped a cozy blanket over her before he dealt with the condom.

Then he was back, pulling her into his arms and holding her as the sunset bloomed then faded and the stars popped out overhead.

When he dropped her off at the house in full darkness, she gave him a quick kiss on the cheek and headed inside.

That's when she realized that for the last hour or more, neither one of them had spoken.

It didn't feel as if they had to.

THE NEXT DAYS PASSED QUICKLY, which was a relief. Busy hands meant Declan's mind was far too occupied to worry about making the right decision when it came to convincing Sydney to give them a chance.

Because he was very firmly of the opinion they already *were* a thing. Not what he wanted them to be, but somewhere on the journey to it.

She was still skittish.

No way in hell he'd be stupid enough to relate her directly to a horse in real life, at least not where she could hear, yet the same principles were involved. Don't go too fast, don't introduce new elements too quickly.

Whether Sydney liked it or not, they already had a solid base. Sex wasn't enough to sustain a relationship, but it was a fine starting place. If it took him keeping her in bed until she realized she never wanted him to leave, he could handle that.

Jinx came home from horse camp on Sunday, absolutely thrilled with how much she'd improved. She phoned to let him know she was back but was staying for supper with the Stone family. "If that's okay?"

"It's fine with me. Did you mention this to Petra or Aiden?"

She hesitated for a second. "I did, and they approved, but I kind of felt like I should ask you, too."

Declan knew about the plans to make Jinx officially part of Aiden and Petra's family, and if this wasn't a clear sign that it was time to clarify things, he didn't know what was.

Still, for now, he followed along like usual. "It's okay with me. Call when you want to come home and I'll pick you up. I wouldn't mind saying hi to Sasha's parents."

"Got it. Bring Dixie? I've missed her. *Love-you-Deck-bye.*"

The last four words came out as a smeared blur, but they lit something inside him big and bright.

The next second fear rolled in again. If anything happened to that girl, he would never forgive himself.

They needed to make changes around High Water because they all had too much to lose, and it wasn't fair to any of them to have their loved ones at risk.

It was a small gathering at the family table that night. Jake had taken the ranch hands to work on their roping skills. Tansy went to visit her sister Ivy so Jeffrey could spend time with his three cousins.

Petra and Aiden held hands under the table and pretended they weren't.

Kevin arched a brow, the scarred slice on the side of his face turning his amusement into a very pirate-y expression. "You do know we can see you, yes?"

"How's your boyfriend?" Aiden returned, trying to divert attention. "Isn't it time we officially met him?"

"Agreed," Declan said as he scooped up a serving of the roast chicken and potatoes that had been cooking in the slow cooker all day. Tansy was back in charge of the kitchen, and they were not starving. "I think you should invite him over."

Leaning back in his chair, Kevin folded his arms over his chest and put on his stubborn face. "How come all of a sudden I'm the one in the hot seat?"

"You're the psychiatrist; you tell us," Petra teased.

"That doesn't mean I can read minds," Kevin reminded them.

"Means you know better than most when people are avoiding things they should do, though." Declan lowered his head and looked straight at his brother. "For example, there's a conversation that needs to happen with a certain teenager. I think you should do it soon."

Petra shivered, hope in her eyes. "You don't think it's too soon?"

"No." Declan turned his gaze on Kevin. "Invite Edison over this coming week. Anytime I've met him, he's been like a big puppy dog. He'll be good for you. We'd like to welcome him."

"You don't think it's too soon?" Kevin winked at Petra as he echoed her concern.

"No."

Aiden snickered. "And you, big brother? What's the thing that you're procrastinating from doing—"

Declan's phone rang, which was such a rare occurrence they all started in surprise. He ignored Aiden's question and thumbed the call on. "Jinx?"

Her shaky voice rang out on speaker. "Deck, Tyler's hurt. We took him up to the loft after supper because he wanted to show us something and he fell down some weird shaft."

"Do his parents know?" Declan shot to his feet and headed for the door with Aiden and Petra hard on his heels. Dixie whined, pacing nervously as she looked around expectantly for Jinx.

"Yeah. And I called Sydney on the direct number she gave me, and she's on her way. I'm scared."

"We're coming over. You stay with Sasha and we'll be right there."

He didn't tell her it would be all right because there were no guarantees.

And wasn't that the most pessimistic, cold-hearted thought?

Somehow Sydney beat them to Silver Stone. By the time Declan, Petra, and Aiden followed the ranch hand waiting for them into the barn, it was clear things had gone very wrong.

Caleb was searching along a wooden wall below the loft. Tyler's crying could be clearly heard through the wood, but there was no sign of him.

"What the hell?" Aiden leaned his ear to the wall. "Service shaft?"

"Something like that." Caleb dragged a hand through his hair in frustration. "But not one that I ever knew about, and it's not on the blueprints."

"We can tear the wall down," Declan offered.

"We started to, and he screamed louder. Says there's a stick that stings him when we move anything on this side."

Stings? The hell?

"Caleb, we have an idea." Tamara Stone stood at the top of the stairs, her face ghastly white. "Sydney says she's going to him."

Christ. Declan raced up the stairs on Caleb's heels.

A small gathering huddled at the top. Caleb's brother Luke was there as well as Jinx and Sasha. The girls sat to the side, arms around each other as they rested out of the way on a haybale. Petra hurried to them, and the girls grabbed her tight as she curled her arms around them both. Dixie shoved her nose into the middle of the huddle, offering worried kisses.

Sydney was methodically tying a rope onto the handle of the medical kit she carried with her. "Once I see what's happening down there, if possible, I'll give the go ahead for the guys to rip a path straight to us. If not, I'll immobilize Tyler as necessary and you'll have to bring him up this way."

"You're going down now?" Declan asked the instant he got close enough to speak without shouting.

She glanced his way and stepped closer, then shocked the hell out of him by calmly undoing his belt buckle and stripping it from his belt loops while she spoke. "The EMTs are at least fifteen minutes out, and I'm here. I'm the only one with the necessary training *and* small enough to fit. I'm sorry, Tamara. I look forward to having your assistance once we're no longer dealing with an enclosed space."

Declan stole the belt from her fingers as soon as he figured out what she was doing. "Let me." He quickly used another rope to create two loops for her legs and a higher chest section to control her vertical position. "Modified climbing harness. We've used it in emergency situations before. It'll hold."

He held it for her and she stepped in without any hesitation, waiting quietly as he cinched it tight. Without taking too long, he double-checked the knots were bomb-proof, because while she needed to do this, she also needed to be safe.

Caleb looked up from where he been calling reassurances down the shaft to Tyler. "You ready?" he asked her as Aiden came forward to take the flashlight from his hands to free him up to move.

Sydney nodded. "I'll go down, figure out what we need to do next. I'll call for the bag if necessary."

Declan couldn't stop himself. He caught her by the wrist and held her still for a moment. Every bit of his heart was in his throat. "Be careful."

"I will." She stared right back, letting him see her fear and her determination.

He nodded. She had this, and he'd have her back.

Then she was off, hurrying to the edge of the shaft and sitting with her legs dangling. "Hey Tyler, It's Dr. Jeremiah. Jinx's friend. I'm coming down to see you."

The announcement was greeted by a wail and a sob and a long drawn out, "*Mommmmy*."

Tamara let out a sob then buried her face against Caleb's chest.

The fear in the man's eyes as he met Declan's gaze—it was the hopelessness of knowing a precious life hung in the balance.

"We've got this." Declan pushed aside all his own doubts and fears and offered up a rock-solid faith in a miracle. If he willed it to be true, that might give Caleb the power to believe it as well. "We won't let him down."

Luke Stone stepped forward to grab Sydney's rope, but Declan took it from him. He looped it around his back then handed the end to Luke. "I'll control her descent. You act as anchor."

"Got it."

She didn't do anything fancy like a rock-climber stepping off a cliff. Sydney scooted forward until he had the slack between them removed and the rope took her weight.

"I'm coming down now, Tyler. There might be some dust that falls, so squeeze your eyes shut."

"M-m-my arm." It came out between teary gasps.

"Then don't move it. Don't move at all. They're going to lower me a little bit more. It's really skinny in here. Aiden, shine that light a bit more to the right. That's it. I can see you now, Tyler. I'm just above you. Declan, stop."

He braced and kept the rope motionless, Luke steady at his back.

Tamara wiped her eyes then took a deep breath. She squeezed Caleb's hand then moved so she could peer into the shaft. "You listen to Dr. Jeremiah, okay, big guy? You're my brave boy."

Sydney cleared her throat. "Change of plans. We need another harness so we can bring Tyler up. That'll be the smoothest journey."

Which meant something was really wrong down there and she didn't want to say it where the kid could hear.

"Can we take the wall down?" Caleb asked hopefully.

"No. Don't think that's a good idea. Tyler, can you turn your head toward me, please? That's the way. Yeah, your left arm is probably hurting. You don't need to move it, just look at me."

And then she started calling out words like dilation and numbers that made Tamara nod. Declan kept his attention on holding Sydney steady in position. The rope between them vanished into darkness, but her weight remained a steady assurance she was there, just out of sight.

Caleb had his belt off in an instant, knotting the rope from the medical bag firmly onto it, ready to feed it down the shaft. "Belt coming."

"Great. Listen for when I tell you to slow down—slow, slow, and stop."

Tyler's crying continued, but he was mostly sniffling between ragged bursts. "I want my mommy."

"Got it, kiddo. I'll get you ready to zip up to your mom and dad, okay? You ever get knocked over when you play with your friends?"

"Yeah."

"In a minute, when I say now, it might feel like somebody really big knocks you over. Just so you're expecting it. And if you want, you get to say a really bad word, just this once. You want to know what it is?"

Sniffles followed. A few more whimpers. "Yeah."

A hushed whisper rose, then a childish shout of pain.

"Don't worry up there, that's me putting the belt on him." Sydney spoke over Tyler's continued crying. "You're okay, Tyler. Your daddy is going to lift you the tiniest bit. Slowly, Caleb. More, more. *There.* You've got his whole weight. Lift him up. Go ahead and say the magic word, Tyler."

"Ro-o-o-to-ba-gaaaaaa."

While Tyler sobbed and shouted nonsense, Sydney controlled his ascent with calmly given orders.

As Tyler's dark head popped into view, Sydney called from below. "Tamara. Possible dislocation of the left glenohumeral joint. He's guarding the limb and in significant pain. Noninvasive abrasions to his legs."

"Got it. I'll stabilize until the EMTs get here and we can head to the hospital." Tamara's voice trembled just enough to betray the mother beneath the nurse as she swooped in and lifted Tyler out of the way. She and Caleb hurried to the side where she put their son on a hay bale to examine him.

What had been the distant sound of a siren was distinctly closer now, and Aiden headed off to meet and guide the paramedics to the loft.

"Ready to come up, Syd?" Declan asked.

"Slower than Tyler, please. I'm not as small as him, and there are some interesting nails to avoid."

Shit. "Tell me to stop anytime."

Declan lifted hand over hand, the journey seeming to take forever. But then her head appeared, and she held out a hand.

Caleb was waiting. He caught her wrist and lifted her the rest of the way out before enveloping her in a bear hug. "Thank God you were here."

She patted his back, meeting Declan's eye over his shoulder. "Glad I could help. Now you've got an interesting mystery to deal with."

Caleb let her go, and she held out a hand for the flashlight. She shone it downward into the hole.

Stepping to her side, Declan wrapped an arm around her waist even as he peered into the shaft at what seemed to be shimmering diamonds. "What is that?"

"Glass. Whatever this was before, someone tossed a ton of rubble down the shaft before they sealed it. Including windows in their metal frames. Most of them broke at least a couple times. That's not the worst part, though, nor the nails that go straight through the walls into the space." She clicked off the light and the area below them continued to glow, small bright lights flashing every now and then.

Caleb's face went white. "Are those *electrical* shorts?"

"Think so," Sydney confirmed. "Between the metal frames on the windows, and the electricity with an unknown source, taking down the wall was a game of Russian roulette. You need to turn off the power in this part of the building and be prepared before you break down the wall. Tyler was lucky he got caught on a small ledge on the way down instead of hitting the bottom of the shaft."

And Sydney was lucky she hadn't gone down to rescue the boy and ended up dead.

Declan caught her by the wrist, forcing calm into his words. "You okay?"

"I'm fine."

Still, he examined her hands and arms, checking she hadn't been hurt and was ignoring an injury to be brave. Only once he was satisfied did he pull her to his body, holding her close as his heart raced a million miles an hour.

The conversation at the dinner table drifted in his mind unbidden. What had *he* been holding back on? Making them a reality.

Screw being patient, it was time for this to happen. The idea of losing another person he cared about still scared the hell out of him, but not being with her?

It was like being dead when he didn't have to be.

Between one breath and the next, everyone moved. The paramedics arrived and prepped Tyler to head to the hospital. Sydney volunteered to go with Tamara and Caleb. Petra and Aiden guided Jinx and Sasha out, and suddenly only Luke remained, eyeing Declan closely, the hired hand at his side swaying uneasily as if he'd rather be anywhere else.

"Everything okay? Want help taking care of the wall situation?" Declan asked.

"Thanks, but first, Raj here wanted to speak with you," Luke said quietly. "I think you need to hear this."

7

———

*R*aj took his time glancing around as if making sure no one could overhear them before shoving both hands deep in his pockets and fixing his gaze on a spot to the right of Declan's shoulder. "I didn't want to say anything if I'm wrong and get an innocent man in trouble, but if I'm right, you need to know."

"I won't condemn anyone without solid proof, so go ahead."

The man fidgeted uneasily until Luke placed a hand on his shoulder.

Raj dipped his chin in a determined nod. "That young hand you've got working for you—Logan. I met him last week at horse camp. Seems nice enough. Steady worker. But he reminded me of someone..."

He hesitated for long enough Luke gave him another nudge. "Go on," he encouraged.

"Before I came to Silver Stone, I worked at a boarding stable outside Calgary. Lots of high-class people kept animals there. Some not-so-high-class, but they had money. One was a lawyer type who got in trouble—turned out he was helping keep gang members out of prison."

"How does that connect to Logan?" Declan asked.

"When the guy got arrested, investigators came by with pictures. Wanted to know if we'd seen any of the gang members hanging around. Trying to make connections, I guess." Raj glanced briefly at Luke, then back to Declan. "Your ranch hand was one of the faces they showed me. I'm pretty sure. But it was nearly a year ago, so I could be wrong."

Christ. They'd suspected Logan had a rough past—the kid showed up at High Water nearly beaten to death. "I'm glad you said something. I'll get to the bottom of it. But he won't be in trouble unless he's guilty of something. That's a promise."

Raj exhaled in relief. "Good. He's a decent kid. I'd hate to see him in trouble. I ran into him when he was warning off a couple of the older campers who were sniffing around Sasha and Jinx."

"What?" Luke's voice sharpened. "I never heard about this."

"Because nothing happened. The girls weren't in danger. Logan made sure of it—told the guys if they stepped out of line they'd answer to him. Kid's small, but wiry. I wouldn't want to scrap with him."

"Thanks for sharing that." Declan offered his hand and gave Raj a firm shake. He turned to Luke, because as much as he wanted to head home and ask Logan what the hell was going on, this had to come first. "Now let's turn off the power to this section of the barn and deal with your problem."

He didn't stick around too long. Just long enough to help open the wall and discover the disaster that lay beyond—wires snaking from a dozen directions, broken glass everywhere, and what looked suspiciously like felt lining.

The Silver Stone foreman was now on the scene, and he

swore softly. "I'm not positive," Tucker said grimly, "but that could be asbestos." The foreman took in the group of helpers who had gathered. "That's it for today. We tarp and seal the opening until we can get an inspector out. Power stays off. If you're working in this part of the barn, get used to using a headlamp."

Luke patted Declan's back as he spoke quietly. "Thanks again for all your help. And you know we've got your back if this thing with your ranch hand needs handling."

"You're good neighbours," Declan replied. "I'll let you know. But I don't think it'll come to that."

Except he fully intended to have a conversation with Logan. Immediately.

When he got home, Dixie stood outside the stall where Jinx was brushing down Rainbow. Logan was cleaning the neighbouring stall.

Dixie's tail wagged as Declan approached, her world finally in order with Jinx's return.

Jinx dropped the brush and ran to Declan to offer a big hug. "I got a text from Sasha. Tyler's okay. They put his shoulder back in place. He has to wear a sling, but he'll be fine."

Declan hugged her back. "Good to hear. You and Sasha acted fast. I'm proud of you."

Her mood shifted in an instant, and she sniffled. "He wouldn't have gotten hurt in the first place if we hadn't taken him up there—"

"That's a load of horse hockey." Declan's tone sharpened. "How many times do you think he's been up there before? Or Sasha? Or her sister Emma? That shaft's been hidden long enough that Caleb might've even been a little tyke messing around with that disaster waiting the entire time."

Her eyes widened. "Really?"

"I'm not glad Tyler got hurt, but I'm damn glad someone

found that shaft. If that wiring had sparked the wrong way? Could've taken out the entire barn faster than anyone could react."

She stared at him, visibly shaken. He debated sugar-coating it—but decided against it.

"Every old building's got funky wiring somewhere. If you're lucky, it's near an edge. But that shaft was dead center. Would've been like a bomb going off in the middle of the barn. But it's found now and they can fix it. Tyler's young. He'll bounce back like a spring colt."

Jinx eyed him with suspicion. "Is this what's called finding the silver lining?"

He snorted. "Pretty much."

She patted Rainbow. "Had too much energy after we got back, but I think I can go to bed now."

Logan's lean frame disappeared into the tack room. Perfect.

Declan cleared his throat. "Before you go, I need to ask you something."

Jinx closed Rainbow's stall and turned to him. "What?"

"Stay away from Logan for a little while."

She blinked. "Why?"

"Just for now. While I figure some things out."

A flush touched her cheeks. "That makes no sense."

"Sometimes things don't," Declan admitted. "But I want you to stay safe."

"Logan would never hurt me." Her voice cracked. She glanced toward the tack room, concern written all over her.

"Never said he would," Declan replied softly. "Promise me anyway?"

She hesitated then straightened her spine. "Fine. But I trust him. And I want to know what's going on. Soon."

"You will."

She left without giving him another hug, which was how Declan knew he was in deep shit.

He made his way to the tack room. Time to get this over with.

Logan looked up as Declan entered. "Everything okay over at Silver Stone?"

"Got work to do, but they're all safe." Declan leaned casually against the doorframe. "How'd things go at horse camp?"

Logan dropped a bundle of halters then scrambled to pick them up. "Good. Really good. Girls did well. I think Jinx could be a solid cowboy... if she wants to be."

"I heard there was some trouble. You handled it?"

Logan froze. "You had someone watching me?"

"If I did, they said you did the right thing. I'm here to say thanks."

The young man blinked in surprise at what must have felt like a ninety degree turn. "It was mostly bullshit guy stuff, but I didn't want to take a chance."

"Bullshit guy stuff sometimes turns nasty, so I'm glad you acted."

"Hell, yeah." Logan made a face. "I didn't tell the girls. First because they were safe, but mostly because knowing about it would creep them out, and I didn't want them to have that kind of memory messing up what was otherwise a really good time."

Declan nodded. "Makes sense. I won't tell Jinx either."

Logan visibly relaxed and returned to straightening tack.

Declan considered the best approach. "You've been here a while, and we can all see you're doing your best to fit in. We don't demand everyone's background at High Water. That's part of how we help people move forward."

Logan tensed.

"But I need you to think long and hard about anything in your past that might come back to bite us. Anything that could blow up in our faces, like that shaft at Silver Stone. We caught that in time. But an innocent kid still got hurt." Declan spoke clear and sharp, gaze fixed on Logan's white face. "You don't want to be the reason someone like Jinx gets hurt."

Logan didn't move, didn't say anything.

Declan turned on his heel and walked away. Sometimes you had to light the fuse and let it burn for a while. He had a gut feeling Logan would be ready to unpack that baggage pretty damn quick.

SYDNEY GOT BACK from the hospital late Sunday night after being pulled in to help with a few emergencies.

After a Monday spent catching up on everything she'd been putting off for a week, Sydney was more than ready for company by the time she arrived at the clinic Tuesday morning.

Lexie had beat her to the clinic, the older woman efficiently lining up the days' health charts, although she did look up with a smile when Sydney walked in the door. "There she is. Our cliffhanging wonder."

"Hopefully I'll be yesterday's news by the end of the week when something else more interesting turns up. You know, like a sale on ground beef at Independent Grocers." Sydney pulled on her lab coat. "How did things go yesterday?"

"First day with the new hours? It was smooth," Lexie said before laughing. "It was repetitive."

"My goodness, you can say that again," Edison announced as he slipped in the door and overheard the last bit. "Where is Dr. Jeremiah? I thought I'd be seeing Dr. Jeremiah. Dr. Jeremiah told me I needed to speak to her as soon as possible."

"Nonsense. You're exaggerating." Sydney smiled as he made his usual air dance across the reception area toward the staff room. "I'm sure at least one of them called me *the General.*"

That got a laugh out of Lexie. "No one straight up said it, but I did have somebody tell me that they got marching orders from you, and they were following them to the letter."

"Mr. Simms, yes?"

Lexie's brows shot skyward.

"He refused to take the meds he needs for his high blood pressure, so I challenged him to a game of *Battleship.* If I won, he took his meds. If he won, I had to tell his wife he was allowed to have steak once a week."

"Oh my." Edison covered his mouth with his fingers. "Good thing you won."

"Of course I won. I cheated," Sydney deadpanned before dancing out of reach of his flickering fingers. "Okay, let's figure out what's happening this morning, because if everything goes well, I thought I'd do some house calls this afternoon."

They worked together smoothly, but in the few minutes when they interacted, Sydney sensed something wasn't quite right with Lexie. A tiredness lingered in her eyes that hadn't been there the week before.

"How are things, really?" Sydney checked when they paused in the quiet of the noontime shut down.

Lexie answered quickly. "With the job? Everything is great."

"I meant with you."

The woman hesitated. "Just feeling a little homesick over the move, I suppose."

Which made sense, but didn't seem as if that was the whole story. Sydney laid a brief hand on Lexie's arm. "If there's anything I can do to help, let me know. I appreciate the work you're doing, and I'd like for you to enjoy it enough here to want to stay."

"Thanks. I'll be fine." Lexie assured her. "Where are you headed this afternoon?"

"Hutterite colony south of town to start. The ladies are really good about coming in and keeping themselves and the children up-to-date, but some of the elders keep trying to pull a fast one and skip their checkups."

Lexie nodded. "That should be fun and diplomatically challenging. Oh, another thing. Someone mentioned that the grapevine is buzzing about Rodney Greenlee. He hasn't been seen at the coffee shop for over a week."

"That isn't like him," Sydney said, dipping her chin slowly. "Thanks for letting me know. I'll swing by his place before I head back to town."

She headed out, thoughts lingering on Lexie's discomfort.

It wasn't just homesickness. Something darker had flickered in her eyes. Sydney made a mental note to check in with her again in the next couple of days.

After nearly three hours of checkups at the colony, it was close to five by the time Sydney turned down the gravel road toward Rodney Greenlee's homestead. The house, neatly tucked into a dip where the foothills met the Rockies, was usually immaculate—like everything in the old bachelor's life.

So when she spotted the front door swinging in the breeze, unease prickled her spine.

She parked beside his truck and cautiously mounted the porch. "Mr. Greenlee? It's Sydney. I came by for a visit."

Silence.

The usual cacophony of barking from his three dogs was noticeably absent. Her frown deepened as she nudged the door open further. Inside, the house was a mess. Half-eaten plates of food, spilled drinks, clutter strewn across the living room—an unsettling contrast to the man's normally meticulous habits.

No sign of Rodney inside.

She made her way toward the barn, circling around the side where the firewood was stacked. A faint rustling drew her attention. In the distance, she caught the crunch of tires on gravel—someone else pulling in—but her focus locked on the source of the sound ahead.

Another rustle was followed by a low mutter. She slowed, instincts prickling.

"Mr. Greenlee? Hello? You've got a visitor." She rounded the corner and froze.

Rodney stood ten feet away, shotgun raised, hands shaking as badly as his voice. "You can't have it."

Sydney instinctively stepped back, her voice calm but firm. "Mr. Greenlee—it's Dr. Sydney Jeremiah. We've met before, remember? I'm not here to take anything from you."

"Stop. Stop right now." His grip tightened, the muzzle of the shotgun dipping and lifting erratically.

Her brain raced. Drop to the ground or throw herself around the edge of the building? If she had a couple more inches, she could—

"Hey there." Declan's voice rolled in like gravel and thunder.

He stepped calmly into view behind her, hands loose at his sides, body angled just enough to draw Rodney's attention. "Declan Skye. Remember me? I run the animal shelter in town."

As Rodney turned slightly, tracking Declan, Sydney didn't wait. She ducked backward, darting around the side of the barn, breath shallow, heart pounding.

"That's a fine piece you've got there, Rodney. You use that for elk hunting?" Declan kept talking behind her, his voice fading as she ran. "That's a beauty. But I don't think you need it right now. It's only me. Just wanted to check in."

Sydney raced around the barn, praying that whatever was wrong with Rodney he didn't shoot Declan outright before she could act.

She fumbled in her pocket, fingers closing around the emergency syringe she always carried but hoped never to use. It wasn't standard issue, but some of the situations she stepped in were dangerous. A girl had to have a backup plan.

When she crept around the far edge of the barn, Declan and Rodney remained in a standoff. Rodney's back now faced her, and the gun had dropped slightly but was still in his hands.

Declan glanced at her so briefly it was a blink. He lifted a finger subtly. *Wait.*

She held up the auto-injector, thumbed off the safety cover, and let Declan see it before she inched closer.

"That sounds frightening," Declan continued to Rodney soothingly. "Sometimes a man's got to protect what's his. But you know, since it's just you and me here, you can probably put that away."

"Don't know." Rodney's gaze darted to the side. The gun lifted again.

Sydney launched forward. She plunged the syringe into Rodney's shoulder, and he jerked.

A wild scream rang as the gun fired, dirt spraying upward— but the sedative worked fast, and Rodney was close to collapsing even as Declan tackled him to the ground.

"Jesus," Sydney gasped.

Declan rolled to his knees, breath tight. "You okay?"

"I'm fine. I've never seen him like this before."

Rodney was well and truly out, the sedative having done its work. Declan hauled him into a fireman's carry and brought him inside, settling him on the bed.

He stepped away for the few minutes it took for Sydney to check Rodney over. "High fever. That's the cause of the delirium. We need to get him to town, stat."

"Edison's on his way." Declan shoved his phone into his pocket.

She paused in the middle of straightening the bedsheets. "What? Why?"

Declan folded his arms over his chest, tension radiating from his big frame. "Because when I saw where you were headed, I decided I should have a little more information. I called the clinic. Edison told me about your emergency knockout trick to use if things go south. And then Edison told me that if you *did* have to use your syringe, the last place you want to end up is explaining it down at the hospital."

It wouldn't be pleasant to explain, but Sydney considered the risk worth the increase in safety.

"So, you used the drugs, and I called the office. Edison offered to babysit your pin cushion until he recovers. Which means if Rodney is running a fever, he'll have a nurse. And if he's sick enough to need the hospital, Edison will haul his ass down there tomorrow."

She couldn't argue from a medical point of view, but the fact Declan had made those decisions without asking her—

None of it made sense. Inside, an uncomfortable sensation tangled her guts. The echo of past decisions made on her behalf for her "own good."

First, though, how had he known to show up when he did? Suspicion rose.

"What are *you* doing here?" Sydney demanded.

"Saving your ass," Declan snapped. "I'm gonna go clean up that disaster zone I just saw so Edison doesn't have to deal with it."

He walked out before she could say another word.

Edison showed up so soon afterward, he had either left the instant Declan talked to him or had driven like a mad man. Probably both.

He paused in the doorway, clicking his tongue as he examined the shivering body in the bed. "Please tell me Mr. Greenlee was talking about little blue men or something equally outrageous before you took him down like a rabid animal."

"He pulled a gun," she admitted with a sigh.

"Oh, sweetie. No." Edison winced. "Well, that would explain the very rigid shoulders on Mr. Big and Broody out there. Just remember, you're safe, he's safe, and after you two work out whatever is messing with your brains, I really want that still to be true."

A little of her fury faded. "You okay here by yourself?"

"Kevin is joining me," Edison assured her. "From the looks of Mr. Greenlee, I think the fever will knock him out of commission for a little while longer. He won't be doing any more Elmer Fudd imitations today."

"Thanks for this." Sydney accepted the hug Edison offered.

"You bet. Now go home."

She paced into the main cabin slowly, but there was no sign of Declan. Clean dishes were stacked in the drying rack, and the living room had been put back to rights.

His truck was gone. Asshole. Just like him to leave when she wanted to give him a piece of her mind.

She drove home feeling equal parts guilty and angry, which meant when she discovered Declan parked outside her house, she had a fine head of steam built up.

Time for a reckoning. There was only one way he could have shown up at Greenlee's the way he had.

She stomped up the walkway to where he sat in the porch

swing as if he didn't have a care in the world. "You're tracking me."

"Of course I'm fucking tracking you. I told you I would. So are Petra and Tansy. Hell, for all I know, Aiden and Jake have your location on GPS as well."

She didn't like being tracked. Didn't like being handled.

But damn if part of her didn't feel safer knowing someone had her back.

Still, he should have asked. "But they didn't show up, *again*, somewhere I'm trying to hold a professional visit."

"Nope. You're right. So how was that visit going, darling?"

She paused, knowing the situation could have ended badly. "Thank you for helping today."

His eyes flashed. "You need to stop putting yourself in danger."

All her positive thoughts vanished as he hit a hot button. "You need to rethink telling me what to do."

"Yeah, that's not happening. You can't see straight, but I'll help you figure it out."

"You think I'm reckless and foolish."

"I think you're a fucking force of nature."

The words came out like a cannon shot across her bow.

Declan's voice quivered, the intensity turned up to eleven. "I'm so turned on right now I can barely breathe. But I'm also so pissed that I can't see straight." He sucked in a big breath of air as he rose to his feet. "You make my chest hurt with how bold you are. I admire the crap out of you even as you scare me to death. You *are* reckless. You're willing to dive into the most dangerous situations and it usually means you end up a goddamn hero. But that doesn't change the fact that I want to tie you up and hide you away so that you can't stick your damn neck out every fucking day. And the things that I want to do *to* you while I've got you tied up..."

Before she could answer or make any kind of excuse, he caught her to his body and slammed their lips together. A hard kiss, demanding and controlling. She was being consumed like wood being fed into the flames.

He pushed her back to the wall, and she clung to him, the fear and the frustration of the day sweeping away as everything narrowed to the pinpoint focus of being in his arms.

He lifted her off the ground, and she wrapped her legs around him as he pressed his hips against her intimately. The fear that had wrapped itself around her ribs hadn't fully let go— but Declan's kiss stripped her bare. Demanding. Fierce. Freeing.

She clung to his neck and kissed him back, groaning as he rocked, the thick length of his erection hitting every sensitive spot between her legs.

They needed to move this inside. She needed to rip his clothes off and lose her frustrations in his touch. In his taking.

She dragged her fingernails over his shoulders, just about to make that suggestion when the door swung open beside them, and Dixie rushed out with a friendly *woof*.

"Sydney? You home? I came over and was working on my 4-H essay using the articles you gave me— Oh, God, I'm sorry."

Jinx's voice cut off as she darted away, and the door beside them slammed shut.

8

It wasn't his proudest thought, but Declan really wished Jinx hadn't been there. Not because of the embarrassment factor, although that was through the roof, but because he and Sydney both had fire left to burn.

He lowered her feet to the porch. "Sorry. Lost my head," he said quietly.

"Me, too." She looked up at him. "Not sorry about the kissing, but the thoughtlessly stepping into danger. You're right."

They stared at each other for a minute before Declan took a deep breath. "Guess I get to give Jinx a ride home."

"Have fun with that." Sydney remained slightly breathless but more than a hint of teasing coloured her words.

Amusement chased away some of his frustration and the flames still licking over his skin. "You sound so sympathetic."

"Glad it's you and not me, that's all I'm saying," Sydney offered before clearing her throat and speaking louder. "Hey, Jinx, don't worry. We're decent and about to come into the house."

Dixie met them with great enthusiasm, licking Declan's hand and bumping into Sydney's knees as Declan followed into the foyer off the small kitchen. Jinx was entirely too focused on putting her notebooks into her backpack and refused to look at either of them.

"Did you find what you needed for today?" Sydney asked.

"Yup."

"Good. Then maybe tomorrow, or whenever you feel up to it, you can call me and we'll finish the interview portion of your project."

"Sure." Jinx cleared her throat, tossing her bag over one shoulder. "You've done some cool stuff."

"I have. Now, remember my pet peeve?"

"Put my bag on properly," Jinx said immediately, slipping on both straps. "Fine. I should go."

"I'll give you a ride," Declan said.

"You don't need—"

"Jinx. Please get in the truck." He kept his gaze steady until she flounced out the door. "Syd, I'll talk to you later."

"Okay. Thanks again for your help today." Her lips quirked. "Have a nice trip home."

"Remember that Tansy isn't the only one good at revenge," he muttered softly as Sydney stuck out her tongue then winked.

Jinx moved like the wind. She popped Dixie into the backseat of the crew cab and settled in the front passenger seat before Declan made it off the porch. He took a deep, deep breath, then headed into a small and intense hell.

He got onto the highway before breaking the silence. "Awkward?"

"So much," Jinx said, teenage angst in every syllable.

Dixie whined and shoved her head over the backrest until her nose hit Jinx's cheek as if checking to see what was wrong.

"It's okay," Jinx told her quietly. "I'm just being silly. Lay down."

Dixie obeyed, and suddenly the entire thing tilted toward the funny side of the equation.

The fact Jinx was icked-out by what she'd seen and not terrified the way she would have been last September when she arrived? Declan could get up on the stage at Rough Cut and dance a jig in front of everyone to celebrate.

They still needed to have a chat.

He cleared his throat.

"You're going to make us talk about this? Really?" Jinx whined.

"I really am," he returned. "You've seen Petra and Aiden kiss before."

"And Tansy and Jake, yes. Plus I know how sex works, so don't, for God's sake, think you need to have *that* talk with me."

"You don't think I should be kissing Sydney?"

"I already knew you guys were kissing," Jinx confessed.

Really? "Yeah? That's not common knowledge," he admitted.

"I kind of spotted you one day just after Christmas. Sneaking into the barn."

"Sorry. We were usually more discreet."

"Ha," she laughed. "Today was discreet?"

"We were outside her house, which is in a pretty remote location." Such a strange conversation, but as long as Jinx kept talking, so would he.

"It's just...*that* was a little more...*heated* than most people do in public."

"Sex can get that way."

"Ugh, please." She gave a full body quiver that was clearly at least eighty percent dramatic effect.

Declan snorted. "You know this is a really awkward conversation for both of us."

"I know." Jinx stared at his face. "I thought maybe you weren't getting together with Sydney because of me."

"The hell?" He shook his head. "Not true."

"Because you had to be careful around me and that sort of thing. And I appreciate it, but I feel so much safer now. I don't want you to avoid being together if you want to."

"It wasn't you. It *isn't* you. Sometimes—" He was going to get revenge on Sydney for making him have to do this, whatever else he did. "Back to awkward conversation territory."

Jinx sighed. "Just say it."

"Sometimes adults get together for fun and not forever."

She made a gagging noise.

"You asked," he offered dryly.

"Not asking anything else." Jinx stared out the window, probably because it was safer. "Just so you know, I think you two would be good together."

"Maybe. But that's a thing for us to figure out. So, sorry for surprising you, but I expect you'll keep what you saw to yourself. It's not really anyone else's business, and I don't think Sydney would like everyone talking about her."

"Agreed."

He parked outside the house and they both headed for the porch. Dixie pranced in wide zigzags, sniffing happily now that she was home. Jinx hesitated for two seconds before giving him a quick hug then vanishing into the house with the dog.

Twists and turns. The upside was confirming that Jinx was well on the way to being over parts of the abuse she'd suffered before coming to High Water. That was a thing to be very grateful for.

The instant he stepped inside, his brothers hit him with synchronized rebukes.

"Deck. Answer your damn texts."

"Where the hell have you been?"

"Everything okay? Declan demanded. "What happened?"

"Shit, nothing," Aiden admitted, slowing down and looking slightly guilty. "Just couldn't get a hold of you."

"I was busy, and since you didn't actually call me or hit the panic button..." Declan shrugged. "What's up?"

"Invite from Caleb Stone," Jake said. "We're headed to Silver Stone in fifteen minutes for supper and poker."

"Okay." Declan frowned. "Good thing I'm home."

"I got the call and accepted for us all," Jake admitted. "You're always around."

Not really, but... Declan eyed his brothers and spoke softer. "Think it's safe for all three of us to head out and leave the ranch?" Since Kevin would also be away. Not that they knew that yet.

Aiden nodded. "The ladies, including Jinx, are headed over to Petra's brother's place. They're doing some prep for the *we got married* celebration for me and Petra next week." His grin flashed bright. "Glad to have a party to look forward to."

"Even gladder that you're already married," Jake quipped.

"Amen to that," Aiden agreed.

Twenty minutes later, Declan was freshly scrubbed and shaking hands with his neighbour. "Good to see you again with no emergency in the background."

"Agreed." Caleb gestured them all toward the side of the house where two large barbecues were sending delicious smoke signals into the air. "Nearly ready, and the beer is waiting and ice cold."

"How's Tyler doing?" Declan asked.

"Great." Caleb shook his head. "He's already tired of the sling and nearly broke his leg falling off the ridge pole of the goat pen roof."

"Damn."

"Right? Tamara gave me hell because I'm the one who told him, when he was higher than a kite on painkillers, mind you, that he'd be leaping around like a goat before he knew it, and the kid took me literally."

Declan outright laughed even as he patted Caleb on the shoulder. "Glad he didn't come to any harm."

"Thanks to Sydney, and thanks to your level-headed response."

"Didn't do anything special," Declan protested.

"You did more than you think. At the time, and after, helping Luke and Tucker." Caleb held up a hand. "No more. Tamara's got something lined up as a thank you for Sydney, and those steaks on the grill are my tip of the hat. You want to call it a reward for being a good neighbour and nothing more, that's fine."

"Always appreciate having good neighbours," Declan returned, accepting the beer Luke offered him. He tipped the bottles together with a *clink*. "To fences that connect instead of separate."

"Hear, hear," Luke cheered.

After the stress and sexual frustration of the past days, it was good to simply relax and hang out with his brothers and friends. As he carved into tender ribeye steak and baked potatoes loaded with sour cream and bacon, Declan spoke with each of the Stone brothers, including the youngest. Dustin had to be barely older than Logan but carried himself like a much older man.

Solid people, family to the core. A connection much like the one Declan had with his brothers. After years apart from each other, it was good that they'd ended up being able to work together so well.

That had been the dream, but it was something to be

thankful for.

Thinking of Sydney's comment about telling people the things that were important, he made a note to share his thoughts with his brothers sooner rather than later.

Walker Stone raised his beer bottle in the air. "As a nod to Caleb, who is now learning the hard way that raising sons is far different than raising daughters. To sons!"

A cheer of "*To sons!*" went up, and Caleb lifted his beer in salute.

"It's too true," Zach Sorenson announced sagely. "Girls tell you when they're about to do stupid shit, boys just do it."

"Not sure why you're wearing that wise old man face. Your kid is barely three months old," Luke complained. "And a girl."

"Five sisters," Zach said with a sigh. He tilted his head knowingly. "Five. Sisters." He turned his attention on Aiden. "And you married one of them. God help you and thank you at the same time. You're either a saint or a fool."

"Fucking lucky," Aiden quipped. "That's all I know."

Laughter and witty snark flowed as fast as the beer. Declan found himself damn near grinning when they headed home hours later.

"Smile any harder and you'll break your face," Jake warned, but he smiled as well.

"Both of you are far too happy," Aiden complained.

"Our pockets are full, and yours are empty. That should explain the expressions." Jake winked at Declan. "Good to get out with you guys like that. The Stones are a great family."

"They are, but the truth is we've got something special, too," Declan affirmed, glancing into the rearview mirror to include Aiden. "Glad that High Water is working, or at least the parts we can control. Glad I get to do this with you both."

"Me too,"

"Agreed."

They poured out of the truck, about to head their separate ways, when a figure stepped into the porch light. Logan summoned them forward.

"Come on," Declan quietly told his brothers. "If this is what I think..."

"Can I talk to you? All of you at once is damn intimidating, but what the hell." Logan included them all in his wry examination. "May as well get it over with."

"Here?" Aiden shrugged and sat on the steps. "What's this about?"

Jake sat next to him and Declan leaned on the railing.

Logan stared upward for a moment. "When you guys found me, you didn't ask any questions. I appreciated that for a lot of reasons. Not sure what to say, not sure how much to say." He met Declan's gaze. "Still not sure on a bunch of it, but I don't want anyone hurt accidentally because of me. High Water is the best place I've ever lived, and I don't want to screw this up, not for anyone."

Declan dipped his chin but waited.

The young man kept rolling. "Just to get this out there—I've never done anything wrong. And there's no reason anyone would come after me, so I didn't think being here was dangerous to anyone. I mean it. I wouldn't have stayed otherwise."

"Go on," Aiden encouraged softly. "What's the story you need to share?"

Logan swallowed big. "I never got tangled up in trouble, but my brother did. Dean is a whiz with numbers. He did the books for our old man's yard care company, but then he found a job that paid better. *Way* better. When I asked for more info, Dean kind of hemmed and hawed, but I finally got it out of him that he was working for a company that doesn't play by the rules."

"Like?" Jake asked.

"Money laundering for one. I didn't ask for any more details," Logan said quickly. "And then Dean left the house, and I haven't seen him since. That was last summer."

"Doesn't sound like the end of the story, though," Declan said.

"I wish it was." Logan sighed. "Early this year, he did something that pissed them off then ran."

"Damn. I bet that didn't go over well," Aiden murmured.

"Not at all. We look a lot alike, Dean and I. A couple of the gang nabbed *me* and thought they could beat information out of me, no matter how much I insisted they had the wrong guy." Logan met Declan's gaze for a second then looked away, but the glimpse was enough to show the depth of the pain the kid still carried. "They finally found someone far enough up the chain who actually knew Dean and figured out I wasn't lying, so they dumped me in a ditch off the highway."

"Outside Heart Falls?" Jake asked.

Logan shook his head. "Highway 2. I moved west for as long as I could—at some point I lost track of what was happening and woke up here."

"Christ. That's a long haul." Aiden shook his head admiringly.

It was impressive, and the entire story explained a lot, but Declan thought back to one other issue that Sydney had shared. Getting beat to hell explained the condition Logan had been in when he arrived.

It didn't explain it all. "The scars on your legs?"

Anger twisted Logan's face. "My dad had issues."

"Enough said." Aiden rose and extended a hand. "Thanks for sharing, but for me, I just need you to keep headed the direction you're headed."

"Agreed," Jake offered another handshake.

"I want you to talk to Kevin, though," Declan said quietly. Logan bristled, but Declan stuck to his guns. "It's a lot, dealing with what happened to you, and he's here to help. Let him do his job."

Logan glanced over the three of them. "So I get to stay?"

"Hell, yeah," Aiden offered. "You do all the shit jobs. You don't get to leave."

Jake snorted. "I'm off to bed. Night, all."

Declan stayed for another moment, the quiet night sounds rising up in a summer symphony. The leaves on the saplings in the nearby coulee rustled peacefully as he rested a hand on Logan's shoulder then headed them in the right direction. "Feel good to get it off your chest?"

"Sort of." Logan glanced around. "Still figuring stuff out."

"Says all of us, all the time," Declan offered wryly.

Logan paused at the door of his room. "Sorry I didn't tell you sooner."

"You had your reasons, but it's good to have people you can share your troubles with." Declan offered another back pat. "Like Aiden said, keep headed the right direction."

"I will." Logan thrust out his hand.

Declan took it and used it to haul the kid in for a brotherly hug. "You're doing fine."

After all the massive highs and frustrating lows, it felt good to finish the day on a positive note. The only thing that dulled the celebration was the silent room and empty bed he crawled into.

He'd give anything to have Sydney curled beside him.

~

OVER THE NEXT TWO DAYS, Sydney spent a ton of time

kicking her own butt. For a smart woman, she hadn't thought things through very well.

She'd gotten away from the mishap at Greenlee's far better than she deserved. Didn't mean she'd stop her visits, but when something seemed off, she needed to slow down and use her head instead of blindly rushing forward.

Far more worrying was the growing urge to simply drive over to Declan's and demand a change in their relationship. It was an impossible thought, and it irritated her like a bit of sand caught between two toes. It was always on her mind, but she didn't have time to stop and shake out her boots.

Even if she did, she had the sinking feeling the scratchy echo would still linger.

"If you've given up on sleep, I need to warn you it's not doing a thing for your beauty routine." Edison leaned a hip on the counter beside her in the clinic staff room and eyed her judgmentally. He circled a finger in front of her face. "You usually have that whole barely-out-of-grade school, peaches-and-cream thing going on, but right now, you need to change something up, sweetie."

She didn't have to look in the mirror to know he was right. "Working through a bunch of things," Sydney informed him. "Nothing about the clinic, though."

"Not worried about the clinic. I'm worried about you," he admitted. "You're a fantastic boss—at least when you're not risking life and limb. And I've worked with you long enough to sense when something's off."

One thing Sydney disliked immensely were straight-up lies, so she avoided them whenever possible. "Again, it's not the clinic, and thank God you're here because you're a lifesaver." She glanced into the main foyer where Lexie was welcoming a client. "Thank God for Lexie because she's lightened my load immensely, and I think we're doing more for the community. That's a good feeling."

Edison nodded slowly. "I'm glad to help. But to casually throw it out, that gentleman I'm seeing isn't only a great dancer with a sexy body. He's pretty easy to talk to, if that's the kind of thing you're looking for. Or if counseling is the kind of thing that makes you immediately say *hell no*, you might want to consider why and talk to him anyway."

"Thanks for the advice. Now go get caught up on those vaccination records," Sydney ordered, pushing Edison on the shoulder to rotate him toward the door.

"Getting my excellent advice out of range, but I'll be back," he promised. "Like a big ol' boomerang of caring."

Sydney snickered. "Boomerangs have a far higher rate of contribution to concussions and cranial impact trauma than most people expect."

He stuck his tongue out as he left her to finish eating her lunch.

Edison was a smart cookie. Too smart, and his comments got Sydney thinking in the direction of her biggest dilemma. She wasn't emotionally ready to make a decision about Declan, but her body had already voted, and her heart kept trying to call a referendum.

Her phone buzzed, and she answered it on autopilot, blinking to discover her grandmother on video chat. "Grandma?"

"Hello, darling." Grandma Belinda's bright smile lit up the screen, her dark brown hair now laced with silver. As she adjusted the camera angle, Sydney's mother, Marie, popped into view. "You get a two-fer today. Have time to chat?"

"For a few minutes." Sydney twisted to make sure the staff door was closed then propped up the phone so she could continue to eat. "Lunch break, so excuse me if I stuff my face."

"No problem. Marie is visiting while Grandpa Nate is away, and we realized neither of us had talked to you in a while." Grandma Bel smiled at her daughter. "She's also wiping the floor with me at cards every night—but that's nothing new."

Her mom winked, but Marie's gaze lingered on the dark shadows under Sydney's eyes. "How are things in Heart Falls?"

"Busy," Sydney admitted, "but getting better now that I have a second doctor in the clinic. It means the workload is getting lighter, and I'll eventually have some of that mythical thing I've heard about called 'free time.' Good friends in the area, lots to keep me moving."

"Good to know. Nice you found a new doctor. Immigrant? New resident getting rural hours?" her grandma asked.

Once again the truth was the only thing she could say. "Grandpa Nate recommended her. Someone he met... somewhere, but I can honestly say she's fitting in really well."

On the screen, her mom and grandma exchanged quick glances before both turning back with very fake smiles. "Oh well, it's good to hear that he's been helpful," her grandma said. "Shoot. Hang on a minute. My neighbour is coming to the door, and if I don't answer it right away, she'll take it as a sign I've fallen over and need the paramedics to come and save me."

Grandma Bel vanished from the screen, leaving Sydney looking at her mother's face.

Marie leaned forward. "Can I help with anything?"

"I'm fine, Mom," Sydney snapped.

Her mother raised a brow.

"I'm fine," Sydney repeated, a little less attitude in her tone. "Some personal stuff, but I'll be okay."

Marie nodded slowly before meeting Sydney's gaze straight on. "I know you and I don't always have the same priorities, and that's okay. But the thing you need to remember is I absolutely want what's best for you, however you get there. Right now, it looks as if the personal stuff is weighing you down."

With her mom's comment on top of Edison ragging on her, Sydney clearly needed to do something about her appearance or she'd be scaring the patients. "I'll figure it out."

"Of course you will," Marie returned instantly. "That's never the difficulty. The question is if you'll ever willingly let other people help you carry the burden while you figure it out. I'm always there for you."

Which was something Sydney knew in theory. Actually opening up and saying something, even to the woman who gave birth to her—that wasn't a skill Sydney had ever cultivated. "I know that. Thanks, Mom."

Thankfully, Grandma Bel was back, and then the two of them told Sydney all about the garden show they were helping to organize in two weeks' time. Sydney ate her sandwich and finished her lunch, enjoying the conversation on one level while feeling totally detached on another.

The connection between the two of them. That mother/daughter link where they finished sentences for each other and interrupted with new stories and happy thoughts—

She didn't have that with Marie.

She didn't know if she *wanted* that or if it just made her ache in ways she couldn't explain.

"Thanks for the call, Gram. Good to see you, Mom." *That* Sydney could honestly say as she accepted their air kisses and finished the call.

She tucked the phone into her pocket, cleared her throat, and switched gears. There was always something that needed doing.

Out at reception, Jenny pulled Sydney to the side. "I have a note on the calendar that Tessa Turm is due this week. I keep track of all our patients so I can send them baby cards, but I think something's wrong."

"What kind of wrong?" Sydney demanded as she leaned over the computer screen.

"She transferred her prenatal care from this clinic to the one in Diamond Valley. There's a note on her chart that you suggested she should get to know the doctor there. The Turm farm is halfway between Heart Falls and Diamond Valley, so it made more sense to drive north all the time instead of south to see you. She should've been having her prenatal visits there, but when I called the clinic to find out if she's had the baby, they said they haven't heard from her. *Ever.* She hasn't been in for any prenatal care, not even these final two weeks."

Shit. Sydney took a deep, steadying breath. Out of all the medical situations she had to deal with, pregnancy and labour were at the absolute top of her *I hate it* list. "Can you phone to find out how she is?"

"I tried," Jenny said. "Her voice mail is full, so I can't even leave a message to tell her to give us a shout."

"Guess I'm making a house call, then," Sydney offered with as much enthusiasm as she could muster.

The trip to the farm would take a good twenty-five minutes. She debated for less than a second before punching through a call to Declan. It would be easier to warn him where she was going rather than him dropping everything the instant she crossed whatever radius he had the GPS warning set for.

She was positive he was still tracking her, because of course he was.

You've reached Declan Skye. Leave a message and I'll get back to you when I can.

Thank goodness. "Hey, Deck. Since we never did really

talk out the whole *you're tracking me* thing, I assume you're about to discover I'm leaving town. I'm headed to the Turm farm. Mrs. Turm is pregnant and I haven't seen her for a while. I don't expect any problems, but I'll be cautious. Please stay home."

She hung up, surprised at the sense of comfort humming in her chest. It felt strange to make that kind of call, and yet—

It felt good to know someone cared.

Which dropped on top of the contact from her grandma and mom, and her mom's insistence that Sydney needed to learn to ask for help. And wasn't that a fucked-up mess.

Yeah, it was just a big ol' slew of emotional bullshit Sydney wasn't keen on having to deal with. Shut it down, tuck it away. Focus on the next thing to do and do it brilliantly.

The work drill was something she needed to do this trip especially, considering this was a pregnancy visit. The whole shut-down part.

The longest gravel driveway in the world led to a tidy bungalow sitting beside a massive barn. A single, small blue car was parked outside the house with no sign of anything else. Tessa's husband was obviously not home.

Still, Sydney took her time. She looked around carefully even as she greeted the dogs that eagerly met the truck, tails wagging, barking happily. "Hello, guys. Yes, hello. Where is Tessa?"

Everything around the barn and arena remained quiet as Sydney made her way to the house. Before she reached the front door, the sound of weeping and crying made her quicken her step.

She jerked the front door open. "Tessa, it's Dr. Jeremiah. I'm coming in."

Her announcement was met with another shriek of pain.

Sydney rushed forward, everything outside the here and now shoved aside.

9

———

Sydney followed the noise, the cries of pain speeding her step until she found Tessa in the primary bedroom. The woman clutched the footboard of the bed with one hand, the other cradling her extended belly. She had her head down and was weeping and screaming in turn.

"Tessa, it's Dr. Jeremiah." Sydney stepped into view, but Tessa barely acknowledged her presence. "I need you to take a deep breath and let me check you over."

"This is not happening," Tessa insisted between gasps. "I don't want to have the baby now."

"Let me take a look," Sydney insisted, her nerves crawling as Tessa continued to wail.

Unfortunately, this was no false alarm.

"You're well into labour," Sydney assured Tessa. "But you still have a ways to go. The best thing is if you can keep moving a bit. Have you called an ambulance?"

"I'm not calling an ambulance. This happened before," Tessa told her. "And then it stopped. I'm not leaving home. Danny will be here soon, and then it'll all be okay."

"Glad to know your husband's on his way, but I'm calling the ambulance," Sydney began.

"No," Tessa shouted. "I won't go in it."

"That's your right, but my choice is to have medical backup." Sydney tried not to cringe as another contraction hit and Tessa's volume went back up past ten. "I'll be right back."

She was gone for all of twenty seconds, cutting the call to 911 short after she'd given the necessary information.

"Breathe," Sydney instructed again, having finally herded Tessa into the kitchen to set up camp.

Another quick check, and Sydney changed her mind about the time frame. This was looking as if delivery was only minutes, not hours, away. "You know, it's a rare baby who actually arrives on their due date."

"Not due yet," Tessa complained for the umpteenth time. "Danny would never have gone away if we knew the baby was coming."

"This is why prenatal care is important," Sydney snuck in, just on the off chance this was baby number one. Its future brothers or sisters might have a better chance of not being such a surprise. "Let's keep you as comfortable as possible until the ambulance arrives."

Tessa gritted her teeth together. "I'm not having the baby until Danny gets here."

Good luck with that one. "Right now, you're not in charge. The baby is, and that's a good thing."

Tessa began another nerve-racking scream that set Sydney's hair standing on end. Somehow she smiled and talked the woman through the contraction, but the ambulance could not get there soon enough.

Everything was going well. At least that's what she kept telling herself.

Yet every single class that Sydney had ever taken about the

things that could go wrong before birth, during birth, and after birth flashed through her mind like some twisted medical horror flick.

This is why I am never ever doing this myself, the parts inside of Sydney's brain reminded her sternly.

Another contraction faded, and in the modest silence of Tessa's panting moans, the distant sound of a siren cut through the air.

Which is when Tessa gripped Sydney's arm tight enough to cut off the circulation, her fingernails digging in. "Oh my God. Something's wrong."

Sydney shut down the panic and took a quick check. "You're fully dilated. If you want to push, now is the time."

Tears poured down Tessa's cheeks. "I want Danny."

Me too, Sydney thought.

A few more twists and Tessa was in position, squatting beside the kitchen table. "He'll be here as soon as he can," Sydney reassured her. "Now when the next contraction hits, it's time to push. Hold onto the chair," she ordered, moving from gentle encouragement into straight-up bullheaded dictator.

The baby beat the ambulance by a half-dozen siren wails. Miraculously, Danny arrived a few seconds later. Sydney was still checking vitals and clearing the baby's airway when Danny burst in. She barely had time to hand off instructions to the EMT before Tessa collapsed into his arms, his presence finally turning Tessa's screams into a good old crying jag.

Sydney stayed until the EMTs gave the all-clear for Tessa and the baby to remain at home under Denny's supervision. The new family promised to head into the doctor's office the next day for a well-baby checkup.

Sydney's ears were still ringing as she got into the truck and followed the ambulance back to the highway. It turned north, and she headed south, the adrenaline flooding her system slowly wearing off.

She pulled off the highway on the first side road that was safe and moderately private. She barely made it out of the truck before she lost what remained of her lunch.

A few minutes later, she stood on shaky legs, wiped her mouth, then made her way to the back. She dropped the tailgate, once again climbing on board and looking out over the scenery to calm her nerves.

"I hate this feeling so much." She didn't even sound like herself, her voice creaky and hollow.

Her hands were unsteady as she lifted her water bottle and forced down more liquids. Her muscles trembled, nerves jangling like elastics pulled too tight.

No use fighting it any longer. Sydney wiggled farther back into the truck bed. She curled her arms around her legs, rested her forehead against her knees, then let the tears come.

It wasn't always this bad, delivering a baby. She'd assisted with the arrival of Petra's niece, and while the fear factor had still been high because of everything that could go wrong, there'd been a steadying link between Zack and Julia. A joyful connection that flowed into the room and lifted them all up.

Things still could have gone wrong in a flash. Like things had gone wrong for Sydney's friend back when she was still in school.

She cried until her ribs ached then wiped the tears from her cheeks and stared out over the rolling foothills. Sitting there in the quiet, nothing but the occasional bird song or the rustle of leaves to keep her company, she felt completely alone.

The inside of her head liked the relief from Tessa's caterwauling, but inside her heart, she ached.

At the edge of the tree line, a small furry body appeared, followed by another. Rare to see them out in the daytime, the coyotes moved swiftly and surely from one side of the clearing to the other. It was a small pack, five in total, but they looked healthy, alert—watching each other's backs without question.

The longer Sydney watched, the more she realized everyone seemed to be telling her the same thing. It was time to ask for help.

Oh, she wasn't ready to throw in the towel, but in moments like today? When she knew damn well what was wrong, yet had no idea how to fix it—

And while she knew to the core of her being that both Tansy and Petra were there for her, they weren't who she wanted right now.

They'd touched on the edges of it the night they'd done the silly speed dating.

She needed Declan's calm and his anger, and she knew that she'd get both. He'd listen without interruption, and then he'd be as righteously furious at the world as she was, and she needed that.

There was no solving some problems, but right now she needed not to hold the burden by herself.

Sydney hauled out her phone and once again tried to make contact.

For the second time that day she got sent to voice mail, but this wasn't something she was going to explain to a recorded device.

"Hi, Deck. Just wanted to let you know I'm safely headed back to Heart Falls. Hope to track you down, so I'll be swinging by High Water in a bit."

She left it at that then sat for another fifteen minutes, staring at the sunshine reflecting off the distant mountain peaks. Just looking out at the world that was so much bigger than her and letting herself feel small.

She didn't have all the answers, and maybe she didn't need

to. Not if she was finally ready to stop carrying everything alone.

~

FOR ONCE, Declan had a solid sleep, unexpected because he was still worried about High Water and still tied up in knots over Sydney. And there hadn't been a chance for the two of them to do much more than offer a passing hello since their interruption a few days earlier.

Still, refreshed and relaxed, he'd gone into the house and found five-year-old Jeffrey up and ready to talk the ear off anyone who would listen.

"Me and Daddy and Papa are going to the zoo. And there's going to be roaring lions and bears who *grrrrr* and I get to see snakes." Jeffrey caught hold of Declan's sleeve, and shook it as if making sure Declan had a firm grasp of all the details. "Snakes and spiders and *monkeys*."

"This sounds like an important trip," Declan responded evenly. "Do they have any horses?"

Jeffrey opened his mouth as if to answer then closed it. He frowned, little boy confusion all over his face. "*Do they have horses?*" he asked.

"They might have wild horses. You should go ask your daddy," Declan offered without a hint of guilt at the evil suggestion.

Jeffrey didn't take the bait. Instead of running off to jump on his new parents' bed and wake them up, Jeffrey climbed into Declan's lap and proceeded to list all of the animals that he *did* know were at the zoo, including, eyes widening, "Zebras!"

It was the sweetest thing. Declan was grateful to have the kid around, adding his enthusiasm and joy to their days. He liked kids well enough, but it was kind of nice that he got to enjoy his brothers' newfound families as an uncle to people with personalities rather than having to deal with the squawking new-arrival type.

If his siblings did end up with babies, he'd be the best uncle possible, but the teeny, easily breakable ones had never really been his thing. He liked them Jeffrey's age and older.

Declan interrupted Jeffrey's ramblings to get him a glass of juice and pour himself a cup of coffee. He was flipping French toast while Jeffrey kept up a mile-a-minute monologue when Jake and Tansy showed up in the kitchen.

"Look, we've got ourselves a new short order cook," Jake teased. "Sunny side up with a rasher of bacon, please."

"What's a rasher, Daddy?" Jeffrey demanded, dancing on the stepstool next to Declan. "Is it itchy?"

"It's bacon." Tansy said reverently, balancing her crutches under her armpits so she could clasp her hands together and smile up into the heavens. "It's the food of the gods."

Jeffrey's little jaw dropped and he whispered intensely, "God eats bacon?"

Declan snickered as he flipped the bread in the pan. "Before you have fun answering that, can I offer you two sleeping beauties some breakfast?"

In the end, Declan fed the entire family including the two temporary ranch hands currently staying over at High Water. Jake and Jeffrey got ready to head out to join Tansy's dad, Malachi, for the trip to Calgary and the zoo. Aiden decided at the last minute to tag along, and the three of them took off to town, a chorus of animal noises filling the air around them.

"I'm spending the day at Sasha's," Jinx announced, absently scratching Dixie between the eyes. "She's training for her final competition, and I'm helping her with timing and moving props."

"Be back in time for supper," Petra reminded her. "I'm in the office most of the day, getting caught up on our accounts."

"I'm going to be a woman of leisure," Tansy informed them all, settling onto the couch. "Or start breakdance training. One of the two."

Declan had smiled as he headed out to spend the morning with the hands in the animal shelter, enjoying the easy labour.

And now, hours later, Declan swayed lightly in the saddle as he rode. Even the clouds overhead seemed to move in time with Cobalt's leisurely rhythm. No rush. No reason to hurry.

Cobalt dipped her head and tugged lazily at a strand of grass, chewing around the bit as she strolled forward a few more steps.

Declan laughed as he patted her withers softly. "You trying to say you plan to snack by the stream?"

She shook her head, nickering at his words, clearly content as she continued to pace the trail with no direction needed from him.

It wasn't a spot he'd come to that often, but it was clearly one of her favorites. The instant he'd left the house after lunch and headed into the open fields, Cobalt had picked up her pace and unerringly selected the right route to end at the small oasis beside the meandering stream.

Never failed to give him a kick of pleasure that animals too had their preferences. Considering he liked to let them choose their path whenever he could, maybe he and Cobalt had been out to the spot more often than he realized.

It wasn't that far from the High Water ranch house, but it was tucked into a tight little hollow, and now at the end of summer, everything was deep green and full of life.

A wind chime dangled from an extended aspen branch, far enough out over the water someone would've gotten wet putting it up. It hadn't been him, but it could have been. Sadie loved wind chimes, and he could imagine himself putting them up to surprise her.

It was the kind of place she would've loved. Maybe that's why even though she'd never been there, he felt her presence so strongly.

Which made it a great place to come when he needed to talk and think and kick his own butt.

Declan dropped the reins and loosened the cinch on Cobalt then found a spot to sit and relax. To spend an hour just being silent. No interruptions, no conversations, although he had to admit he was thoroughly enjoying the addition of five-year-old Jeffrey to the household.

He closed his eyes and let the sun fall on his face as the morning repeated itself through his mind.

Sleep might have caught him for a moment or two, and he stretched, batting away a leaf that had fallen from a tree overhead and brought him back to the here and now.

Rest done, time for the gut-spilling.

"The guy Jinx rescued a while back, Sadie? He's grateful for the roof over his head and the chance to start over. It's hard to think ill of him, but at times, I'm not sure what to believe." He tossed the leaf toward the stream and watched it swirl in a small back eddy before gently floating away. "If I go with my gut, which is what you'd tell me to do, I think Logan's a good kid. I just don't know why it seems as if I'm still missing something."

He wasn't usually the one who needed every answer. That was Jake's job—planner, organizer, master of backup plans. Declan was okay with going with the flow, like the leaf currently headed out of sight to its next destination.

It knew it would be okay.

"High Water is a good idea and a good place. I believe that." Declan leaned forward, hands clasped, elbows resting on his knees as he admired the grove. "Good people live here. And I'm working to convince Sydney to become more a part of it than she already is."

It almost felt confessional. Sadie was dead, so she certainly didn't run his life. He didn't need her permission and he wasn't really asking for it.

More like affirming what had gone before. The connection between them and the lessons she'd taught him over the years they'd shared. "Sydney's got something big on her heart. I can feel that too." He laughed at himself. "But I suppose this is one of those times you'd tell me to stop talking to the wrong person."

Which is what Sadie usually said while shaking a finger at him. Anytime he'd complained about someone in town ignoring the rules or not doing their job right.

He smiled at the memory.

Smiled bigger because the next image that arrived was even brighter and hotter. *Sydney* shaking a finger in his face.

Yeah, he definitely had a type.

Moving on was hard, but right.

"Definitely a few changes coming," he said firmly. "Still think High Water was a good idea, Sadie, but we're gonna need to tighten the reins a little."

He leaned into the reclined angle of the bank. The grass beneath him was cool and refreshing, and water bubbled over rocks at the bend in the creek only a few meters away.

"You'd have seen this coming, I bet. You'd have warned me. Not that you would've warned me off, but you were good at seeing what might happen so we'd be ready for it."

Except neither of them had seen her cancer coming. It was something that happened to other people. It was something that people got over.

Sometimes the memories filled him with frustration. But today, oddly, he had a sense of peace.

It wasn't what they'd wanted. It wasn't what *anyone* wanted, but Sadie had simultaneously fought *and* planned. When she died, Declan had found she'd gone through all her things and left notes and gifts for all her family and friends. He hadn't known she was doing it.

Back in the here and now, Declan rose and headed for home. The quiet time had refreshed him, and he was ready for anything.

A few minutes later when Cobalt rounded the corner of the trail, finally rising out of the hollow, Declan's phone pinged with far more dings and bells than should be legal.

"There are moments I envy past generations not having a beacon in their pocket." Still, he tugged his phone free since Cobalt was doing the driving anyway.

He listened to both messages from Sydney, slightly bemused that he hadn't heard the GPS alarm go off when she left town. Definitely no cell service in the hollow. He'd have to remember that.

The tone of her voice in the second message made him sit up a little straighter, though. Declan tapped his heels into Cobalt's sides, hurrying her along a little.

If Sydney had headed to the ranch house, she was probably there by now. He tightened his grip on the saddle and kept Cobalt moving at a steady pace. Whatever Sydney wanted, he was grateful she'd been willing to tell him she was coming over. It was time for them to deal with the—

Shit.

He'd absently opened an unread message. Petra had sent one only a minutes ago, which was odd. She and Tansy both teased that he was the worst at responding and usually resorted to phoning. Either she was feeling chatty or hoping he'd heard from his brothers.

But the instant he clicked the link open, all amusement evaporated.

Blackbird. Barn.

That's all the message said, but Petra knew exactly what that meant. It was a call for help and a warning not to arrive with guns blazing.

Whatever was happening at High Water, he needed to be there—*now*.

10

———

*S*ydney sent off a quick note to Petra to warn that she was coming over, not really expecting a response.

She knew her friends loved her—but showing up unannounced at High Water as if she lived there? That still felt wrong. A remnant of the rules that her grandparents had laid down while she lived under their roof and attended university—

No, her grandfather, not her grandma.

Oh, Grandma Bel still wanted her to be polite, but Grandpa Nate definitely had *opinions* about the way things were supposed to be done. Funny how knowing some of Grandpa Nate's beliefs were outdated didn't stop them from shaping her instincts.

Turning down the road into High Water, Sydney checked for the usual ever-present activity. She wasn't sure how many ranch hands were in residence at the moment, but there always seem to be somebody in the yard or moving to and from the barn to the house.

She knew there were no rentals in the artists' studio over

the dorms and residence. With Tansy's leg still in a cast, the place wouldn't be taking new bookings for a while. They'd only had a few already in place that they coordinated with the new cook at Buns and Roses to take care of the catering.

Sydney was just about to park when a shot of anger pulsed up. Whoever the jerk was taking two parking spaces for their truck and not bothering to pull out of the road between the residence and the barn needed to get some lessons on—

Shit. She slowed then stopped completely. That license plate was familiar. Or more, the odd way the license plate was not clearly visible at a glance was familiar.

Leaving her truck running, she slipped down to take a closer look. The plate was coated in mud and dust, even though the rest of the bumper was mostly clean.

The last time she'd seen plates like that was the night she'd come to dinner and the troublesome new guy had been there. The one Declan had to restrain, and who Jake had sent packing across the country using his police contacts.

An eerie calm flooded in, and the hours of sadness and tangled confusion disappeared in an instant.

This was what her brain did. Problem solved and saw the next thing to do. That truck was too damn familiar, and maybe she was wrong, but after the reminder from a few days ago, sometimes being overly cautious wasn't a bad idea.

She walked back to the open door of her truck, keeping her step steady and her head up, just in case she was being watched. She reached and turned off the engine and left her vehicle blocking the truck in place.

One more casual stroll put her at the stranger's passenger door which opened easily. She checked the glove compartment.

No registration, no insurance papers. Which was smart, because no one should keep them there.

She opened the console between the front seats and a gun glistened back at her.

A mental landslide of swear words hit as she took a quick glance around at the thankfully still empty yard. She grabbed the gun, held onto it tightly as far away from the trigger as possible, and left the vehicle, closing the door firmly behind her.

The rain barrel at the edge of the ranch house caught her attention. Inspired, she walked briskly to the far side of the house where a matching barrel sat. It only took a moment to lift the lid and toss the gun inside.

If that was a legally owned firearm, she'd pay to have it fixed, but considering they were in Alberta, and it was a *handgun* that was not properly secured?

She didn't think it was likely.

While she was at the back side of the house, she took a quick peek in the windows, both relieved and afraid to discover no one in the kitchen or living room, or visible through the bedroom windows that she had to stand on her tiptoes to look into.

Mentally, she counted cars. Petra's was there. Tansy's loaner from her brother-in-law that she was borrowing since her SUV was toast was there, as well as Declan's. Kevin was MIA, and she didn't know the other two trucks, but they were probably ranch hands. They were parked in the right spot, out in front of the dorm doors.

No idea about Jinx, but she'd lay odds the girl was at the neighbours.

Sydney slowed her step and checked her phone. She made sure the sound was turned off then considered if it was worth the risk to text anyone. It could all be her imagination, but the need for caution still screamed in her head.

Hoofbeats sounded in the distance. She turned—and there

he was, Declan charging in like a goddamn knight. He slowed, pointing imperiously for her to stay where she was.

He joined her at the corner of the house, dismounting and tucking himself and his horse as close to the back wall as possible. "We've got trouble," he said softly.

"There's no one in the house," she told him quickly. "One strange truck in the yard that is clearly owned by an asshole. I found what I'm guessing is an unregistered handgun in the console that is now safely out of the picture."

She looked up at him, waiting expectedly.

He dipped his head slowly. "Got a message from Petra there's trouble in the barn, and we need to be careful. She only sent the warning signal word, so I think her phone isn't on her anymore."

"We can know quickly enough." Sydney shook her phone in the air. "Your tracking program. Because I assume you also tagged Petra?"

His eyes brightened. "That's brilliant. And of course I tagged everyone in the damn family. Got the app, may as well use it."

The good part was that in under a minute they knew both Petra's and Tansy's phones were in the barn. The bad news was they were stacked so close together they were probably in a pile on the ground.

Declan considered. "One truck?" he asked. "Crew cab or single bench in the front?"

"Single."

He checked the screen one more time then shoved his phone into his pocket. "I figure that means only two guys. Whatever they're up to, it's Tansy and Petra in there alone with them."

"What about Logan and the two ranch hands you have?"

"Kevin took them all with him to do some work out at Red

Boot ranch." Declan looked Sydney up and down. "I don't know why I'm asking, but are you okay getting involved?"

The fact he'd asked instead of simply telling her to stay out of it kept the *try and stop me* from escaping. "I'll follow your lead," she promised. "How do you want to do this?"

He motioned to the back of the horse. "Hop on up. We're going to send you in one way so I can get in another." His face went stormy. "You got your magic pass-out drugs on you?"

She patted her pocket. "Always."

Declan leaned over, linking his hands into a step. "Up you go."

He waited until she was in the saddle, reins in hand before he laid a big hand on her thigh and squeezed. "Walk Cobalt around the back side of the barn and go in through the arena. If the overhead door is closed, open it then mount back up before entering. You can get away quicker on horseback if you need to, or use Cobalt to stomp anyone who gets in your way. You want to get the of attention of whoever is in there so I can get inside unnoticed. But don't take chances."

She listened as he gave her a few more instructions then nodded firmly. "*You* stay safe," she ordered. "No heroics."

"Hopefully we discover this is all some big misunderstanding." He squared his shoulders and lifted his chin. "But be ready for anything."

As per the plan, Sydney shook the reins gently and got Cobalt headed around the edge of the barn. It was an ominous sensation to have to casually ride past a place where people could be watching her.

She fell into that place of calm again up to where the barn door was open, and she confidently headed Cobalt into the entrance.

She stopped right in the doorway. "That was a good ride,

girl," she announced loudly, patting the horse's neck. "I'll have to borrow you again next time."

A lanky man in his midthirties stepped forward from one of the stalls, smile firmly place. He tipped his baseball cap back and grinned at her. "Hey, there. Let me give you a hand."

"Oh, hello." She smiled but kept her seat. "Thanks. This is my first time renting one of the horses, and I'm not sure where everything goes yet."

"First time? So you don't know everyone here?" He caught the reins and began to guide her toward a stall close to where he'd appeared from.

"Ten rides starting today," she announced perkily. "Plus I get to do the horse care, you know brushing them and whatever it's called. I love horses. Don't you love horses? Of course you do. You wouldn't work here if you didn't. What a great job you have."

She kept the chatter up, bubbly and brainless as she slid off the horse and quickly ducked under Cobalt's neck to her right side. Just in case the guy planned to grab her.

"How'd you hear about our place?" he asked.

"Just moved to town—I'm the new receptionist at the clinic, you know—and my landlord told me this was the place to call." After a quick peek up into the loft area, Sydney frowned at the man pretending to help her. "Do you know where the brushes are?"

"Sure," he said. "But I just thought of something. You're new, but have you seen my buddy around? I've been trying to track him down for a while."

Sydney pretended great interest in the guy's phone as he held it forward, and a clear image of someone who looked very much like Logan popped into view. Not Logan though—the eyes were the wrong colour. "He's cute."

The guy choked for a second. "I guess?"

Above them in the loft, out of sight of the stranger, Declan appeared, silent as a ghost. When he drew his fingers across his throat, she got the message.

"Wait, I might know him. Let me see again," she ordered, slipping her hand into her pocket as she doubled back under Cobalt's neck. She thumbed the protective cap off the injector. "You're too tall," she complained, laughing innocently. "Or I'm too short."

"You think you've seen him in town?" The guy leaned over more as he held out the phone again.

Sydney hummed softly, then pointed at the screen with her left hand. "That looks like—"

She jammed the muscle relaxant against his neck then stepped back, crowding into the corner of the stall and putting Cobalt's head between them.

"What the fuck?" The stranger whirled with a snarl, all pretense of being a nice guy falling away. His eyes widened, the quick-acting relaxant hitting his system so fast his legs collapsed, and he crumpled to the ground in a heap.

DECLAN HAD CRAWLED in the upper window of the barn and made a quick trip around the perimeter of the loft. It was only after he'd spotted Tansy and Petra safe but trapped in neighbouring stalls that he'd signaled Sydney to go ahead and use her knockout meds.

His entire body tightened as he waited mostly hidden from view in the loft, unable to do more than watch.

Thankfully, Sydney was both brave and quick, and within seconds of the man landing at her feet, she'd grabbed Cobalt's reins.

His horse was justifiably upset at the body sprawled

under her legs. Then again, if the guy got stepped on, that was his problem for having come in where he wasn't welcome.

Sydney knelt to check the man's pulse, but she glanced up at the loft, waiting for the next signal of the options Declan had shared.

He dropped a handful of zip ties from the loft, speaking quietly. "Stall Cobalt next door, tie this guy up, then lock the gate. Stay hidden—someone's in the office."

"Tansy? Petra?"

"Safe."

He took off for the stairs that would drop him just outside the office door. Silently he paced around the spots where he knew the floorboards would creak underfoot.

He made eye contact with Tansy and Petra individually and offered both of them a finger pressed to his lips and one hand raised in the *wait* sign.

Tansy grimaced, casted leg stretched out on the hay bale she rested on, and flashed him a thumbs-up.

Petra planted her hands on her hips, clearly frustrated, but she too dipped her head in agreement.

From the noise inside the office, the man inside was searching through every filing cabinet and every desk drawer, not even caring he might be overheard. Low curses rumbled from him as he worked.

Declan took a second glance into the room to gauge the best way to rush forward, but luck was not on his side. He locked eyes with the stranger rifling the office.

"Who the fuck are you?" the man demanded.

May as well go for it, Declan decided. He took a step forward, blocking the doorway. "I'm the one who needs to ask that question. Why the hell are you tearing apart my office?"

"You work here?" The man's expression lightened. "Just

trying to find some information, man. Tell me what I need to know, and I'll get out of your hair."

"Don't know that I want to give you anything considering how poor your manners are," Declan drawled. He folded his arms over his chest and stared down at the man who was a good five inches shorter than him. "This how you usually ask for directions—breaking and entering?"

"Fuck this," the stranger muttered, and too late, Declan remembered Sydney's warning about the gun.

She's going to give me so much shit—

"Back up," the stranger ordered, pointing a dark handgun squarely at Declan's abdomen. "Mac. Where the hell are you?" he shouted.

"You mean the guy who took off in the truck?" Declan had his hands raised as he shuffled backward. "Christ. He had the pedal to the metal and took off like his ass was on fire," Declan lied.

The stranger kept moving toward him, and Declan kept backing up, barely keeping his shit together when he stepped out of the door and spotted Sydney pressed to the wall, inches to his left.

"Bullshit," the stranger said. "Since you work here, I assume you'll be able to give me a little more help than those useless bitches. You got someone here named Dean?"

Declan hesitated in his step, wondering if he could swing quick enough to knock the gun out of the man's hand, when Sydney moved, hard and fast.

The crowbar in her hands slammed into the man's forearm. The gun fell as the man screamed. Declan was on him in a second, wrestling him to the ground and pinning him in place.

The entire takedown was far too reminiscent of having to overpower Russ.

"Bloody idiot," Sydney muttered. "And yes, I mean you.

Here. I found some more zip ties on the bench where I grabbed the crowbar."

"Good job staying safe in the stable," Declan grumbled as he accepted the long strands of plastic.

Sydney put her knee between the man's shoulders and helped restrain him. "Right? Lucky for you, I've got selective hearing." She waved her phone. "Want me to call 911?"

"Yeah." Declan paused. "What about your knockout special—gonna be a problem?"

Sydney shook her head. "Some of the effects will have worn off by the time they get here, and self-defense on home turf is always the proper answer. It's iffier when I'm an uninvited guest at someone else's home like Mr. Greenlee's."

The stranger, with his ankles and knees lashed together and his hands immobilized behind his back, continued to curse and utter threats.

Declan snatched up a rag and shoved it in the man's mouth. "You eat with that mouth? Enough."

"I'm grabbing the girls," Sydney announced. "If you've got this under control."

"If we don't find keys, we'll need to cut the locks." Declan stood, fisting the back of the man's shirt and dragging him toward the stalls. "I'll give you a hand. I'll just tuck this trash into the stall next to where you left the other one so it's easier for the police when they get here."

CHAOS at its finest reigned for the next two hours.

The police came; the police left with the promise the two invaders would be safely locked up for the foreseeable future. Tansy and Petra reclaimed their phones and got a hold of their guys, who were luckily already on the way home.

In one of those never-ending type of days, parts of the story were repeated over and over, especially once Jake and Aiden got home and reassured themselves everyone was really okay.

With Jeffrey temporarily out of the way, passed out in his bed from the excitement of the zoo day adventure, the rest of them met at the kitchen table to catch up.

"We were out in the barn taking care of the rescue animals," Petra said. "Next thing, I hear someone talking to Tansy—quiet at first. Which, fine. Didn't expect anyone else to be in the barn, but people do show up with strays at times. But then her volume went up, and she told him to mind his own business and get the hell out of the barn."

"Damn leg cast," Tansy complained. "Couldn't move fast enough. He hauled me into the stall and dumped me inside."

"You did call out *Blackbird*," Petra pointed out. "Gave me enough time to text Declan the heads-up signal before the second guy surprised me."

Aiden's glare tightened.

"Neither of them roughed us up," Petra assured him. "It felt like they were trying to be sneaky—then gave up and went full-on brute force instead."

"I think they weren't really supposed to be doing what they were doing." Tansy waved a hand. "Sorry, that made no sense, because obviously— I mean, they weren't looking for information because someone told them to. More like they'd an idea on their own and were feeling it out."

Interesting idea, but Declan kept the story moving forward before it could get derailed. "Sydney and I got Petra and Tansy unlocked and waited for the police to come. Turns out the breaking and entry charges were more than enough to get things started because there were warrants on file for both their arrests."

All eyes turned to Petra.

She held her hands up innocently. "Don't look at me. I didn't have time to shove any lies into the system."

"So we won't have a return visit from those two anytime soon?" Jake clarified.

"Nope," Declan confirmed. "It's still a mess, though, so if you could check with your friends and make sure Russ wasn't tied to this, I'd appreciate it."

"And we need to talk to Logan," Aiden said firmly.

"Agreed." Through the window, Kevin's truck was visible as he made his way down the drive, returning home with all the hands. Declan debated the wisdom of immediately hauling the kid up in front of the entire group, but none of the ladies would leave, and no one wanted to wait.

"This is our home too," Tansy said softly. "And he's part of the High Water family. Family meetings are part of the deal."

"Let's handle this fast—before folks show up expecting supper," Petra said.

"I'll grab him," Jake offered, slipping out the door.

11

While his brother hurried to fetch Logan, Declan floated a quick idea. "Revamp supper plans? We can fire up the barbeque and do burgers."

"Sounds great. We have tons of ingredients for salads," Tansy offered. "And I can whip up a sauce for macaroni and cheese in the same amount of time it takes you to heat up the grill."

Supper plans dealt with, Declan turned to check on Sydney, suddenly aware no one had questioned her continuing presence in the discussion.

She belonged.

Everything got quiet as Jake and Logan stepped into the house.

Jake settled next to Tansy, taking her hand in his.

Logan stood quietly in front of them. "Jake said something happened today that you need to talk to me about?"

"Deck, you go ahead. Easier for one person to tell it all," Petra suggested.

Logan listened quietly as Declan gave a quick summary of

the day's events, the young man's face growing whiter and whiter. "I'm so sorry. I really don't know why they want Dean."

"They're looking for something," Petra suggested. "Has he ever sent you anything? Asked to visit?"

"He has no idea where I am. And if he did message, I sure the hell wouldn't have given him directions on where to find me." Logan met Declan's gaze. "They didn't drop me anywhere near here, I swear. I walked forever before I collapsed."

"I believe you," Declan said.

Logan straightened up, resignation on his face but pride as well. "I'd never do anything to hurt any of you. Never, so I'll just get my things together and leave."

The front door flew open and Jinx stormed in. "Bullshit."

Declan rose to his feet. "Jinx—"

"He's not leaving. He didn't do anything wrong," Jinx all but shouted as she raced to the table.

"Hello to you, Jinx." Petra raised a brow. "Eavesdropping again?"

"Bad habit," Jinx admitted. "One I learned long ago to protect myself the best I could." Before anyone else could speak, she got right up in Logan's face. "So you're saying that if the guys who abused me showed up at High Water and caused trouble, you'd want me to leave?" she demanded.

"Of course not. You didn't—"

"Exactly. *They're* the assholes, not me." She jabbed a finger right into his gut. "Figure it out, hotshot."

Logan gasped but didn't take his eyes off her.

She rolled her eyes massively. "*You* didn't do anything wrong either, except maybe be related to someone who is making bad decisions."

"But Tansy and Petra could have—"

"They didn't," Declan cut in before Jinx could. "Jinx?

Come here and let someone else get a word in edgewise. Because we never intended to let him leave."

"Oh." Jinx blinked. "Okay."

She bumped Logan's shoulder hard as she passed, stopping beside Declan to offer a brief, fierce hug. "He's an idiot," she whispered.

"Who means well. Now sit and be polite," Declan ordered.

Oddly enough, it was Tansy who took the lead. "Like they said, you're not leaving. I get where your head is at, but you're not responsible for anyone's actions but your own. The things that *you* choose to do. And right now, it seems you're choosing to be a part of High Water. Yes?"

Logan looked as if it was a trick question. "I don't want me being here to cause problems."

"Ditto," Petra said brightly. "I don't want my presence to cause problems, but it's entirely possible at some point, someone will show up and muddy the waters. And if that happens, we'll deal with it."

Jake cleared his throat. "Tansy has a broken leg right now because of my past coming to visit. You want me to leave?"

The kid looked closer and closer to tears. "You guys use two by fours when you want to get your message across."

"We can use something even bigger if it hasn't sunk in yet." Tansy leaned back in her chair and folded her arms over her chest. "The only way you get to leave High Water is when you're a hundred percent fit and you have somewhere else you want to go. We're not going to keep you forever if this isn't right, but stop trying to run away. It's exhausting for us."

For a second, Logan's lips twitched. "I'll do my best to stop being tiresome." He turned his attention to Declan. "But can we put some safeguards in place to stop this from happening in the future?"

"We'll do the best we can, but like Petra said, life is

unpredictable." Declan glanced around the table at his family. "Let's talk about vetting our ranch hands a little more thoroughly."

"We talked once about having some of my friends from the force get to stay for a while," Jake reminded them. "Extra people on site who we can trust explicitly would be okay. We can brainstorm what other kinds of additional security we'll need to put in place as time goes on."

"The longer High Water exists, the more people know it's here." Aiden shrugged. "That's just a fact."

"And one we have to be comfortable with." Declan stood and made a move before Logan could back off. He offered a hand, and this time Logan was the one to move forward and accept an embrace.

People moved in different directions to get dinner ready. Declan caught Sydney heading for the door. "You're staying."

She shrugged lightly. "I was out on a call this afternoon. I need to shower and unwind. Thought I might do that at home."

"None of us mind if you stay." He examined her face, trying to see if this was what she really wanted or if she was just taking an easy out. "*I* would like you to stay."

She lifted her gaze to his, and for the first time that day, without her blustering energy as a distraction, every line on her face declared how bone-tired she was.

"Syd, grab a shower, and stay for supper." The command came from Petra, sliding across the room and wrapping an arm around Sydney's waist. Without another word, she guided her friend back across the room to the women's quarters.

Declan didn't know if he was more worried by Sydney's quiet acceptance or the questioning look in Aiden's eyes as his brother watched the entire exchange from a distance.

Screw it. If his brothers were aware of his plans, Declan might have backup.

Scratch that. If they all knew he wanted to get together with Sydney, he absolutely would have one hundred percent support from them and their partners.

They moved dinner outside by the fire pit, the makeshift table covered with quickly assembled salads and burger fixings and the massive pot of macaroni and cheese Tansy had miraculously produced.

All through the meal, though, Declan's attention was riveted on Sydney.

A gentle bump to the shoulder got his attention back on Jake. "Tansy and I have plans tonight, but first thing in the morning, how about you, me, and Aiden talk through some options. Once we have some specific ideas we can have a family meeting, but I'd like to start with the three of us."

"Sounds good." Declan checked Petra and Tansy quickly. "The girls don't look worse for wear after the excitement."

"They're tough," Jake agreed. "I just don't want them to have to be."

"Amen."

After the food was gone and most of the cleanup done, Sydney said her goodbyes to the girls and headed to her truck.

Declan had been watching closely and timed his interruption perfectly. "Come for a walk with me?" he asked.

"Deck, I'm tired," Sydney began.

He held out his hand. "Just to the barn. You look like you could use some kitten therapy."

Her lips twitched, but she slipped her fingers into his and let him guide her toward the animal rescue. "Is this a little bit of the hair of the dog that bit you? Returning to the scene of the crime so it's doesn't become a frightening spot?"

"I should've thought of that, but no," Declan admitted. "This really is about the kittens."

The current batch were old enough to be at the super-entertaining stage, but it was late enough in the evening they were tired. Instead of pouncing all over Sydney, the little black and white female he dropped in her lap meowed prettily as she stretched her back and then eased her head under Sydney's palm, begging to be scratched.

They sat on hay bales directly in front of the wide double loft doors that Declan swung open to the west. The sun had reached the top of the mountains, and sunset glows filled the sky with streaks of gold and orange.

For a long time, neither of them said anything. Just petted the kittens and stared at the sky. Side by side, Declan was content in a way he hadn't been in a long time. Not even that afternoon, because now he was with Sydney—

Declan finally broke the easy silence. "Thanks for letting me know where you were headed today."

"Yeah, maybe I should have let you drive out and join me." Sydney let out a huge sigh. "Nothing dangerous to me," she offered quickly, "but it was a tough one."

Declan snuck his arm around her waist and eased her body against his, holding her there in a gentle embrace. "Want to talk about it?"

"Not really," she said. "Other than to confess I do not like delivering babies."

Huh. He hadn't seen that one coming. "Everything okay?"

"Baby and mom are fine," she assured him. "Just my least favourite doctoring drill, especially in nonmedical settings."

He didn't know enough to be able to offer advice, and frankly, she didn't seem to be looking for it anyway. He pressed a kiss to the top of her head and held her little tighter. "I'm sure you were brilliant as usual."

"Of course," she said, twisting to look up at him and offer a tired smile. "Thanks for this. In spite of everything, it has been a good day."

He stared at her sunlit face, the glowing colours hiding some of the dark circles under her eyes and the tired lines bracketing her mouth. She was still so damn beautiful—but clearly hurting. And that couldn't continue.

Not changing it up this instant, not on top of everything that had happened that day, but soon.

Later that night, after the kitten cuddling was done, he escorted her to her truck and waited patiently as she crawled behind the wheel.

As she drove away from High Water, Declan firmed his resolve. He needed to adjust his approach and find a way to change her world. She deserved more.

OVER THE NEXT WEEK, it was far too easy to fall back into the old habits Sydney had learned over the years. If she ignored the frustrating moments and focused on the task at hand, the world around her would fade away and she didn't have to think.

Didn't have to long for what she couldn't have.

The clinic was hopping, the house visits she made went well—if grumpily received by the usual cranky old-timers.

Lexie continued to be a gift beyond measure, although there were times Sydney caught the woman staring into space with a decidedly unhappy expression.

They all had growing pains to deal with when moving to a new situation, Sydney supposed. But nothing in Lexie's demeanor said she wanted to talk about it.

Sydney's phone pinged at the same moment Edison's did.

"*Woohoo*, it's party time," her nurse announced enthusiastically. He tromped over to her and laid both hands on her shoulders. "You *are* in a party mood."

Sydney laughed. "Of course I am. It's Petra and Aiden's official wedding celebration. There's a lot to party about."

"*I* know that. I just wanted to make sure you remembered," Edison offered with a slight sniff before finishing cleaning the examination room. "Sometimes you get the oddest ideas in your head. You're not allowed to decide tonight's the evening you absolutely have to drive out to Charlie Miller's to make sure he's not doing something weird with mud again."

"Trust me, tonight I want a dose of my friends. Not another visit with the mud-cures-everything brigade." Sydney smiled at Edison's snicker. "Enough work talk. I'll see you there."

"With bells on," Edison offered with a grin.

His expression made Sydney wonder if he'd turn up literally decked out to jingle.

Pulling into the parking lot at High Water, Sydney couldn't believe the rush of people wandering the yard, excitedly chattering as they milled about.

"Welcome to wedding chaos," a bright and cheery voice called.

Tansy was seated in a spot of honour beside the house, a cascade of helium balloons arched over her head.

Sydney came forward to hug her then accepted the card Tansy held out. "What's this?"

"Petra decided they needed something more than food and dancing. It's a bingo-slash-scavenger hunt."

Sydney settled in the chair beside her. "Is that why people are running around with cameras?"

"Uh-huh. You have to take a picture of whatever's in each square. Petra has a printer set up in the artists' studio. Fern is sticking the pictures into a grid on the wall, and in the end, we vote for who interpreted their items best."

"A box-grid display of memories. Sounds like someone recycled your wedding-in-a-box idea."

"Anything for my best girl," Tansy offered with a grin. "Here—I saved my favourite card for you if you're interested. If not, food and drink are upstairs. Petra and Aiden were by the fireplace last I saw."

Sydney took the card, hugged her friend again, and strolled slowly around the yard, taking it in.

There were a lot of Heart Falls residents who'd come to offer their congratulations on this fine first day of August. Jinx and Sasha zipped past, Sasha's little brother riding on her back as they spoke eagerly about something. Probably whatever they were trying to accomplish next on their bingo card.

Edison had made it to the ranch before her, and he stood beside Kevin, eyes sparkling as they chatted quietly. Kevin had his back to the barn, arms folded over his chest as his gaze stayed fixed on Edison's face.

She wasn't about to interrupt that conversation, although her curiosity was at an all-time high. They were a cute couple in some ways, but Edison was so bouncy compared to the far more stoic counselor of High Water.

"Sydney. Come give us a hand." Tamara waved her over

Sydney joined the cluster of sisters by the firepit. She knew them all, but it was interesting to consider how the connections in the community twisted together.

Tamara was Sasha's stepmom. Julia was Petra's sister-in-law. The oldest sister, Karen, was married to a man Sydney had treated her first year in Heart Falls. And Lisa was married to the local veterinarian, a regular visitor to High Water. "Look at you having a family reunion. What can I help with?"

Lisa grinned, somehow balancing the baby on her hip in spite of her massive baby bump. "We're working on our bingo card. We need a photographer."

"Sure." Sydney held out her hand for the phone then took a few steps back, following their instructions as she snapped a picture. Three of them held shovels with small chunks of charred log while Lisa dangled little Mason to the side and pointed at his belly. "No idea what you're up to."

"It's for the 'Make a pictorial representation of your name' box." Karen rested her hand on a smaller belly than Lisa's. "That make more sense?"

Sydney considered for a moment then laughed. "The baby's belly thing threw me for a minute, but that's not what you're pointing at. Coal-*man?*"

"Yes," Lisa shot a fist into the air. "We rock."

"Ha. That's great."

"Thanks for your help." Tamara took the phone back from Sydney. She tilted her head toward the artists' studio. "I saw you'd arrived. Come on up and let's grab something to eat. We haven't had a chance to visit for a while."

In the end, Sydney landed in a chair beside Tamara, a plate balanced on her knee as they chatted easily.

"Jinx says that you've had a busy summer," Tamara said.

It was hard to fight a grin. "Is that what she says?"

"When she's around the family," Tamara said earnestly. "When she's chatting with Sasha? The story gets a little juicier."

"Really?" Sydney didn't think that Jinx was the type to share stories. Like the fact she'd caught Sydney and Declan fooling around.

Tamara's lips twitched. "I didn't mean to overhear the conversation, but sometimes teenagers forget adults exist." Her expression softened. "I've been getting to know Petra, and I've known Tansy for what feels like forever. I'm probably guilty of thinking you and I are better friends than we are just because of how much they talk about you and how much they clearly love you. So, forgive me if I'm overstepping, but... What's up between you and Declan?"

Dammit. If people in town thought they were an item, this was going to end poorly. Rumours could ruin everything.

The longer she was silent, trying to figure out what to say, the more Tamara's expression fell.

"Sydney? Is something wrong?" The sincerity in the other woman's voice just about broke the dam.

"It's...complicated," Sydney finally said, watching the ebb and flow of laughter and conversation all around them. "I think he's a fine man."

"But still complicated," Tamara said thoughtfully. "Okay. I can understand that." A small snort escaped her. "In case you never heard this particular bit of gossip, I came to Silver Stone as the nanny. Ended up marrying my boss."

"Complications of a different sort, but yeah. I can see that would've taken some juggling."

Tamara nodded. "Juggling. Mistakes. A whole lot of frustration. But I'm glad neither of us gave up."

Sydney blinked.

"Because again—yes, I'm overstepping—but I've seen you two. Maybe it's because I was a nurse, and I still have the tendency to be a little too snoopy, but there's something between you. More than casual interest."

Denying it seemed wrong. Admitting it, dangerous.

Sydney stayed silent.

Tamara glanced across to where her husband Caleb stood chatting with the Skye brothers. "I'll drop the topic now, but say this first. I've got your back. You need anything, you ask. And if you don't know what you need, we can talk about that. But for now we should grab a drink, and I want to go and annoy my husband for a while."

They gathered up their plates and made their way to the side counter just as a bell rang loudly.

Petra shook a dinner bell above her head. "Everyone! The party's not over, but we need your attention for a sec."

Julia and Zach wove through the crowd with glasses in hand, making sure everyone had something to toast with.

Standing at the front, Aiden and Petra smiled at each other before Aiden turned to the crowd. "Our wedding was a little unorthodox. Which, if you know anything about Petra, is typical."

A cheer went up along with a ripple of laughter.

Petra stuck out her tongue for a moment then eased in and pressed a kiss to his cheek. "So while the wedding happened back in the winter, we wanted to take this moment to celebrate with all of you. Our friends, our family, and a big important part of our future."

Aiden took his turn again. "Coming to Heart Falls was the right thing, not only because we found all of you, but because Petra's brother was brilliant enough to already live here, so it brought her here as well."

"You're welcome," Zach called. "Invoice is in the mail."

Laughter rippled through the yard.

Petra grinned. "Coming to High Water was scary. But I knew I was coming home. I just didn't know I'd find the one person who would make it perfect." She turned to Aiden. "You are my heart. I love you."

"Love you forever. Forever and a day," Aiden replied.

They kissed. The cheer that went up was deafening.

"If you'll all raise a glass with us," Aiden called, "this is our official 'we got hitched and we want the world to know it' party."

"To Petra and Aiden!" Tansy shouted, leaning into Jake with Jeffrey on her hip.

"Auntie Petra and Uncle Aiden!" Jeffrey echoed, holding his glass of orange juice high.

The toast echoed through the crowd, delight ringing in every voice.

Sydney stood on the edge of the gathering, watching the joy, the love, the *certainty* flowing through the crowd like sunlight.

The temptation to step forward, to reach for that kind of future—God, it was strong.

But she still didn't see a way forward. Not while she was beholden to Grandpa Nate's money. But knowing it and accepting it were two different things, and the difference was starting to tear at her.

Maybe that was part of what Tamara had seen.

Sydney wanted more.

12

Declan's plans to take Sydney by storm were messed up the very next day when Petra's brother Zach gave him a shout and asked for help dealing with a horse issue for Red Boot ranch.

The trip took the two of them out of town for five nights on the long haul to Winnipeg to pick up horses Zach's dad had received in some sort of odd research trade.

They stopped four hours out of Heart Falls on the way home to grab a final meal before completing the trip. Drizzling rain had followed them all the way across the prairies, and it was nice to finally sit down with a hot coffee and watch the shitty weather instead of white knuckling through it.

"Thanks for being a good sport about the horse run." Zach leaned back in the booth and pushed his empty breakfast plate away. "It's not been the nicest trip ever."

"You just drive to the conditions," Declan said easily. "Run it by me again—how did your dad end up with the horses?"

Zach snorted. "He's an inventor, remember? Somebody owed him information and decided to donate his entire research project in the hopes Dad would take over and finish. Only, that's not that kind of researcher my dad is. The horses are in good shape in spite of whatever nonsense their previous owner was putting them through."

Now it made more sense. "Okay. Yeah, I couldn't figure out how your dad was using horses, let alone getting them into his laboratory."

It was midafternoon by the time they got back to Heart Falls, and nearly supper when they'd finished unloading the horses into the barn, all of them cared for with Cody Gabrielle's help.

"You guys cut it close," Cody cautioned as they closed the final gate.

Declan thought for a minute, but nothing came to mind. "For what?"

"Shit. Tonight is Chance's bachelor party," Zach said with a quick glance at his watch. "Half an hour and I'm good."

"I'll need a little longer," Declan admitted.

Cody gave him a warning glance. "Don't even think about heading back to High Water and ghosting on the rest of the night. Your brothers already said that they would be here."

"Tell them to bring you some clean clothes, and you can shower here at the bunkhouse," Zach suggested. He offered his usual enthusiastic grin. "It's not like we have to impress anybody. As far as I know, our agenda is steaks and beer and some good old-fashioned teasing of the groom-to-be."

In under an hour, Declan found himself seated in a comfortable chair with a beer in hand and a mouthwatering scent teasing him from the nearby grill.

"We missed you," Jake offered, settling into the chair at his side.

"No, we didn't," Aidan rebutted. "It's not as if Declan's the noisy one I have to ignore most of the time."

Declan quietly grinned into his beer and kept his mouth shut.

"Oh, so you're saying *I'm* the noisy type?" Jake demanded.

"Just telling you the next time you and Tansy are fooling around in the hayloft, we need to set up some kind of warning system. Like a sock on a doorknob, because there are some things I just don't need to hear." Aiden winked at Declan where Jake couldn't see.

Instead of getting cranky, their middle brother's expression bloomed into a wide smile. The happiest smile Declan had seen him wear in a long time. "I'd apologize, but I'd be absolutely lying," Jake said.

"Ass."

"Jerk."

A deep rumble of laughter bubbled up and Declan didn't even try to stop it. He met both of his brothers' eyes in turn. "I'm really happy for you both."

He wasn't bitter. Not even close. But damn if their good luck didn't stir up the want in his own chest a little more clearly.

Aiden raised his glass, but Jake examined Declan more seriously for a moment. "You know we want good things for you as well, right?"

Declan pretended not to understand. "I've got a great steak and a drink and I'm pretty damn comfy. Thanks, anyway."

His brother opened his mouth to say something, but was interrupted by Cody rising to his feet and announcing a toast to the demise of his brother's imminent solo status.

"He's the best type of brother," Cody began. "One I would've picked myself, but I didn't have to because someone else in my family was smart enough to make that choice." Cody glanced around, smiling at the friends there. "So we have to first say thanks to our mom and dad for being smart enough to put us together as a family."

Chance nodded his head and raised his glass. "To your mom and me Da. Best possible folks a man could choose." His eyes danced with merriment as he took over being host. "And raise your glass to the Fields family, who are brave enough to welcome not only one but *two* of the Gabrielle men into their fold."

Overhead, lightning shot across the sky in a ragged flash and a blast of thunder drowned out the ensuing cheer. The roiling black clouds moved eerily as the wind picked up, and everybody grabbed their chairs and headed into the big ranch house.

Safely inside, some people were setting up with card tables and a group headed downstairs to a rec room with a pool table and foosball tables for more active entertainment.

They were a great group of guys, but after a week of being out of town, Declan was itching for something different. It'd been too long since he'd seen Sydney, and enough was enough.

He leaned in and spoke quietly to Jake. "What are the girls up to tonight?"

"Bridal shower for Rose," Jake informed him. "At Ivy Stone's place on the edge of town." His lips twitched with amusement. "You plan to crash it?"

Tempting, but no. "There's a couple things I need to do while the ladies are occupied," Declan offered smoothly, not mentioning that it was things he needed to do at Sydney's house. She'd be occupied tonight, and that was all he needed to know.

Jake raised a brow but didn't say anything. At least not until he put down the deck of cards in his hand and followed Declan to the door, waiting quietly while Declan pulled on his coat and hat.

Declan raised a brow at his brother. "Need something?"

"Just to catch you up." Jake's amusement vanished and in place was his serious brother from the police force. "Sydney did a couple of house calls this week that made her nervous. She called me to follow along as backup. Nothing bad happened, but that's when I found out you've been tracking Sydney for a while now—with her permission."

"So?"

Jake breathed out slowly. "So, when a woman who is nearly as bossy and controlling as you asks you to keep an eye on her, I think you need to acknowledge she might be asking for more than just someone at her six."

"You're not telling me anything I haven't thought of," Declan said. "But straight from the horse's mouth, she said what we're doing is enough."

"Which I get, but it doesn't line up," Jake insisted. "I'm not telling you to think something's there when she's told you no. I'm saying something seems off."

"I hear you," Declan agreed. "And if I need Tansy and Petra to offer me support, I'll ask."

His brother smiled. "That's all I wanted to hear. We've got your back, bro. Whatever you need, whatever the pace—we've got your back."

Which was exactly what he expected, and as Declan made his way through the storm to Sydney's house, he felt a whole lot more hopeful than he had any right.

Didn't matter how keen he was to mix up their relationship. If she said no again, he'd listen.

But first, she was going to listen to him. He was going to make it crystal clear exactly what he had to offer and then hope like hell it was enough.

~

"I can't believe you're making me play this game." Rose all but glared at Tansy. "*You're* the baker—

"And clearly the candlestick maker, too," Fern added with a snicker. "Or something like that. You suck at this game."

"Laugh it up, sweetheart." Rose eyed their youngest sister with mock annoyance. "Someday soon you too will plan a wedding, and we're saving up all our badness to torment you."

"Not going to happen," Fern offered with a grin. "Cody and I plan to shack up happily for the rest of our lives, no ceremony needed."

At Sydney's side, Petra leaned in closer. "I wonder if I should inform Fern I overheard Cody talking about buying her a ring..."

"You heard that or hacked their emails?" Sydney eyed her friend. "You're scary at times. That's all I'm saying."

"Not my fault if people decide to talk about stuff I don't need to know when I'm right there. In the Red Boot ranch tack room, behind a half closed door," Petra admitted, looking a smidge guilty. "In my defense, I *was* trying to overhear some clues as to what to get my brother for his birthday this year."

Sydney wasn't falling for it. "It's August. Your brother's birthday isn't until December."

"I like to plan ahead," Petra insisted.

Laughter bubbled up from the middle of the room where the game had continued.

The amazing turn out for the bridal shower filled the house to bursting, but the crowd was expected, considering Rose had lived in town since she was thirteen. There were teachers from the school, and the new cook from Buns and Roses. Edison had been invited to both parties, but had instantly chosen the bridal shower over the bachelor party.

A nice collection of generations were represented, with Rose and Tansy's mother in attendance along with their

Grandmother Sonora and other older ladies. They were the ones who'd organized the classic bridal shower games like the one currently tormenting Rose.

The tray in front of her held a dozen different bowls filled with white substances. Rose was trying in vain to identify them.

"You have the salt correct, and inexplicably the rice flour, but nothing else." Her mother shook her head. "I thought after all these years of helping out at Buns and Roses you would've learned some cooking basics."

"I know plenty. You open the pantry and reach for the packages that are clearly labeled chocolate cake mix, pancake batter, cream of tartar." Rose wrinkled her nose. "Although for the life of me I couldn't tell you what on earth to put that last one in."

They partnered up to name the nearly identical powders. In the end, Edison and his teammate scored the only ten out of ten.

He batted his lashes. "I am multitalented," Edison offered perkily.

"And oh so modest," Lexie intoned.

"That too," Edison agreed.

Into the amused laughter, Tansy motioned for Petra to bring something forward. "Just to prove I'm not totally a pain in the butt, I warned Mom this had to be a two-step game. Ta-da."

She gestured toward a second tray. This one held more than a dozen small canning jars, each one filled with something green and leafy.

Rose leaned forward with suspicion before she let out a little gasp of delight. "These are herbs."

"Plant-based challenge! If you don't beat our butts, I'll want to know why," Tansy said firmly.

Edison snatched up a jar in either hand and waggled his

brows. "We have ways to make you talk," he intoned with villainous glee.

It took almost no time for Rose to have a completed list in her hand and a gloating smile on her face.

From her comfy corner chair, Sydney had quietly observed as the merriment unfolded. Outside, a storm had rolled in from over the mountains, turning the sky charcoal and making the nearby trees sway. The house sat next door to the local cemetery, and in it, the small twinkle lights that hung from trees and between fence posts bobbed and danced like lanterns held in ghostly hands.

Sydney breathed in deeply, soaking in the moment of calm.

Lexie settled beside her, a plate filled with snacks resting in her lap. "They're good people."

"The best," Sydney agreed. "Are you having fun?"

"I am. Although it is kind of odd that they're holding two parties tonight. I thought it was becoming the norm to have a joint event. The last shower I attended, Michael and I brought—"

Lexie cut off. She snatched up a chip and loaded it with salsa before shoving it in her mouth. She stared up at the corner of the room as if pretending she hadn't spoken at all.

Confusion was the highest thing on Sydney's mind. "Who is Michael?"

Rapidly chewing and swallowing Lexie shrugged. "No one. Just someone I was seeing at one time. It didn't work out."

No. There was more to the story, and Sydney had a horrible premonition she knew what trouble had been haunting Lexie all along. "Michael Jeremiah?"

Lexie's expression crumpled.

On her other side, Petra stiffened. She'd been watching the center of the room but now turned her attention to Sydney and Lexie. "Relative of yours, Syd?"

"Oldest brother," Sydney confirmed. "Lexie? What's going on?"

The rest of the room was filled with the noise and amusement of the games as people wandered into the kitchen for refreshments. With unerring talent, Tansy made her way over and settled on the arm of Petra's chair. "You guys look way too serious for a party."

"Is there somewhere we can go for a little privacy?" Sydney asked Tansy.

"Sure. This way."

Lexie didn't meet any of their eyes, but she also didn't try and run away, following them into a neat and tidy home office.

"What's up, Lexie?" Sydney spoke softly but firmly. "If you were dating my brother and things didn't work out, why would my grandfather recommend you so highly? Or is something else happening here?"

Lexie looked absolutely miserable. "Mr. Jones suggested it would be in all of our best interests if I got more experience elsewhere."

"Best interests?" Sydney didn't want to jump to conclusions, but a whole lot of bouncing in her brain headed toward *oh shit* territory. "Tell me if I got this right. You're fully certified and working at Toronto General where my brother also works. The two of you get involved. Suddenly, my grandfather decides you needed to work in a different province."

"Mostly right." Lexie lifted her gaze off the floor, frowning as she met Sydney's eyes. "Your brother is in line to receive an invitation to become a part of a very prestigious research event. But it involves travel, and—"

"And if you and Michael were getting serious, he might turn down the research in order to stay with you." Sydney didn't make it a question. She was damn sure that's what her grandfather had thought.

Lexie nodded.

This was more than messy—it was manipulative, and it stank of Grandpa Nate's brand of control. "Does my brother know why you left?" Sydney asked.

"If I told him, he might've told me to stay—and that would've defeated the whole plan," Lexie said softly.

Tansy's gaze jumped between them all. "So your grandfather broke you up because he's organizing life plans for his grandson? Why would you go along with that?"

"How could I stay knowing that being involved with Michael would damage his long-term career?" Lexie demanded with a hint of heat. "We were getting serious, but we hadn't made any commitments yet. I thought a clean break would be the best. There's still a chance we can be together at some point in the future."

Petra shook her head. "It doesn't seem like something you should be deciding by yourself. But I don't know. Maybe I'm wrong."

At her core, Sydney was rattled—shaken in a way that made old memories claw to the surface. "You two don't understand." She caught hold of Lexie's hands, squeezing tight. "Grandpa Nate has this way about him. He kind of runs over you with his well-meaning, virtuous-sounding ideas, and you go along for the ride because there doesn't seem to be any other solution."

A frown creased between Lexie's brows. "Did he meddle with you? Is that why you're living in Heart Falls?"

No. It was far more subtle than that. "I moved to Heart Falls of my own free will," Sydney assured her, suddenly needing this conversation to be over. "It's okay, Lexie. We need to talk about this more in the future, but it doesn't change anything about what I know to be true. You're a fantastic doctor, and I'm grateful to have your help at the clinic."

Relief relaxed Lexie's face. "I'm very happy to be there."

"But you'd be happier if you could be with Michael," Sydney suggested.

"That's impossible, but yes." Lexie straightened her shoulders. "For now, this is my choice. I *want* to stay in Heart Falls and work for you. But I'll think about talking to Michael, when it's appropriate, in spite of Mr. Jone's insistence that I not get in touch."

He'd done it to Lexie. He'd done it to Michael. And now, looking at Lexie's downturned eyes, Sydney realized how many people had been nudged, rerouted, or redirected by Grandpa Nate's *well-meaning* hand.

Sydney offered Lexie a hug then sent her back out into the party.

When Petra and Tansy would've left the room as well, Sydney waved them down.

Inside her, a storm churned—nearly as chaotic as the one now battering the walls outside the little house.

"That was one of the wildest things I've ever heard," Petra said.

"Hold onto your socks." Sydney met Petra and Tansy's eyes in turn. "She isn't the only one Grandpa Nate is messing with. But he's damn good at it, and to be honest, he's meddled in ways I don't know how to stop."

13

---

oth her friends went still, their attention snapping on her like a spotlight. "Your grandpa. How is he messing with you?" Petra demanded.

The concern on Petra's face was echoed in the soft squeeze of Sydney's arm by Tansy, and Sydney took a deep breath as she looked at her friends.

How much was she willing to tell them? How much was she willing to share?

She knew a lot of their secrets. But this felt different— maybe because she was supposed to be the smart one, which made it harder to untangle from logic or pride.

The soft grip on her arm released and the next thing she knew, Tansy bopped her one on the shoulder. "Spill the beans now," Tansy ordered with a glare.

"Yeah. You've got that Sphinx look on your face," Petra said, frowning deeply. "That's your hiding-something-big face —and now's not the time to bottle things up."

"Just figuring out what to say," Sydney protested.

"If it's about your grandpa, start with this: 'He's a meddler of epic proportions.'" Tansy suggested.

"Say it," Petra wheedled, dragging out her words. "Come on—Say. It."

Which meant Sydney was actually laughing slightly when she spoke. "My grandfather...has strong opinions about what a woman's role should be."

Tansy blinked. "Okay. That's not the direction I expected this to go."

"I thought your grandpa encouraged you to go into medical school," Petra said, her confusion deepening. "I'm sure that's what you told us at one point."

"He did. He and my grandma were instrumental in me attending university when I did." She looked at both her friends. "I was sixteen when I got accepted, and our family home was four hours away from the university. Grandpa and Grandma lived a fifteen minute bus ride away. Having their house as a home base was vital, especially when everyone around me was a lot older. So I lived with them from age sixteen until after I completed medical school and my residency."

Petra eased her hip back on the table and folded her arms over her chest. "Enough beating around the bush. What's the connection between the look on your face and us finding out Lexie is here because he's keeping her apart from your brother?"

Even talking about it made her stomach churn. "Grandpa wants the absolute best for his grandchildren. For us three girls, that meant jobs that piqued our interest and kept us mentally challenged. The worst possible life choice was to get tangled up with some guy too soon. Because somewhere down the road when we did decide to get married, he assumed that meant we planned to toss aside all our training and become proper wives and mothers."

Now Tansy looked confused. "It's possible to be a doctor *and* married *and* a mother. I mean it would be busy as hell, but life gets busy, no matter what."

Petra slid an arm around Sydney's waist and squeezed her for a second. "No, this is something bigger. Syd, I know you respect our friends who are homemakers. Why do you have that look in your eyes when you say it while talking about your grandpa?"

"Yeah. Why is your grandpa so irrational about this?" Tansy was nodding now. "And you know, if you lived with him for a bunch of years starting when you were sixteen, whatever his hang-ups are might've become your own."

Sydney all but growled in frustration. "I'll have you know it took me a couple of years of deep thinking to figure this out," she complained.

"Just don't take a couple of years to tell us about it," Petra said.

Sydney stepped away and paced for a moment before turning to face her friends. "My grandpa has a problem with women giving up their careers to become homemakers because that's what my mom did. She fell in love and gave it all up, and instead of the brilliant law career she could've had, she chose to stay home."

Petra shook her head. "Your mom and dad raised five amazing, extraordinary children. She might not have been working in a hospital or a courtroom, but she definitely did something of great value."

"And I know that," Sydney insisted before making a face. "I know that in my head, and that's why I have no issues with our friends who choose family as a career. But somewhere deep down, the idea of doing that myself makes my stomach churn.

Like it'd be betraying everything I've worked for—even when I know better."

Silence fell for a moment as Sydney stared at the ground and tried to get her pulse to slow.

"Syd, This is something you need to talk to someone about," Tansy began quietly.

"I know," Sydney snapped before adjusting her tone apologetically. "I know, sweetie. It just didn't seem worthwhile because right now I have the clinic and I need to—"

A quick knock on the door was followed immediately by Lexie's arrival. "Sorry for interrupting, but Sydney? I just got a call forwarded from the emergency line at the clinic. Mr. Nagy phoned and he sounds delirious. Should I send an ambulance to find out what's wrong?"

Dammit. "A patient I saw this week who cut himself while chopping firewood," Sydney explained to Tansy and Petra. "He might've got an infection. Or he might've decided to medicate himself with that bottle of whiskey like he was doing before I saw him." She considered for a moment. "He lives hell and gone in the foothills. I'd hate to send the EMTs out if what he needs is to be told to go to bed and sleep it off."

"If you plan on going out there, I'm coming with you," Petra informed her.

Tansy bumped Petra's side. "There's someone else willing and able to accompany our lovely doctor friend on her house visit."

"Oh, of course. He's perfect." Petra pulled out her phone and her fingers flew over the keypad. She paused and met Sydney's gaze head-on. "I assume you have no issue if Declan accompanies you? In case you need some grunt labour lifting a body into bed?"

Just what she needed. Declan Skye in her space when her brain was already tangled and confused.

Still, there was no fighting her friends when they got in this kind of mood. Sydney put on a happy face. "Tell him to meet me at the clinic. I'll grab supplies and we'll head out."

"I'll leave another message with Mr. Nagy, asking him to call back." Lexie offered. "In case he becomes lucid enough to check his phone."

She vanished from sight, but as Sydney headed toward the door, Tansy caught her arm and held her in place.

"This conversation isn't over," her friend warned. "You've been keeping secrets, which is absolutely your right. But this secret is making you completely miserable, and that's not allowed. You're our friend, and we won't let *anybody* be mean to you."

"Not even yourself," Petra chimed in from the opposite side.

"You're such jerks. Why do you have to be my friends?" Sydney mock complained. She gave them each a quick hug before extracting herself and tilting her head toward the door. "I need to go do my doctor thing, but yes. We will talk about this more. And I'll think about—"

"You'll think about what *you* want. You, Sydney Jeremiah, person of extraordinary intellect with a big old ginormous heart." Tansy dipped her chin firmly and pushed Sydney toward the door. "We'll make sure that happens—don't think for a second we won't."

The best and the worst part of it was Sydney knew she could trust them to follow through. Which was both heaven and hell.

Friendship. Bossy and loving and painful all at the same time.

Sydney hurried to grab her things and head to the clinic.

$\sim$

> Petra: Sydney has an out of town emergency
> visit and needs you as back up. It's not a high
> speed situation, but meet her at the clinic
> ASAP. Confirm you got this.

THE MESSAGE WAS the last thing Declan had expected. Thankfully, he got it before he finished the message he'd been about to send, warning Sydney to expect him at her house.

> Declan: I'll be there.

The roads in Heart Falls were a wash of puddles and mud. It took less than five minutes to get to the clinic, but she'd beat him there. The lights were on, shining through the glass windows of the reception area. Rivulets of water ran down in shimmering streaks.

He pushed through the unlocked door carefully. "Syd?"

"Nearly ready. Come and grab this bag." She lifted those amazing silvery grey eyes to meet his. Concern was written on her face and dark shadows lingered. "Are you okay driving?"

"Sure." He picked up the oversized duffel bag she'd indicated and eased it over his shoulder. "Got everything you need?"

She lifted a bag of her own then gestured toward the door. "This is it. Let's go. I'll give you directions once we hit the highway. We head south to start."

The storm was no longer kidding around. In the thirty seconds it took to get from the front door of the clinic into his truck, both of them were drenched.

Declan grabbed a towel from the back seat where he'd put them earlier and handed it over. "Dry off."

"You don't want me to get your seats wet," she teased.

"It's wet enough outside. We don't need it raining in here," he agreed.

He clicked the seat warmers on, making sure hers was set to high, then focused on reaching the highway safely.

The wipers flipped back and forth at such a rapid pace it brought back the memory of the metronome Aiden had broken when he was a kid. The *thump, thump, thump* sounded so quickly it damn near made Declan's heart race in an attempt to keep time.

"Thanks for coming with me," Sydney said quietly, gaze fixed firmly on the highway ahead of them.

"Of course."

"Sorry to pull you away from the bachelor party."

He snorted. "I left a while ago."

"Well, shit. I interrupted your relaxing evening?"

"Hardly." He hadn't intended to tell her this quickly, but it seemed the appropriate time. "I left the party to go and do something important."

She didn't say anything, but her gaze lingered on his face.

"I was at your place," he confessed.

Sydney snickered. "Well, there's me messing up what should've been a lovely booty call."

"Wasn't a booty call." Declan cleared his throat. "I wanted to see you after being gone all week. Not for sex, but to talk. To spend time together."

He waited for her to shoot the idea down, but she didn't.

Risking a quick glance to the side, he discovered Sydney was still staring at him, but this time her expression was more like a child looking longingly at a toy in the window.

Something they really wanted but knew they couldn't have.

Driving in dangerous conditions was absolutely not what he wanted to be doing while having an important conversation. He forced his gaze back to the road. "Syd? Where are we going?"

"Township Road for the turn is coming up," she warned.

"The first five km are straightforward then we follow a forestry service road for a bit."

Okay. He really needed to focus on the road, but this was not the end of the conversation.

Time to give her a break, though, and stick to something simpler. "How was the bridal shower?"

Sydney eased back in the passenger seat, extending her legs as she let out an enormous sigh. "The party part was good."

"Implying some other part was bad?"

"Hello, complicated life," she offered. "What about you?"

"When I left the bachelor party, Cody was trying to convince his brother to shave off his moustache."

She gasped. "Not the day before the wedding."

"I think Chance was pulling his leg about being interested in the idea, but hopefully he doesn't do anything that makes Rose want to kick his ass on their first day married." Declan peered through the rain that descended in light gusts and then in downpours that made it look as if a river was being dumped through a sieve. "When Sadie and I got married, she insisted any parties happen at least two weeks before the big day."

"I can see why, since the goal of the bachelor party seems to be to cause havoc," Sydney said.

"What's the worst prewedding story you've heard?" Declan asked.

Sydney adjusted position. "The worst is the group of pre-med students who took the very drunk groom-to-be down to the clinic and wrapped his leg as if he'd broken it."

"The hell?"

"Oh, yeah, it was terrible. Funny in one way, if you can picture the poor guy standing at the front of the church in an ankle-to-hip, rock-solid cast."

"She still married him?" Declan asked. "Sadie would have

married me, but she might have broken something over my head for being an idiot before the big day."

"The wedding went ahead, but the worst part was they didn't tell him the cast was a fake until three days into the honeymoon."

Declan felt slightly guilty for being amused. "Poor woman. I hope somebody paid for them to get new wedding photos somewhere down the road."

"It was her brothers who did it, so yeah. There was payback."

The truck hit a pothole Declan hadn't seen in time, and the entire cab rocked violently. Sydney gasped then didn't make another sound.

"Sorry."

"Don't apologize," she reassured him. "I would've had to turn back over ten minutes ago."

The next twenty minutes she directed him. The road became steadily steeper and more and more soupy as the rain turned the gravel road into a sea of mud.

When they finally pulled into the yard of the old-timer's cabin, Declan was happy to put the truck in *Park* and release the death grip he had on the wheel. "How do you want to do this?"

Sydney peered out the window. "He's got a little porch, so grab our bags and head out there. Knock to see if he answers, then open the door if he doesn't."

They did a mad rush between the parked truck and the fifteen steps to the porch, and Declan's jacket still clung to him like a second skin.

Sydney wiped water from her eyes and tightened her ponytail before putting her knuckles to the door. "Mr. Nagy? We've come for a visit."

A chorus of barking erupted behind the door, followed by

frantic clawing. At least the dogs inside were excited to say hello.

She knocked three more times then tried the door.

When it swung open easily, two mid-sized mutts rushed forward, bumping their heads into Declan and Sydney before weaving their way around their legs. They barked and licked and otherwise acted excited to help.

"Down," Declan ordered, hand stretched over their heads.

One of them whimpered slightly as he dropped onto his haunches, but the other disappeared into the house, tail wagging furiously.

"Let's see what's happened," Sydney said.

"I go first," Declan said firmly.

She stepped aside, brushing another streak of rain off her cheek. "Be my guest."

The house was empty. Unlike previous mountain cabins Declan had visited, this bachelor kept his organized. There was a cold pot of coffee on the counter, three-quarters full, and a few clean dishes in a drying rack. The airtight stove held the remains of a dying fire.

Declan pushed into the back bedroom section of the house, knocking on the door before pushing it open. "Mr. Nagy? You okay?"

The bed was unmade but empty. A quick check into the other room showed an office space that was also unoccupied.

Sydney shrugged. "Must be in the barn."

They both pulled up their collars and headed into the storm. The wind snapped at their clothing, blasting them with moisture as the rain lashed sideways, stinging like slaps.

The barn was empty, the shed was empty. The dogs following at their heels seemed not the least bit concerned about where their master was.

"His truck is here," Sydney said, worry colouring her voice. "Did he go wandering in the trees?"

A loud crack of thunder shook the barn, and Declan pulled Sydney to his side. "If he is out there, we're not looking for him. Not now in the dark and the rain."

"I know."

He crouched to pet the dogs. "Where's the boss? Hey, boys. Where's the boss? Go find him."

One took off like a shot, and Declan headed to the door to watch as the dog went straight to the truck and sniffed before coming back and whining.

"He's not in there," Declan assured the dog. He looked at Sydney. "See if we've got any reception."

She pulled out her phone and made a small noise. "I have no bars, but there's a message from Lexie. Must've come in while we were bouncing on the road." She read it, her eyes widening. "Well, *shit*."

"What's up?"

Sydney made a face. "The hospital called the clinic because we're the physicians on file. Nagy was checked in half an hour ago. A friend dropped him off."

"Well, that's good." Declan breathed a sigh of relief that the man wasn't lying out there under some bush in the storm.

She nodded. "I'm glad he's there. But..."

She stared at the rain soaked landscape. At the puddles that had turned into streams that were now flowing down the road.

From the doorway of the barn they clearly saw the lightning strike hit a tree to the side of the road. Electricity crackled on the air, and the hair on Declan's arms stood on end as the deafening *crack* boomed.

The wind howled in his ears, but even at a distance, the creaking and rumble of the tree falling was louder. It leaned to the side, pulling part of the embankment with it.

A swirl of mud rushed down the side of the mountain and across the road.

Sydney gasped. "What—"

From farther up the mountain, another deep rumble started, and the ground underfoot wavered.

Declan caught her by the waist and pulled her into the middle of the open arena. Far enough away there was nothing within striking distance.

Far enough from the barn so that if it collapsed they'd be safe.

The rain let up only enough to let them see the hazy outline of the steep mountainside to the west. Between one breath and the next, the side of the mountain seemed to have been sliced off like a hot knife into butter. Trees remained vertical but began to flow down the hillside, like a surfer riding a wave. The surreal sight ended abruptly when the shifting tree line hit the horizontal level of the road, and with a great crash and thunder, tall spruce tipped and tumbled like bowling pins, leaving massive roots jutting skyward.

The slide felt endless, though it likely lasted less than a minute.

Sydney leaned into him, and Declan tightened his grip around her soaking wet body as the full damage finally registered.

Behind them, the barn was intact, and the house was fine. But the road down the mountain simply didn't exist anymore.

14

———

he dogs disappeared into a shelter tucked into the corner of the porch. Declan ushered Sydney through the door, their soaked and mud-coated shoes abandoned outside.

The cabin was pitch-dark except for the faint glow of embers through the glass of the airtight stove.

Sydney cursed softly. "Of course. The mudslide took out the power lines to the cabin."

"We need to stoke the fire and we need to find out what there is for food that we can borrow while we're here." Declan rubbed his hands together and blew on them. "Which do you want to do?"

"The fire is yours. I know how to deal with the damper on my firebox, but not all of them are the same and I don't want to smoke us out."

He nodded and headed to the black cast-iron stove set into the far wall.

Sydney turned on the flashlight app on her phone. "I'll look for flashlights, as well."

"Check the top of the fridge, if you can reach. That's a common place to keep the spares."

"Is that a jab about my height, buster?" Sydney teased as she went into the kitchen, flicking the kitchen light out of habit. She poked quickly in the fridge to keep the cold in before checking the cupboards. There were jars of jam, rice, pasta, and a half-loaf of bread that wasn't too stale.

The coffee in the pot on the counter, though, she poured down the drain with a shudder. She kept trying to break the old-timers of the habit, but had failed to convince them she knew what she was talking about. She'd once found actual mold growing on the surface of the liquid, but chances were as soon as she was gone, the man had used a spoon to scoop the evidence into the wastebasket then reheated and drank the rest.

Waste not, want not, could go a little too far at times.

She'd just spotted an oversized flashlight tucked beside the fridge when the crackle of wood catching fire in the stove reached her ears. She propped the sturdy light source up against a bowl, lighting up the entire counter, then crossed her fingers.

Water flowed easily from the tap, and she quickly filled a stovetop-friendly kettle to make them tea.

The wind howled so hard that the entire cabin shook, but they were safe. And given a little time, they'd be toasty warm.

A shiver took her from top to bottom just as big hands landed on her shoulders. Declan tucked her back against his warm body. "It's okay. We'll be all right."

Sydney pivoted on the spot. "Not worried about that, honestly. Just cold."

He nodded, lifting a hand that held a thick Hudson's Bay blanket with its distinctive rainbow stripes. "Wrap up for now." He eyed the kettle. "I hoped he was on a spring-water system. No problems with pressure?"

"Ran clear and cold," she told him.

A hum of approval rang out. "Gravity fed. Good to know we have all the running water we want, just no heater."

"Thus the kettle."

Declan eyed her for a moment. "The fire is going, so I thought before I dry out, I'd take a look around and make sure everything is secure for the night."

She hesitated. "Is it safe?"

"I'll keep away from the hillside, and I won't stay in the barn any longer than I have to." He tucked his fingers under her chin and lifted so she was looking up at him. His smile was so faint others might think he wasn't showing any emotion, but she saw it. Saw that he was more relaxed now than he'd been the entire drive up the mountain.

She dipped her chin. "Okay. Get back here quickly so I don't have to go out there after you."

"Yes, ma'am."

He brushed his lips over hers, a soft, quiet caress. One hand pressed to her lower back and kept her near as he sweetly nuzzled and kissed.

When he finally pulled away, she was a little light-headed.

Declan stopped at the door and grabbed a rain slicker that hung there as well as what had to be Ted Nagy's ten gallon hat. He tucked the brim down tight, took a breath as if bracing himself, then opened the door and stepped into the gale.

Sydney moved around the little cabin, taking stock of the rest of their supplies. There were a surprising amount of blankets in the hall closet as well as towels folded neatly on a shelf above the bathroom door.

She carried a supply of towels to the door and went looking for dry clothing that might fit Declan.

Red and orange flames were flickering over the freshly stocked wood she'd placed in the stove when the door opened, and with a swirl and a scream, cold air ushered Declan into the room.

"Everything's fine," he assured her immediately. "I fed the dogs, and they bunked down in the barn with the rest of the animals."

He took the towel she offered then began to strip right then and there.

It was tempting to watch the floor show, but it somehow didn't seem right. Thoughts of her grandfather's interference and the fears Sydney carried were too big and loud to let her slide off into mindless pleasure.

So she busied herself pouring him a cup of tea and adding a spoonful of sugar, making sure he had a prime spot to sit.

Big solid feet clad in grey woolen socks landed beside her and then he sat, easing across the floor until he leaned on the couch, arm right up against hers. He reached his hands toward the fire and wiggled his fingers. "It's the middle of August, and it feels like snow on the air."

"Oh Lord, no."

He snorted. "No, not at this elevation. But I wouldn't be surprised if we find that the tips of the Rockies are painted white when we get far enough back to see them."

She passed him the mug of tea, and he wrapped his hands around it gratefully. "We won't see them for a while, though, will we?"

"Not if we want to drive out," he said. "Once the storm runs its course, we can hike down to an accessible point to get picked up. Either that, or we have to get a helicopter in."

"I don't think either of us is important enough to need a helicopter rescue," she said dryly.

"Speak for yourself." He stared into his teacup, lips twitching slightly as he hid his gaze from hers. "I'm damn near royalty. At least that's what my horses tell me."

Unexpectedly, amusement bubbled up. Sydney shifted closer until their sides connected, and she leaned her head on his shoulder. "Glad if I have to be trapped in the storm it's with you."

He pressed a soft kiss to the top of her head. "Ditto."

Sydney stared at the fire for a moment, sipping tea and letting herself think. The quiet around them grew. The only sound was the ticking of the metal as the fire heated the stove. It wasn't awkward or painful or confusing. The heat curling from the fireplace was soft fingers offering peace and contentment and acceptance.

But in her core, that knot of discontent remained. The ugly worries were not going to simply go away if she ignored them.

Physician, heal thyself. It wasn't possible, she knew that.

There were times when if you wanted an injury to heal, you had to first exorcize the source of the infection. Clean it up, no matter how painful the process.

"My head is a mess right now," Sydney confessed quietly. "On the inside," she added when he leaned over with concern to examine her closer.

"Messes on the outside I sometimes know how to deal with. Messes on the inside?" He cupped her cheek with his big hand. "I can be a good listener. Don't know how much advice I can give, but I can listen."

"Maybe when we get to the part where it's called for, instead of giving advice, we can just toss out ideas." Sydney rubbed her face against his hand, suddenly reminded of the kittens demanding to be petted.

"That I can do."

The next minute she found herself airborne then settled into his lap with the blanket cocooned around her shoulders and his gaze intense on hers.

"You asked about the bridal shower? Well, turns out the

fantastic helper my grandpa sent me is also my brother's ex-girlfriend."

Declan was silent for a minute before declaring, "The hell? Your brother doesn't live anywhere near Heart Falls."

His confused expression made Sydney snicker in spite of the tension in her gut. "I knew my grandfather was the meddlesome sort, but I didn't know the extent of it. Seems my brother might be in line for a great career opportunity, so Grandpa kindly removed the distraction of a steady girlfriend. But he did it in a nice way," she pointed out quickly. "Offered her up like a cherry on a sundae to me to help at the clinic. So I win, because I get a great helper, and Lexie wins, because she gets a great job. And Michael wins because now he can take the opportunity when it's presented without being torn about leaving behind someone who means a lot to him."

"That's dirty." Declan's opinion was very clear in that moment. "We're not talking teenagers, are we? Because you're the youngest, so this is someone in their late thirties or early forties, yes?"

"Definitely adults." Sydney took a deep breath. "And as infuriating as I find it, I don't have a leg to stand on because I've been taken in just as hard by him."

This time Declan didn't say anything. Just waited, concern creasing his brow.

Oh boy. "My grandfather owns the clinic."

"Your clinic?"

"Heart Falls Family Care. Yes, the one that I run, and that Lexie works at. We get paid for services through the usual Alberta health care system, but there are still costs related to setting up a medical practice. There's the usual time lag between output of costs and getting payment. Grandpa Nate has been footing that bill, which means he's the head of the clinic, and we're staff. I draw a salary, same as the other employees."

Declan nodded slowly. "Okay. I've no idea how things like that run other than we've got a pretty damn good situation here in Alberta." He tugged on a lock of hair falling past Sydney's cheek. "What does this have to do with not having a leg to stand on?"

The worst part was not screwing up the courage to tell him this, but realizing it was only the first part of what she needed to share.

Enough. She'd been scared and holding out for so long that none of it mattered anymore. She needed a new path forward.

She took his hands in hers and held on tight. "My grandpa told me he would fund the clinic as long as I remained fully committed."

"Damn easy. You're one of the best doctors I've known in my entire life."

"That's sweet, and I appreciate it. But let me define *fully committed* the way my grandpa does," she warned, gripping Declan tighter even as she lost the courage to meet his gaze. She stared at their hands and noted her knuckles were turning white. "A doctor whose first and only responsibility is to the job. No boyfriend, no steady relationships, and definitely no getting married." A sharp stab hit her in the rib cage as she realized another truth. "Hell, if he could've outlawed girlfriends, he probably would've."

Oddly, under her, Declan began to quiver. She glanced up to find he was actually chuckling.

He shook his head. "How on earth could he think you being involved with somebody would mean you'd be less committed? That's not who you are."

She didn't want to say it. Saying it made it real. But not saying it had left her choking on silence for too long.

"As much as I want to be with you... I can't. Because choosing you means letting Grandpa cut off my funding. And if that happens? Everything I've built here, everything I've worked for, disappears."

WHAT SYDNEY WAS SAYING—THE importance of the situation—Declan knew exactly how much this meant. It was her job, her livelihood, and a steady paycheck for other people as well. Not to mention the huge difference she was making in the community.

He heard all those unspoken things, but one part struck him as straight up the biggest thing to focus on.

"You want to be with me?" he asked quietly.

She swallowed hard, pain twisting her features. "Part of me doesn't know how I get up in the morning without you there. Another part of me wants to run away as far as I can because I don't want to hurt you. And I'm really afraid I will."

A muscle jumped in his jaw. She had no idea—none—how much he could take, as long as it meant she was still in his life.

Screw it. Declan pulled her fully into his arms and held her. Let his embrace become a barrier locking them together and locking out the world. The storm still raged against the roof. Rain smacked into the windowpanes like kids on a candy high let loose with drumsticks. But they were here, together, and that made everything right.

Sydney tucked her head under his chin and cuddled in. She stuck her hand under the soft flannel shirt she'd found for him, the front gaping open because he was a far bigger man than the owner of the cabin. Declan didn't give a flying flip what he was wearing because Sydney was holding onto him, and it felt as if she would never let go.

Which wasn't what her words had said.

Since he'd never been that good with words himself, he'd learned a lot about watching people's conversations and the things they said with their bodies. Sydney was saying pretty damn clear she knew where she wanted to be.

In his arms.

He pressed another kiss to the top of her head.

Start with the important stuff. Don't assume she knows.

Once again Sadie's words echoed in his head. Yeah, and once again, she was right.

Declan didn't change his grip, just tilted his head so his lips brushed Sydney's ear. "I want to be with you."

She stilled, her breathing deep and even, as if she were fighting to keep it that way.

"I think about you first thing when I get up in the morning and last thing at night before I go to bed." He pressed his lips to her temple. "And in between I think about you and smile. Sometimes I think about you, and I get hot and bothered."

A sharp exhale of amusement escaped her.

"Okay, yeah. A lot of the times when I think about you, I get hot and bothered. But it's not just how much I enjoy being with you physically. I want to *be* with you, Syd. I want us to be together, and I'm sorry that your grandpa's rules mean this isn't something you simply get to decide on your own. That's not right."

"It's not, but I don't know how to solve it."

"Me neither. Not yet, but maybe we can do that idea-tossing thing between us. And if we're not smart enough on our own, we've got other people in our lives who are smart in different ways." Declan cleared his throat. "Since I seem to remember being raked over the coals for assuming there's only one kind of smarts out there."

She nodded, but even as she sat up straighter, she seemed to be withdrawing. "There's more."

"This is life," he uttered in a deadpan tone. "There's always something else to complicate things."

This time when her lips quivered, he wasn't sure if she was fighting tears or laughter.

"Do we need to make a list? Because that's Jake's type of smarts. Not mine."

This time she did laugh. "I don't have any notebooks with me."

He shrugged. "Worst-case scenario we use toilet paper as a notepad."

She pressed her lips together in an attempt to hide her smile. "I'm trying to be serious."

"You're succeeding in being serious," he told her with all earnestness. "Only Sadie would tell me the more serious the conversation, the more we need to say fuck it and find things to laugh about."

Sydney nodded, her eyes going soft. "Sadie sounds like she was amazing."

"She was," Declan agreed. "But so are you. She would've liked you, a lot," he added quickly.

Surprise arrived. "You think so?"

"Absolutely." Declan tilted his head to the side. "Tell you what. Let's take a break for a minute then come back here. This serious talk can go on for as long as it wants since we've got nowhere to go."

Another hard gust shook the cabin, and Sydney nodded as she scrambled to her feet. "Dibs on the bathroom."

"Don't use all the toilet paper," he offered dryly.

She blinked at him for a minute and then snickered her way off down the hall, the flicker of firelight trailing after her.

Okay. It was a little like walking through the barn with

kittens racing underfoot. He needed to keep his pace steady and firm so she'd know he was there for her.

Chances were, even giving her a little breathing space, she'd put those walls back up and find ways to cut this conversation short.

Nothing doing. This was too important to give up just because it was awkward.

By the time Sydney returned, he'd spread out a couple of blankets in front of the fireplace and put some pillows down so they had places to relax a little farther from the heat that was now pouring from the very efficient airtight stove.

He really didn't have any solutions, because he'd never heard of this kind of situation before outside of far-fetched TV plots. But what he did have was family he could count on, which meant Sydney's worries about the clinic might not be easy to solve, but they were solvable.

Which meant digging deeper.

As expected, when Sydney sat back down, she settled kitty corner to him, leaning against the couch. The glow from the stove was the only light in the room, throwing dancing shadows across the cabin walls and highlighting the rosy colour in her cheeks. It looked as if she'd washed her face, and she lifted her chin, determination in the gesture.

She was about to bolt. Maybe not physically out the door, but it was clear as anything she'd decided whatever it was she was hoping for was impossible and she was ready to bail.

Which meant the only great solution was to get a step ahead of her.

"Can I ask you for help with something tangling me up?" he asked quietly, speaking the second she began to open her lips.

Sydney swallowed whatever it was she had been about to share.

"What?" Nervous and twitchy as if expecting him to blurt out something she'd regret.

Maybe. Maybe, but it would be the truth. And truth was powerful. That's what their stepfather Jeff had told them, and so far it was one of the greatest lessons Declan had learned from the man.

He met Sydney's gaze straight on. "I'm scared because the last two women I've loved left me. But at the same time, I don't think I have a choice anymore. I'm falling in love with you, Syd. And I don't know what to do."

15

———

She couldn't believe her ears. Sydney stared at Declan. "You can't say something like that."

He raised a brow. "Which part of it? Confess that I'm afraid?"

"You can't—" Her heart pounded harder, and Sydney discovered she'd pressed a hand to her chest, fingers numb over her racing heart. "*Declan.*"

He deliberately folded his hands in his lap. "I'm no wordsmith, but it seems with the mess we have to wade through tonight, I should keep the parts I know simple and straight up. I meant every word. I'm falling in love with you—hell, I'm *in* love with you, and that scares me shitless."

Sydney closed her eyes, the electric pulse racing through her making her light-headed. "You can't be in love with me."

He chuckled. "Nice try. Tell me another one."

A flash of something other than confusion made her lean forward and offer him a heated glare. "I'll admit I'm drawn to you. I've had more than fun this past year, and if it were up to me, I'd be advocating hard for us to date for real. But I just told you how messed up my situation is."

Declan waved a hand in the air. "We'll talk in circles if we're not careful. So let's get this straight. Yes, I heard the bullshit your grandfather put in place. That's a huge, complicated fuck up, but it's also something I'm damn sure can be solved when we put our heads together with the rest of the family." He shifted position, sitting awkwardly in a modified cross-legged position at her side. "So let's pretend it's not an issue. Let's focus on us because that's a big enough ball of trouble all on its own."

"Okay, fine. But you can't go tossing around words like love," Sydney rebuked. "That makes my brain crazy."

He shrugged. "Talking about emotions without naming the emotions doesn't work for me." He made a face. "Seriously, how come I'm having to play the emo card?"

"Because we don't say those type of things in my family," Sydney offered bluntly.

Confusion danced over his face. "You say you love Tansy and Petra damn near every time you're around them."

She leaned back and took a deep breath. "That is because Tansy is so...*Tansy*. The little brat made me repeat it back to her one day about a dozen times in a row before she let me out of that deathtrap of a van she used to drive." It was Sydney's turn to shrug. "After that I started telling her I loved her proactively to keep her from turning into a Disney princess in public, dancing around me like I was a maypole while she sang *I love you, I love you, I love you*."

Declan's lips twitched hard.

She reached over and slapped his arm. "It's not funny."

"Wasn't laughing," he said, eyes widening.

Oh really? "You were too. I know your laughing face, and that was absolutely a *laughing at Sydney* face."

"Okay. I am amused." He looked up, thoughtful. "Repetition and training. I can deal with that."

Wait, what? Sydney put two and two together and got another reason to glare at him. "You are not training me like a dog to say *I love you*."

"Hopefully not. I'd kinda like you to say it all on your own at some point. Which does not have to be today," he continued. Declan caught her fingers in his. "Back to me being totally serious. We've spent enough time together this past year, so whether you believe it or not, I'm way beyond just caring about you as a friend. But I'm also being brutally honest when I say that scares me. The last woman I felt like this for was Sadie."

When big strong Declan's voice grew shaky on the final words, Sydney figured she was done for. "I'm not getting through this conversation without crying like a baby," she warned.

"Hopefully you didn't use all the toilet paper."

Dammit. She was still on the edge of crying, but now she was laughing as well.

"That does have to feel scary." She softened her tone and really thought it through. He'd said the two women he'd loved—

Sadie. And...

"Oh, Declan. Your mom didn't want to leave you. Neither did Sadie."

"I know that, in here." He tapped a finger to his temple. "But in here?" He laid his hand over his heart and shook his head.

Fine. It seemed this was the night of true confessions.

Sydney dug down deep and let it out. "I've got some issues with a couple of key life areas. Some of it I'm sure caused by Grandpa Nate and his attitude, but there's another one that no one knows about."

God. Was she really going to tell him?

"You want to sit at the table to talk?" Declan stroked his thumb over her knuckles. "You want to cuddle on the couch? What would make this easier, darlin'?"

Sydney tugged him to the couch, sitting beside him and leaning her head on his shoulder. It would be easier if she didn't look at his face. "Remember I said I don't like doing deliveries?"

"Yeah." He linked their fingers together, and his thumb moved in a steady rhythm like a mini heartbeat, back and forth over her thigh.

"First two years of school I didn't make a lot of friends because of the vast age differences, but there was one girl, on the younger side as well, and so brilliant. Stacy was a shiny star who made everyone rise up and do better."

He leaned against Sydney's side and let her be quiet for a moment, just listening.

"Brilliant, but also beautiful, and she fell in love. Middle of her third year she and her engineer-in-training boyfriend decided they wanted to get married." Sydney could picture it still. "It was a beautiful wedding. Early March, snow everywhere. They were both still in school, but it was doable. Until year four, when she got pregnant."

Beside her, Declan stiffened. "Oh, hell."

"The really sad thing is Stacy was very much pro-choice. She could've chosen to have an abortion, but she and Peter really wanted the baby. By the time Christmas finals rolled around, Stacy was diagnosed with gestational diabetes and preeclampsia. She was still pretty upbeat. They decided because her schooling would take another seven years to finish, and Peter was one term away from being fully certified, she'd stay home with the baby after it arrived, and somewhere down the road she'd go back to finish."

Declan's big arm snuck around the side of her, creating a protective wall. "Things went wrong?"

"She died." Sydney's voice broke. "The baby was in intensive care for three weeks, but he made it. Now Peter has a little boy to raise all by himself, and everything Stacy used to tell me she looked forward to doing is gone."

The protective arm around her shifted her until her face was pressed against his chest, still avoiding eye contact but holding her so she didn't have to hold herself. "I'm sorry you lost your friend. I'm sorry for all the tomorrows she didn't get to have with her husband and baby."

His voice was deeper, choked with tears. Of all the people in her world, he could more than understand the pain she felt.

She touched her hand to his chest softly. "I'm sorry you lost Sadie. And your mom. Sometimes it just hurts too much."

He held her quietly before finally speaking. "It wouldn't hurt as much if we hadn't loved them so deeply."

Sydney lost it. The tears poured out until she felt as if she were washing the inside of the cottage as much as the storm was flooding the countryside.

Even when the tears eased enough for her to draw a ragged breath, the tight knot at the back of her throat was still there.

She had to finish. She had to let him know every barrier that lay between them.

"I am never doing that." Her voice cracked but held firm. "I am *never* getting pregnant." She drew in a ragged breath. "It's not that I don't like kids—I love all my friends' babies. But I can't. I just *can't*—"

"And you never have to," Declan assured her. "There's no rule that says anyone has to procreate, thank God. Although I wish sometimes there was an approval process and people couldn't become parents unless they passed some sort of exam."

Once again a laugh escaped when she least expected it. "You make it really hard to wallow in my tears."

"Oh, hell. You go ahead and cry as much as you want. I figure I've filled a bucket's worth a couple times in my life. There are days where I'm tempted to start again. But then those are the times Sadie would remind me I've a lot to be grateful for as well."

Sydney made a rude noise.

He cleared his throat. "She didn't say it the wrong way. It wasn't one of those Pollyanna always-looking-at-the-bright-side bullshit things. More like remembering to be grateful that I got to have the time I did with my mom. That I've got the memories I do with Sadie. That I got to experience life and take in the things they both taught me that make me into a better man. I can't wish that away. And that's what I'd be doing if I wished I didn't hurt as much as I do for losing them."

Sydney's breath was shaky, but at least she'd said that one thing. "I have to apologize."

He pulled back and let her look up at him. "Better not be for crying in my arms."

She shook her head. "I'm guilty of thinking you'd want a kid of your own, and there's no way I can give you one."

The look he gave her. "Sydney Jeremiah. And here I thought you were the smart one."

"What? A lot of guys think it's important that—"

"You look at my family and tell me what you see," he ordered firmly. "Just in case you're still wiping tears from your eyes and things are fuzzy, I'll start you off. We've got Aiden and Petra, who are signing on kit and caboodle to be mom and dad to a seventeen-year-old. Then there's Jake and Tansy raising a five-year-old who is no blood relative, but you tell me they're not Jeffrey's mommy and daddy."

"I know," Sydney protested.

"So if that's one of the reasons you've been keeping yourself from committing to me, toss that bullshit out the window. Because if at some point we decide we want to have more family than we've got walking through the doors of High Water, we can adopt. We can help raise whatever kids my brothers might end up having, and I'll be happy as a pig in mud. As long as I've got you beside me."

It sounded so simple. "I still have issues," she whispered.

"So do I, to be honest." Declan let out a big sigh. "And I'm a bit of a stubborn ass because I've got someone right there at my beck and call at High Water who could help me deal with my bullshit. I could talk to Kevin anytime I want, but I've been pretending it's not necessary."

"Edison told me I should talk to Kevin," Sydney offered quietly. "Guess it sounds like a good idea we should be brave enough to follow up with."

He rubbed his chin against the palm of her hand. "Maybe we can hold each other accountable for that. Once we get off the mountain."

"Deal," Sydney promised. She stared at his face for a moment, looking into those earnest eyes and solemn expression. "Without referring to our toilet paper notes, shall I summarize?"

"Go for it." He held up a finger.

She smiled. "We still have to figure out the Gordian knot problem of my grandfather holding the purse strings and my personal decisions hostage. We will find a way to brainstorm with our brainy bunch when we get home."

He held up another finger.

"Two. I'm not having any children I bear myself, but someday, if I want, I acknowledge there are other options."

"And those options will be discussed when appropriate and never under duress." Declan caught her hand and pressed a kiss to her palm. "And three. There's a man right here who loves you and is willing to try and be brave in the hopes you'll love him back."

"I'll try." The words a mere whisper. "I will."

A full-on smile bloomed on his face. "That's all I ask."

This time it was Sydney who shifted forward. Rising up on her knees and leaning in to connect their lips in a tender kiss.

Tears had dried on her cheeks, the wind howled outside, and there was an ache in her chest from moving so quickly between sorrow and laughter—yet all of that faded away as she fell into his touch.

It wasn't enough to take. She needed to give.

Sydney pushed the open shirt back off his shoulders as she crawled into his lap.

DECLAN HAD NEVER BEEN a big one for talking in the first place, but to have to go through an entire heap of bad memories and fears had left him on shaky ground.

There'd been one shot after another, but right now they got to come back to the parts that were the most real. The most true.

Sydney was going to give them a chance. He'd still have to fight, he figured, but she was a fighter too.

The other thing that was more than real? The sweet taste of her lips on his. The eager press of her hands over his shoulders, tugging at his shirt.

"Good thing we got it warmed up in here." He reached over his head to grab the back of his T-shirt. He yanked it forward and off, offering his naked chest to the delicate scrape of her nails.

"Lord, you're gorgeous." Sydney admired him before leaning forward and pressing her lips to his shoulder. Then his chest, swirling her tongue down to his nipple.

His body tightened, and Declan wished like hell he'd been smart enough to strip everything away before she got started. "Sydney. Let's take this to the floor. We've got the blanket and—"

She nipped, and he swore. A flash of sensation struck like a lightning bolt. The same ones dancing across the sky as the storm continued to rage—they were right there in the living room as far as he was concerned.

"We'll get to the floor," Sydney promised, rising up until her face was inches away from his. Her hands were firm on the waist of his jeans, pushing the button free and catching hold of his pockets. She tugged. "Lift your hips, sugar. I need these off."

Somehow she had undone his zipper, and as Declan leaned back and raised his ass off the cushions, Sydney stripped the fabric free. All the way down his legs and she tossed his jeans onto the nearby straight-back chair.

She trailed a finger down the center of his abdomen, teasing the trail of hair that vanished under the elastic of his briefs. "Just to be clear," Sydney said softly as her hand landed on the thick ridge of his cock. "This is not a booty call."

Thank fuck. He laid a palm on her sweet ass, giving it a gentle caress. "Booty still involved."

She closed her fingers around him, jacking him slowly and deliberately through the fabric. "Sure. But considering the storm outside, I'm feeling a little wild. Didn't want you to think this was the same as all the other times."

Declan opened his mouth to make a point and lost all

concentration as she slid the elastic aside and covered him with her mouth.

She sucked, and the head of his cock slid between her lips, hot and wet and potentially mind-blowing.

He slid his hips closer to the edge of the couch to give her more room, knees wide as pleasure wrapped around him and a groan escaped his lips. "Christ, Syd."

A pleased hum escaped her, and the combination of the vibration and the slow pump over his shaft threatened to make him lose control in an embarrassingly short time.

Declan closed his eyes and took the gift. He trailed his fingers through her hair, pulling it back from her face. He looked down and took it in, and somehow watching made it more intense. The smile at the corner of her lips as she worked him. The wetness on her lips coating his cock. Dirty and beautiful and he was thirty seconds away from blowing up, and that was not happening. Not tonight.

He reached down and pulled her off, laughter bubbling up from her as he kept the forward motion going and simultaneously rolled. They landed on the floor in front of the fire on the blanket he'd spread out earlier. Sydney was still fully dressed, his underwear tangled somewhere around his hips.

She pushed up, resting her palms on his chest as she reclined over his body. "Fancy meeting you here."

"We can play those kinds of games later. Right now, take off your clothes," he ordered, curling up to reach for the waistband of her T-shirt.

"Bossy tonight," Sydney said brightly. She arched her back as she reached behind her for the hooks on her bra.

Declan's hands were already there, and their fingers bumped as he distracted her with a searing kiss. Tongues tangling, her breath hot and heavy as he threw away the lace and lifted her high enough to latch onto her breast.

"Oh God, yes." Sydney's fingers ran through his hair, nails dancing lightly, a steady scratch over his shoulders as he sucked and nipped.

She squirmed, and he let go. She got to work on her pants as Declan dealt with his underwear. Seconds later the very naked woman planted her feet on either side of him, fists on her hips as she gazed down at him in a decidedly R-rated superhero pose.

"Have you come to save me?" Declan teased.

Sydney looked confused for a minute then smiled. "How about we save each other?"

Great idea, except what *he* needed to be saved?

Was her.

Declan lunged, and Sydney squealed. This time when he brought her down, her back was to the floor and he held her knees pinned to her chest, one in each hand.

"First thing I need is a little kitten time."

"Kittens?" Sydney laughed, fingers curling around his wrists as the brightest sound he'd heard from her all night rang out. It faded into a long, low moan that danced lust up his spine as he leaned in and ate hungrily. He licked again, taking in every inch of her pussy, thrusting his tongue deep then easing around her clit. He lifted her knees up and out to give himself more room to work, driving her up until she quivered under him.

"Deck. Do it," she begged.

"No."

He let go of her knees, stretched one arm across her abdomen and slid two fingers into his mouth, getting them wet before reaching between her legs and sliding his fingers deep.

Sydney's eyes widened. "Oh God."

He wished he could watch all the changing expressions on her face, but getting to feel, getting to give, was just as good. He dipped his head and put his tongue back to work, flicking the tight tip of her clit while he stroked his fingers against the front wall of her pussy.

She planted her feet on the floor and arched, writhing against his mouth as her body squeezed tight and her orgasm hit.

Declan hurried. He pulled his fingers free, covered himself with a condom, then lined up his cock and slid them together with one smooth stroke.

A noise of pleasure rippled on the air as Declan held himself on his forearms over her, hips rocking slowly.

She cupped his face, silver dancing in her eyes, pupils wide. "It's good. Oh damn, it's good."

"Hell, yeah."

He gave himself over to pleasure. To the giving between them, the ebb and flow. The teasing touch of her fingers and the hot grip of her body around him.

When he reached down to help take her over one more time, that too was pretty damn perfect.

Declan came, the ache in his body rolling out into relaxed satisfaction. The tangle of emotions and words—all of it smoothed and simplified by this honest physical connection.

She was breathing hard, smiling as she stroked his chest and pulled him to her side.

They lay there in the quiet, the house still shaking occasionally but with less intensity as the fire crackled in the stove. For the first time in too long, it felt as if the storm inside him had softened too.

That's when it hit.

Declan eased up on an elbow so he could see her face clearly. So much soft, tempting skin that was impossible to resist, so he didn't even try. He stroked his fingers gently over her body, meeting her eyes with his. "Remember you said that this wasn't a booty call?"

She nodded. "It's more."

He leaned in and brushed his lips over hers. "It's always been more. Just saying."

Her smile softened, and something unguarded flickered in the depths of her eyes. "I know."

16

————

By the time they got cleaned up, it was late enough to crash. Declan made another trip onto the deck to grab the air mattress from his truck that he'd left out there earlier, and the two of them set it up in the middle of the living room.

"Not that Nagy would object to us using his bed," Declan offered. "It's just that..."

"Say no more." Sydney helped straighten the quilt over the inflated mattress. "I'm sure it would be fine, but this is even better."

For a while she was worried she wouldn't get any sleep with her brain running on overdrive.

But when she twitched one too many times, Declan simply pulled her closer against his body and pressed another kiss to her temple. "Whatever rabbits you're chasing will still be there in the morning. Go to sleep."

Amusement washed away some of the worries racing on repeat. "You really do plan to train me like a dog."

"If it ain't broke, don't fix it," Declan offered. "By the way? I love you, Sydney."

"If you're looking for me to say it back, I demand a full-on Disney princess dance," Sydney said. A trickle of nervousness ran up her spine.

He sighed sleepily. "Don't want you to say it right now. Just want you to say that you're here and that you're trying."

She wished it was as easy to do as it had been with her girlfriends. "Yes, Declan Skye. I'm in your arms and happy to be here."

He took a deep breath, and by the time he let it out, she could have sworn he'd fallen asleep.

She must've followed him immediately because when she woke it was morning. Sunshine did not stream in the windows, and there was no scent of bacon or anything delicious. It was still dark, but when she checked her watch it was past eight o'clock.

The space beside her was empty, and Declan's boots and coat were missing from the hooks by the front door. She opened the curtains and looked out on a sky nearly black with clouds as rain smacked into the windows as if paddling her for being a lazy butt.

He was probably caring for the animals. So she would care for the humans.

She had a pot of oatmeal on the stove and coffee ready when he got back less than twenty minutes later.

Declan accepted the towel she handed him with a nod of the head. "It's still coming down hard. I walked as far as I could into all the clearings, but there's no reception anywhere. We're stuck for at least another day."

"There's more than enough food," she reassured him. "The clinic will be fine even if I miss a few days early in the week.

Lexie is there, and they can handle all of the office visits. Sorry I'll miss Rose and Chance's wedding, but it can't be helped."

"Me, too. Thanks to Petra's tracking abilities, everyone will know we're together here on the mountain. They shouldn't be worried. Also positive, my brothers have to deal with the chores."

Sydney laughed, bringing him into the kitchen and gesturing toward the coffee pot. "Help yourself. There's orange juice on the table already."

"Thanks. You don't need to do the food stuff all the time. We'll work together for the rest of the day."

"Nothing doing, buster," Sydney complained. "I don't want to be *sent* to the kitchen because, trust me, nobody wants me full-time in charge of their food. But I'll admit I'd prefer to be in here than out in the barn."

"It's quite nice out there once you make it through the rain," Declan said thoughtfully. "I'll take you on a tour later today. If we can find some time in our busy schedule."

"I found a deck of cards," Sydney offered.

"Excellent. That means strip poker."

She scooped up a serving of oatmeal. "We'll need more wood in here to keep it toasty. Since you'll be walking around naked."

"Don't you wish."

Sydney waggled her brows then tugged the brown sugar container toward herself.

For the next two days, they had a break from reality. The weather was the worst Sydney had seen in a long time, but they were quite comfortable in the small cabin. Even taking the wet trip across to the barn with Declan a couple times a day turned out to be enjoyable. As always, there were kittens to be found and the dogs to play with. Nagy only had a few pigs and chickens, which meant not a lot of work but the sweet reward of fresh eggs to add to their meals.

Declan showed Sydney the old-timer's under-the-house cold storage, lifting away a section of the floor in the back pantry. The flashlight flickered over a set of narrow stairs to reveal a dark and cool hiding spot that held a surprising amount of canning.

"The really good bachelors know how to do it all," Declan said easily.

"I've never seen canning around your place," Sydney teased.

"Because I'm not a really good bachelor," he confessed. "I like companionship too much. I liked being married, and I like spending time with my brothers. I'm definitely a herd animal."

Which made Sydney laugh all over again. "So I'm a dog, and you're a cow."

He snorted. "Please. I was thinking horses."

They played some cards and shared meals. By some unspoken agreement, they didn't go back to the problem of Sydney's grandfather. As if putting it on the shelf until they could talk to the rest of the family.

It was too big a box of trouble to unwrap by themselves.

A couple times a day they made love. With every touch and kiss, every caress as Declan drove her wild and took her up and over the top again and again—

It was abundantly clear that he'd shared the truth. It might've started as only sex between them, but it hadn't been that way now for a long, long time.

On Wednesday when they woke, sunshine stretched golden fingers across the floor through the crack in the curtains.

Declan was still at her side, and she rolled in his arms and poked him gently. "Looks like the weather's turned."

"Looks like it." He nuzzled his nose to her neck. "I was

kinda into ignoring the rest of the world. I like having you all to myself."

"It's been sweet," she agreed, "but I want to keep moving forward. I want to problem solve and find out how we fix what's broken."

"Including us," he reminded her.

"Including us," she agreed.

There was no miraculous return of the Internet, and when they walked down the road to the edge of the mudslide, it was clear no one was getting through the disaster without a massive bulldozer and a lot of work.

Declan pulled out the forestry service maps he'd found and spread them across the table, plotting out a route.

"What about the animals?" Sydney asked.

"We'll make sure they have plenty of water and food. Once you and I get out, my brothers or I will come back in on horses or quads if we have to. It's a problem, but it's another one we can solve."

They packed up using the equipment they'd found over the past three days. Food, water, and emergency supplies if for some reason they had to shelter overnight. Declan was convinced they could make it to one of the nearby farms in under four hours walking.

"Somewhere between here and the road we'll be able to send out an SOS," he assured her.

The first part was easy. They followed an abandoned logging road, overgrown and strewn with puddles and debris from the storm. The second part was tougher as they hit a section of forest where a fire had gone through, and Sydney felt as if she was constantly climbing over fallen trees that were just the wrong height. Too low for her to go under, and too high for her to do anything except sprawl her way over, her clothes catching on sticks and twigs.

Declan confidently led them forward, compass in hand. Always willing to help her over any obstacle when she asked.

"Are you sure you're not a wilderness guide?" Sydney teased at one point.

"The horses are supposed to be the ones walking," Declan told her earnestly. "This is not my favourite thing. Except the company's pretty good."

He paused before offering her a granola bar out of his pack, leaning in to kiss her, soft and sweet, the way he'd been doing all week. Sydney felt something inside her expanding, warming her from the inside out.

Her phone pinged. His phone beeped.

"We've got a connection," she said excitedly, as both of them dug through their pockets.

She flipped past a number of old messages to the very bottom one, sent two hours earlier.

> Petra: We saw your GPS markers move away from Nagy's cabin. Jake, Aiden, and I are on the way. Once we get closer, we'll message until we connect. Assume spotty internet, but don't worry. I can see you.

> Petra: By the way, thank God you're safe. We missed you. See you soon.

DECLAN STILL HAD an ongoing love-hate relationship with technology, but over the next two hours he had to admit this was one of the times he was damn grateful for it.

Not only that it existed, even though there were frustrating moments when they lost the signal and once again wandered blind for thirty minutes, but the fact that when they finally popped out onto the forestry service road four hours after leaving the cabin, both Jake and Aiden's trucks were right there waiting for them. It was damn near miraculous.

"Sydney. You okay?" Petra rushed forward, arms outstretched, and enveloped Sydney in an enormous hug.

Then Declan couldn't see her because he was getting an equally enthusiastic rib-cracking treatment from Jake. "Bad time to pick for a house call," Jake teased when he finally stopped pounding Declan on the back.

"Any word on how the old man's doing?" Declan asked.

Petra had her arm linked through Sydney's and was guiding her toward the truck. "He's okay. Lexie said to tell you that whatever the infection was, they caught it in time. Mr. Nagy needs to stay in the hospital for a couple more days, though, because they've got him on an IV."

Sydney dipped her chin. "Sounds about right."

"We'll have to head up tomorrow again and take care of his animals," Declan told his brothers. "And make sure somebody knows about the road."

"Department of highways has already been informed," Jake told him. "When you didn't come home on Saturday, we drove out the next morning to see if it you'd had truck issues. The road's washed out a good distance from the homestead, so we went home."

"Your truck is stuck for a while," Aiden informed him.

"I can deal with that."

Petra had the door open to Aiden's truck and was handing out offerings of water and sandwiches. "If you guys need anything other than this, let me know. Tansy packed an entire picnic. She might think you're not capable of cooking for yourself."

"We're fine," Sydney insisted. "Declan took good care of us on the hike out." She wiggled her shoulders. "I am looking forward to a hot shower."

"Hop in. It was slow going for a bit, but the roads are in decent shape from here all the way home," Jake assured her.

Petra opened the back door for Sydney to crawl in, and Jake pressed on Declan's shoulder to guide him to his truck.

Before anyone could take a step, Sydney caught Declan's hand. She stared up at him with those bright eyes and such a hopeful expression on her face. "I'll ride with you."

The other three froze for a moment, then Petra offered up a wicked grin, nodding happily. "Hop in with Jake. We'll meet you guys at home."

"Wait. Really?" Aiden headed to the truck, Petra pushing him on his back. He pivoted his head to glance behind him, confusion clearing as realization sunk in. "*Oh.* Okay."

Jake had also connected the dots. He grinned widely as he dipped his chin and gestured to his truck. "Other than I'm not giving up the driver's seat, pick your place."

When Declan offered Sydney the front passenger seat, she rolled her eyes. "Right. Because that makes so much sense. My legs are half the length of yours."

Declan debated crawling into the back with her anyway, but she bumped him in the side and then crawled into the back seat before he could protest.

He closed the door behind her, settling in the front beside his smirking brother. "Watch what you say," Declan warned.

"Me? I'm a pillar of society." Jake peered in the rearview mirror and winked. "I'm glad to see you two looking so...well."

"Thank you," Sydney offered primly. "And I'll just repeat what Declan said. Watch what you say right now."

"Absolutely," Jake offered, laughter in his voice.

The rest of the way home he told them about everything that had been damaged in town from the storm. There were a few outbuildings at High Water that needed to be repaired, but other than that, their newer construction had all held up well.

"The community center isn't looking so great," Jake said. "Bunch of roofing tiles are gone, and one section of the siding is banged up to hell where a tree branch swung into it."

"Is the hall still structurally sound?" Sydney asked. "I have a babysitting course to teach there in a week or so."

"As far as I know, it's fine to still use."

For the rest of the story, they waited until they actually got home, and Declan motioned for everyone to join them in the house. "We've got something to talk to you about."

Jake's eyes widened, but he held back until Sydney and Petra were gone into the house ahead of them. "I assume things went well, but did they go so well you have an *announcement* to make already?"

"If it were up to me, we would," Declan admitted. "But while we're now together, Sydney is still skittish. She's got good reasons, so careful with the teasing."

"Petra said the same thing," Aiden offered softly. "But good for you, bro. Sydney is a wonderful woman."

The spot of warmth inside his chest was damn fine, and Declan vowed to work even harder to make this thing between him and Sydney work.

"Thanks, but first we all need your help to solve a problem."

Gathered in the living room, Declan met each of his family's gaze in turn. Tansy and Jake had left Jeffrey with Kevin in the barn before returning and claiming one of the couches. Aiden and Petra settled on the other, and Sydney pulled the oversized ottoman into a triangle with the other two seats so she and Declan could sit together and face them.

"Remember that thing we found out about Lexie?" Sydney began.

"About your grandfather being an interfering interferer?" Tansy suggested.

Sydney nodded. "He's got a long history of that, and he's messed me up as well. I need your help to find a way out."

The other four listened carefully as Sydney explained the rules for the financial aid that her grandfather could pull at any time.

Aiden made a face. "He doesn't sound like a very supportive man when it comes down to it."

"No, that's the problem," Sydney said softly. "He's very supportive, but in all the wrong ways. Support with requirements isn't really help. It's ownership. And it hasn't helped that for nearly the last nearly fifteen years I've heard a steady stream of how wrong it would be to give up my autonomy and my career to be with a man." Sydney shook her head.

"But now that you and Declan are—" Tansy hesitated, examining them closely. "Please, tell me you're no longer trying to pretend that you're not aware of each other every single second you're in the same room?"

Sydney's jaw fell open. "You knew Declan and I were seeing each other?"

Tansy's grin widened. "Well, I suspected, but you just admitted to it, so thanks for the confirmation."

"Oldest trick in the book," Petra said sadly, shaking her head sorrowfully at Sydney. "You need to learn not to trust her."

"Please. I was so out of it regarding my sister Fern's romance, I'm trying to be more alert these days." Tansy smirked. "Also, na-na-na-boo-boo. I gotcha."

Sydney threw a pillow at Tansy. "Fine. Yes, Declan and I are trying to be together. I have hang-ups, so don't tease him for us moving forward at a molasses-in-winter pace. I did some math on the side while we were stuck in the mountains, and

I've got enough in savings that I can run the clinic without Grandpa Nate's help for three months at the most."

"The options are?" Jake had his notebook at the ready. "You don't tell him that you're together?"

"Not an option." Declan and Sydney said it at the exact same time. Her lips quirked and she squeezed his knee.

"Option two," Aiden chimed in, scratching the back of his neck. "You tell him, he sees reason, and things work out—"

Tansy snorted. "Aiden, you're such an eternal optimist. The man's been running his family like a corporation since forever. You think *reason* is in his playbook?"

"Option three. I tell him, and he pulls his support. Which means I could maybe keep the clinic open until the end of the year." Sydney swallowed hard. "That would mean disappointing a lot of people here in Heart Falls because having a local clinic has made a difference in their lives. It means a lot of old-timers will go back to not getting any care because they're not about to do the drive into town for some silly medical advice. And it means that I would have to take a job at the hospital in Diamond Valley."

"That's an hour and a half away," Tansy protested. "You can't drive that on a daily basis, especially in the winter."

"You're right, I can't." Hopelessness coloured her tone. "I'd have to move."

"If that's what it comes down to, then that's what we'll do." Declan linked his fingers with hers, ready to offer it all. "If the clinic has to close, then you and I will move."

17

———

It was nearly as shocking as if he'd right out announced that he loved her in front of his brothers and her friends.

But what hit first wasn't anger or frustration—it was relief. Pure and overwhelming. He was sticking to his guns, serious about being there for her, about wanting to be with her.

The family murmured around them—questions, half-formed objections—but Sydney only saw Declan. The only thing she heard was the pounding of blood in her ears.

She cupped her hand to his cheek. "It's not quite dancing around a maypole, but damn—that was close."

Declan's lips twitched. "You going to squirm if I say it again right here, right now?"

"You go ahead and say it as much as you want," Sydney offered slowly. "Maybe there's something to that training effect after all. I'm feeling only about a sixty percent rise in panic."

He pressed their foreheads together, staring into her eyes. "No matter what happens, I'll be there for you."

"I believe you."

They sat like that for a minute before Aiden cleared his throat. "Not that this isn't delightful, like watching the mating habits of some rare Canadian wildlife, but do we have a timeline? Or any other ideas to throw on the table?"

For all their ribbing, the eyes of every family member were kind. Every one of them leaned forward, focused intently. Not one person was ready to let her face this alone.

"I can't promise anything, but maybe..." Petra spoke quietly, lost in thought.

Sydney turned to face her. Declan's arm had snuck around Sydney's back, and the two of them sat together, a united force.

Petra wrinkled her nose. "I need to talk to my brother. And if you're okay with it, I'd like to give my mom and dad a shout. Like I said, I can't promise anything, but I might know of some financial possibilities."

"I'm fine with that," Sydney said. She fought to keep from smiling too hard. "I'd better confess my first instinct when you spoke was to assume you were about to offer to hack into some program to find me funding."

"She can always see if there's any dirt she can dig up on your grandpa," Aiden offered quietly before coughing into his hand. "Never mind me. I didn't suggest a thing."

"No, no digging into my grandpa." Tempting as it was, the last thing Sydney wanted was to stoop to his level—interfering where she had no right. "It doesn't seem proper for me to turn around and be rotten back to him. That's not how I want to run my life, and there are enough other things I need to pull in the right direction, so don't tempt me."

Petra raised her hands in the air. "I'll keep you on the straight and narrow. Somehow."

"Good luck with that one," Tansy muttered, whistling innocently when Petra stuck out her tongue.

"I love you guys," Sydney offered impulsively. "And the fact that I can tell you that means more than you'll ever know."

Declan's grip on her hand squeezed briefly. "If we're good for now, I need to grab a shower."

"And I need to stop by the clinic," Sydney said.

"I can drive you home to get your truck," Petra offered.

They went through a round of hugs before Sydney found herself alone in the living room with Declan.

He stood there silently, hands tucked into his back pockets. "I want to be with you tonight," he told her. "Your house, or my place. Either one. I don't care."

She considered. "I'd like that too. I have things I need to get caught up on, and I want to check into some other funding ideas that might be possible."

He nodded. "Let's have supper here with the family. I think Jinx and Jeffrey will want to see both of us."

"And we both made a promise to set up appointments with Kevin." Sydney hated and loved the idea. "There's a lot going on right now, but it might still be a good idea to check his schedule."

The face Declan offered was damn near hysterical. "I kind of hoped you'd forgotten about that part."

"Hey, if I'm going to suffer through it, you're going to suffer through it too. That's what couples do," she teased.

"Sounds about right." Declan closed the distance between them, pulling her into his arms and hugging her tight. "I'm glad we're safe, and I'm glad were home. I know you're worried about your job, but I still think it'll be okay. I still think there's a way for you to have everything you've worked for and a chance at happiness. On your own terms."

Sydney squeezed as hard as she could. "I'm here, and I'm trying," she repeated.

When Declan let go of her and pranced in a circle around

her for a second, she worried that their recent eating habits had caused low blood pressure that had affected his—

"My God, stop it," she laughed as realization dawned on what he was doing—turning her into a maypole.

Declan shrugged. "Damn. I forgot that if I'm a Disney princess, I need to put on a crown or whatever those shiny things are. Next time." He leaned down and kissed her, the gentle touch growing more heated but only for a brief second before he let her go. "Not to freak you out, but I love you."

She let his words flow over her and carry her out the door and into Petra's vehicle.

At home, she had a long, hot shower. Then, freshly dressed in clean clothes, Sydney slipped into the doors of the clinic.

Jenny rose to her feet and rushed forward excitedly to offer a hug. "Thank goodness. That was quite the adventure."

"All's well that ends well," Sydney quipped, taking a quick glance around the waiting room. She dipped her head at the two patients waiting, then headed into the staff room.

She caught up on the record logs from the past two days when Edison whirled into the room and threw himself at her. "Oh my God. That is the scariest thing I've ever heard of."

"Getting trapped in the mountains?"

"With no power," Edison returned. "I don't do primitive. Camping is out, and I need my creature comforts."

"It wasn't that bad," Sydney assured him. "Declan and I found it relaxing."

"Really?" Edison blinked. His eyes widened and a grin flashed out. "Tell me more."

"Save it. Only for a while," she assured him. "Is Lexie nearly done for the day?"

"Last patient is in right now. Let me go finish cleaning up the exam room and then we're all yours. You can tell us all about your adventures with your mountain man."

Only when she had them all gathered—Lexie, Edison, and Jenny—it wasn't her time in the mountains that she talked about.

Lexie's part in the story wasn't Sydney's to share, so she went straight to the punchline. "My grandfather is partially funding the clinic, and I'm not supposed to get involved with anyone. But Declan and I have grown very close, so I'm thinking about telling my grandfather that he needs to change his requirements because I refuse to follow them any longer."

Jenny looked confused. "That sounds very possibly illegal."

"Not illegal, just ignorant," Edison offered indignantly. "Seriously? That doesn't sound very grandfatherly."

Lexie met Sydney's gaze straight on. "It sounds very Grandpa Nate." She swallowed hard. "If the funding does get cut, how long can you continue to run the clinic?"

"We can finish out the year," Sydney told them truthfully. "I'm looking into other options, and it might be that we're fine."

"But it might mean being out of a job at the end of the year." Jenny nodded slowly. Then she shrugged. "I'm low-tech and easily replaceable. I'll stick around, and if I have to find a new job come January, I will. But I hope you figure things out." Jenny reached across and gave Sydney's hand a firm squeeze. "The clinic is important to Heart Falls, and you're doing good things in the community."

"I'll do everything I can to make sure the clinic keeps running," Sydney assured them. "I just don't want to keep anything from you because I'm not the one controlling your destiny. I think that's not something to keep quiet about."

Edison offered her a hug and went to clean the final exam room. Jenny also smiled sweetly and went back to the desk to tidy.

Lexie remained, a haunted expression in her eyes. "You're going to stand up to him."

"I don't know if it's standing up to him if he pulls the carpet out from under me," Sydney said.

The other woman shook her head firmly. "That wasn't a question. I'm telling you that I'll support you however I can because you *need* to stand up to him." Lexie swallowed hard. "I should've, and I've been trying to gather up the courage to do it ever since. Because you were right. I should've talked to Michael, and we could have decided together instead of me simply doing what I was told was in Michael's best interest."

Sydney caught Lexie's fingers. "It's not too late. I bet if you told Michael you wanted to talk he'd be all over that."

"I know. And I want to, but I'm nervous. I wanted to ask if you'd help." Lexie waved a hand. "Not this minute. Right now you're caught up in something else big that you need to deal with."

"Oh, honey. There's always a million enormous things to deal with," Sydney reminded her. "Doctors invented multitasking. If you want me as backup when you talk to my brother, you've got it. Let's send him a message now and set up a time."

A hesitant smile crossed Lexie's face, and her shoulders relaxed the faintest bit. As if having something tangible to do had released some of her pain. "Let's do that."

Declan was out in the barn when Jinx came barreling in. "Declan?"

"In the stall with Cobalt," he called. An instant later, she was there at the gate, standing perfectly still—following the rule to stay calm around horses—but he could see her bouncing on the inside. "We're fine."

Still, he stepped outside of the pen and let her snatch him up into a hug.

"You're not supposed to get in trouble like that," she said, face still buried against his chest.

"Sometimes things happen for a good reason." He patted her shoulders and waited for her to let go. "Sydney and I are dating."

"Get out." Jinx jerked back, her jaw hanging open. "And everybody's allowed to know?"

"Hell, yeah." Declan cleared his throat. "Heck, yeah."

Jinx laughed—a sound like bright sunshine dancing on the air. "You are too funny sometimes. I'm glad you're home safe, and I'm happy for you and Sydney. Is she coming over for supper?"

"She'll be here. She said she wanted to see you and Jeffrey."

"Of course, Jeffrey. He learned a new word while you were gone." Jinx stepped away and offered him a big smile. "Just wait until he pulls it out at the dinner table. It's a funny one."

"I look forward to it." Declan turned back to his horse but caught the tail end of someone slipping away. Logan, probably.

Logan, who seemed to always be around whenever Jinx was. Declan didn't like it, but he understood it completely. Jinx was a bright shining penny to the young man.

That night at the table, plates were piled high, fruit punch and beer flowing freely. Declan looked down the table and counted eleven family and friends. Gratefulness rushed in at having this type of meal to contrast with the sweet, quiet ones he'd shared with Sydney.

Both special. Both experiences he needed in his life.

Jeffrey had asked to sit beside both Declan and Sydney, which put the little tyke directly between them as he chattered away a mile a minute. "Daddy said that was lots of mud. So much it was a mountain of mud. Sounds really squishy."

Sydney answered him seriously. "A mountain of mud indeed," she agreed. "And lightning and rain and wind. It was a very big storm."

"Sounds perturbing." Jeffrey dipped his little chin intently then tried to shove an entire soft taco into his mouth.

Jinx snickered, catching Declan's gaze. She spoke softly. "So perturbing. You were perturbed, weren't you, Declan?"

Tansy laughed, avoiding everyone's gaze as she stared at the ceiling light and pretended to be busy chewing.

"That kid is going to have the vocabulary of a university professor by the time he starts grade one if you keep this up," Jake warned.

"Do you find that perturbing?" Tansy offered. "It's actually a scintillating goal to reach for."

"Stop," Jake groaned.

"Daddy? Are you okay?" Jeffrey leaned forward intently.

"Just fine, bucko. Eat your supper."

After cleanup, they broke into small groups for a while but ended up meeting again around the fire pit.

Declan pulled out the small bear figure he was whittling and began to draw small shavings from its back, creating the texture of fur. Sydney sat next to him, listening as Jeffrey told her a long story about the adventure he had taken that involved being a knight on horseback, and that Jinx and Sasha had taken him and Tyler Stone into a magical land.

The two ranch hands had called it a night, and Kevin had already gone to bed. Jake lifted Jeffrey in the air and flipped him over to suspend him by one ankle as he carried him around to give all his aunties and uncles a kiss good night on the cheek.

Tansy stretched her leg to the side and offered Jake a wicked smile. "You got him riled up. You get to put him to bed."

"Yup." Jake didn't look one bit remorseful.

It was family, with a layer of sweetness made even better by the fact Sydney was there in an entirely different way than she'd been in the past.

Oh, she was still there for her friends, the three of them chatting easily about plans for the days ahead. Worries pushed aside—for now.

But Sydney was now there for *him* as well, and he knew it. Right down to the tips of his toes.

"I'm glad you have her."

Declan glanced to the side. How had Jinx moved quietly enough to sneak up on him like that? "Nothing is set in stone, so don't go jumping the gun. Okay?"

"I won't. But I can almost see the way you guys are connected." Jinx made a face. "And I don't mean that other stuff that I interrupted before."

Declan kept his expression as blank as possible. "Of course you don't."

She grumbled for a minute. "You think it's funny."

"It's funny," he assured her, offering a hug before she headed to bed.

In the end, he and Sydney were the final ones by the fire. She picked up a log and added it to the coals. "Just a little longer," she said.

He shifted so she could lean into him, the two of them watching the flames dance. "Something on your mind?"

"I messaged my brother this afternoon," she informed him. "Michael. The one Lexie was dating."

"Oh. What's up?"

Sydney tightened the linking of their fingers, using her other hand to stroke the connection. "Lexie asked me to be there while she explained what Grandpa Nate did."

"That was a quick move." He couldn't imagine it would've been easy. "How did it go?"

"Michael was appropriately shocked. But then thankfully

when he got mad, it was at our grandpa, and not Lexie. Although he did give her hell for not telling him up front."

"That sounds positive."

"It was." Sydney let out a deep breath. "I thought the conversation might be terrible and heartbreaking, but after the initial shock was over, Michael's biggest demand was for her to never leave him out of the picture again."

"That's amazing. Is she headed back to Toronto?"

Sydney shook her head. "Not yet. And I didn't see this one coming, but Lexie told Michael that while she wants to be with him, she made a commitment to help me. That I was also dealing with some nonsense caused by Grandpa Nate. She wants to see that everything works out well for me, so she's staying until Christmas for sure. Michael is sworn to secrecy. He's not allowed to tell Grandpa that he knows anything."

Damn. This was far more complicated and tangled than Declan liked. But as long as he didn't have to keep all the stories straight himself, he supposed it was all right. "Did Michael get offered that wonder job yet?"

"No, but he's also been pre-warned about that because of not keeping secrets."

"Okay. So now we just have to tackle your funding issue— and then we can do the next thing."

Sydney snuggled under his arm. "For the first time since this whole big ball of trouble started to unravel, I feel as if there might be a chance for things to simply work out instead of falling apart."

He was glad she felt that way, although he wasn't certain.

Michael had been more than reasonable. Grandpa Nate? He was the one who had caused problems in the first place.

Still, it was positive news for now, and as the two of them made their way hand-in-hand across the yard to Declan's apartment, he pushed everything aside except the here and now and the woman he planned to hold all night.

The woman who curled up in his arms, languid and sated after their lovemaking, and proceeded to fall asleep sprawled over his body.

In the morning he happily went out to her truck and grabbed the duffel bag of clothes that she'd left there, whistling the entire trip. He hummed softly as they made their way into the house and enjoyed breakfast served up by a grinning Aiden.

Hell, Declan was one step away from breaking into song after he kissed her goodbye and she headed into town for the clinic. The yard was quiet, the fresh scent of rain lingered. The barn lights glowed softly. Everything felt right.

Of course he should've known better. Feelings like this were too good to last. Only when a man was at the top of the mountain could he get kicked hard enough to rollercoaster all the way down to the valley.

He stepped off the porch and came face-to-face with Logan.

"Declan. We need to talk." Logan stared at the screen of his phone as if something might jump out and bite him. When he glanced up, his face had drained of colour, his hands shaking as he held out his phone. "It's my brother. He sent me a whole shit ton of information...and a USB stick just arrived in the mail. I don't know what the hell to do."

18

———

eclan wasn't handling this one alone. He gathered his brothers and Petra, who was still in the house. With Jinx and Jeffrey off with Tansy at her mom's for the morning, the kitchen was quiet as they gathered around the big, beat-up kitchen table.

Logan shook his head. "I'm sorry."

"Stop apologizing, and let's figure out how to fix this," Jake ordered. "You said Dean didn't know how to get a hold of you."

"He didn't. At least until a couple of days ago." Logan opened his phone and pushed it across to Petra. "He messaged me. Used the wording we used to use when our dad had decided to go on a bender."

Petra examined the phone. "Pick up milk?"

"If we saw that, we knew not to come home." Logan said it flatly, no emotion at all. "I usually still showed up because if I didn't, Dad would just beat the snot out of Dean. At least if there were two of us, sometimes the old man wouldn't start, worried about the odds."

Aiden cleared his throat softly. "The scarring on your legs. That's from your dad?"

"Yeah." Logan sighed. "The times that I sent the message to Dean and ended up alone."

"You saw that message, and you answered it, didn't you?" Declan asked quietly.

"He's an ass, but he's still my brother," Logan said.

Petra scrolled for a second then put the phone down. "You guys didn't exchange more than two or three sentences."

"I gave him my email," Logan pointed out. "I thought it would be better to have anything from him show up there. Then I could ignore it if I wanted to instead of having him interrupting me with a message. I don't want him in my life, but I can't just abandon him."

Even though it seemed to be exactly what Dean had done to Logan in the past.

Petra opened her laptop and plugged in the small black USB stick that Logan had set down. Her face changed in an instant.

Declan lifted his chin. "What's wrong?"

Petra cursed under her breath. "Some of these files are locked down hard—encrypted. But from the folder names and what little I can see, we're dealing with financial data. Lots of it."

Jake leaned in. "What kind of financial data?"

Petra didn't look up. "I need more time to unpack it, but it's not someone's tax returns. There are hints of crypto wallet keys and what might be international transfers. If this is what I think it is, there's enough here to hurt someone—or help the right people stop it."

"The email says he needs to get the information to his past employers. He thinks if he gives them back most of what he stole, they might leave him alone." Logan shook his head. "I don't think he understands how gangs work."

"And now he's messed you up in it. And he knows where you live." Jake stretched his hand out and laid it on Logan's arm. "We'll do what we can, but this will take more than the power of High Water."

"I don't want Dean to get killed, but he made his choices." Sadness slid across Logan's face. "High Water Ranch is supposed to be a place where people can get a second chance and start a new life. That's what I want, and I don't want him dragging any of us into the kind of hell that could ruin it all."

Petra worked methodically, fingers flying over the keyboard of the laptop she'd grabbed. "This is a stand-alone computer system—no internet, no risk of being hacked. No way I'd run this on my main system."

"You know how Dean tracked you down?" Declan asked Logan.

Logan sighed. "I'm using my mom's last name. Dean knew it, of course. I should've used something else, but I didn't want to give her up completely. She was a good mom."

Declan got up and made a fresh pot of coffee. Petra was talking about stripping ID codes, and Jake was contacting a couple of friends on the RCMP force who dealt with gang activity.

It was all outside Declan's wheelhouse, and his mind kept drifting to Sydney—wondering what she'd suggest if she were here.

He watched for a little while longer then ended up rising from the table. "I'm going to go do something useful. Shout if you need me."

Jake rose to his feet and came to give him a pat on the shoulder as they spoke privately. "This might not be your skill set, but you're the reason Logan didn't try to keep this a secret and deal with it by himself. I'm glad you're a part of High Water."

"Me too."

Declan took his time out in the barn, caring for the horses and the couple of rescue dogs. There wasn't as much happening in that section of the ranch since they'd taken it over. And while it was the middle of summer, with Tansy's accident, they'd kept the bookings in the artists' studio to a minimum.

He wandered for a while, taking in the signs of the storm. Doing a little maintenance here and there, like securing loose boards and raking leaves from where the water had gathered in puddles.

By the time he spotted his brothers stepping onto the porch of the house, Declan had come to a place of peace in his head. It sucked that the people who mattered the most—everyone at High Water and Sydney—were facing problems he couldn't fix with the strength of his two hands.

Still, he didn't have to be good at everything. He just needed to be there for them.

He made his way to where his brothers stood and turned to give Logan a slap on the back.

"We're okay?" Declan asked Logan.

Logan nodded. "It's still a mess, but Jake has leads and Petra put something on my phone that will help if Dean tries to contact me again."

"You came to us fast. That was the right call," Declan said, gripping Logan's shoulder firmly.

"Thanks for being trustworthy," Logan offered back wryly.

Time to give the kid something else to focus on. "There's a bit of work you can do on the other side of the garden. Tansy can give you more specific directions, but she and Petra wanted more raised beds for next year, so you can go ahead and build a few more." Declan checked with his brothers. "Anything else for Logan to do?"

"That should keep him busy enough for now," Aiden said.

Logan nodded then took off at a quick clip, head held high.

They watched him for a minute before Jake spoke. "Not quite sure how that kid ended up so good-hearted considering the hell he went through growing up."

"Optimistic hearts take a lot of punishment before they get broken. I'd say he got here right on time," Aiden offered. "He's still got a lot to learn, but he'll get there."

"It's still paying it forward, isn't it?" Declan said quietly. "Making a difference in one life at a time, this time by teaching."

"Seems we need to make a difference in more than one at a time," Jake said. "I'm trying my best to not blow a gasket over the shitty situation Sydney's grandpa put her in."

"We might be able to solve that easier than you think," Aiden said softly. "Petra spoke with her brother. It'll take a few weeks for him to get back to her. I can't tell you more than that, but she crossed her fingers and had a good feeling about it."

"I'll take it," Declan said. He looked around the yard, unsettled energy bouncing in his belly. "I need a ride. Either of you want to come?"

Jake shook his head. "Not this time. I'm waiting to hear from my contacts."

"I'll come," Aiden offered.

In no time, the two of them were on horseback and headed out into the warm sunshine.

There was something medicinal about being out in nature. In doing nothing except stare at the horizon and sway easily in the saddle as Cobalt picked her way down the muddy trail.

Aiden too seemed thoughtful and far more quiet than usual.

"It's been harder than I imagined." Aiden finally said. "And yet so much more than I'd ever dreamed of. Being in the right place at the right time—it's tough."

"We always knew it would be." Declan glanced at his brother. "Wouldn't want to be doing this with anyone else though. You, Jake."

"Petra. Tansy." Aiden smiled. "Sydney."

"Hopefully." He met Aiden's gaze straight on. "She's got my number, and I meant it. If she needs to move, I'm going with her."

"I know. It won't come to that, though," his brother assured him. He lifted his chin. "That was one of the things that Jeff taught us. Family sticks together. We'll find a way to make things right for Sydney. We'll deal with Logan's bullshit. They're family. We're in this together."

It was a bit of a benediction. Declan didn't need to say *amen*—it was already true. He stared into the pale blue sky and entertained himself thinking up ways to get Sydney to say that she loved him.

He'd already figured out that she did, but chasing the words could be fun.

It was intoxicating to realize she'd become the target of a very large, very determined stalker. Or did it even count as stalking when Sydney secretly loved having Declan underfoot as often as possible?

She'd slept at his place, and he'd slept at hers. He'd made sure that she knew when he was headed to the Nagy farm to deal with the animals and help with the road, and he'd still made it home in time to bring her to High Water to enjoy supper and an evening by the fire.

He showed up at lunchtime at the clinic with enough food for the entire staff and a special carrot cake selection for Edison.

"I heard from someone that this is your favourite," Declan offered in that soft, gruff manner that made Sydney's heart ache. "Thank him for it, not me."

Edison blew Declan an exaggerated kiss. "The delivery boy still gets a pat on the back. Thank you."

"Welcome." Declan raised a brow. "You're invited to dinner at High Water anytime you'd like. You know that, right?"

"I know." Edison cocked a hip and offered a flirty smile. "Just making sure Kevin doesn't take me for granted. Sometimes a guy's got to keep the mystery going in their relationship."

Sydney walked Declan to the door, and he paused, glancing to make sure the waiting room was empty before pulling her into his arms. "I hope you coming over to dinner every night at High Water doesn't mean we don't have mystery in our relationship. Whatever that means."

"It means you have a girlfriend who is happy to be fed on a regular basis," Sydney assured him.

Even as he kissed her, she felt his smile against her lips.

Saturday morning after a lovely wake up, sunshine pouring in the window and highlighting the sheets, Sydney took her happily sated self over to the main ranch house. Declan held her hand as they walked, and despite the frustrations still weighing on them, Sydney didn't think she'd ever been happier.

Inside the house they were greeted with a chorus of calls, including Jeffrey, who ran straight up to her and hugged her knees. "Auntie Syd, Daddy's making pancakes!"

"Delicious news," Sydney offered back.

Declan swept the tyke up in his arms. "Are they horse pancakes?"

Jeffrey's eyes got wide. "Made of horses?"

Sydney laughed. "Have fun with this one."

While Declan reassured Jeffrey that it was the *shape* that counted, not the materials, Sydney slid up to the counter and got their coffees started. She caught herself watching him—this mountain of a man talking nonsense about pancakes—and wondered when he'd started to feel like home.

Distraction needed, stat.

She hip checked her friend when Petra entered the room. "Morning. You look far perkier this morning than last night."

"I had a breakthrough on the data." Petra waited until Declan joined them, wiping her hands on a dish towel as she leaned one hip against the counter. "Okay, here's the short version," she said, glancing between Declan and Sydney and speaking softly enough the ranch hands at the table couldn't hear. "The USB stick is encrypted, but it's not military grade. It took me until this morning to get into the root folders. What's in there looks like a series of crypto wallet keys and a document trail—account numbers, deposit logs, even dummy business registrations. Someone tried to hide their tracks, but it's sloppy. He probably copied these from someone high up in the gang."

Sydney blinked. "You're saying it's all money?"

"Dirty money," Petra confirmed. "We're talking money laundering, probably drug related. Most of its traceable now that I know what I'm looking at. Jake's contacts in the RCMP are already working on it. They're planning something — a sting, or at least a quiet intercept. But they'll need someone to hand it off. Carefully."

It still sounded dangerous, but as long as they went through the police, that was a good thing. "Poor Logan, getting dragged into something that's not his fault."

"He's got us now," Declan said firmly. "We'll protect him."

They absolutely would.

Something else had to be said. Sydney eyed her friend closely. "It sounds as if you've been taking hacker lessons. Well done with your on-the-job training."

Petra grinned. "One step closer to taking over the world."

With one trouble moving ahead somewhat smoothly, Sydney pushed the other issue aside and focused on the bright spot in her day.

After breakfast, Petra waved off her help with dishes. "You said you're teaching at the community hall this morning."

"Babysitting course. I'll be there all day, so don't try to drop in," Sydney warned Declan.

"Why would I drop in?" he asked with a completely straight face. "I've already got my babysitting badge. Cut my teeth raising Jake and Aiden. Now I've got Petra and Tansy to keep in line, too."

Petra stuck out her tongue. "Big brothers are the worst." Petra's grin softened. "And by that, I mean the best. Love you, Declan."

"Love you, too, Petra." Declan turned to Sydney and straight up said it again. "See how easy it is? I love you, Sydney."

"You're impossible, Declan." But the warmth in her chest flared.

"Perfect. And now I'm off to do chores. Maybe I can practice telling the horses and cats how I feel." He tipped his chin and headed out the door.

Her friend's gaze burned like a laser. "He's tossing out the L word already. That's got to feel big and scary."

"You have no idea," Sydney muttered.

"Oh, I think I have a pretty good idea, but I also know how this story ends if you're willing to take a chance." Petra tugged

Sydney into a hug. "Deck is a great guy. I'm glad to see the two of you together, and I think you can get over the *I love you* willies eventually."

"Eventually." Sydney escaped as soon as she could, heading home to grab the bags of supplies she needed for the class from her shed.

Something foul had died in there—possibly already rotting —judging by the horrid scent that wafted out the instant she opened the door. She wrinkled her nose but didn't have time to investigate. Instead, she held her breath as she hurriedly carried the oversized red-and-yellow duffel bags that held the CPR mannequins to her truck bed, hoping that the scent would dissipate by the time she reached the hall.

The main floor area was set up for a gymnastics practice later in the afternoon, so the babysitting class had been given the stage area where the annual bachelor auction was usually held.

She breathed through her mouth as she carried in the heavy bags and stacked them to the front of the stage near the curtains. They wouldn't need the mannequins until the afternoon.

By nine o'clock, five tweens were seated in a loose semicircle on the stage, surrounded by foam mats and clipboards. Sydney knew two of them from the clinic and quickly learned the names of the others.

"Roll call," she said brightly. "Let's see who we've got. Hailey, Noah, Addie, Lucas, and Grace. That's my whole crew today?"

Hailey, with pink streaks in her braids, gave a double thumbs-up. Noah adjusted his glasses and muttered, "Present, Doctor J." Addie had her nose buried in a spiral notebook but nodded. Lucas, tall for thirteen, gave a salute, and Grace giggled.

"I'm not going to make you memorize diaper brands or perform surgery on a teddy bear," Sydney promised. "But I do expect you to learn a few important things today—like how to keep small kids from duct-taping themselves to the dog."

That got a round of laughter.

Sydney launched into the first module, safety basics. They talked about age-appropriate toys, what to do if the child started choking, and how to create a safe play space.

At one point, she passed around a bottle of coloured water. "Raise your hand if you think a two-year-old would drink this."

All five hands went up instantly.

"Exactly. Now tell me where something like this might be found?"

Hailey threw up a hand. "In the fridge."

"Under a sink," Lucas shouted at the same time.

Which led to a whole discussion of where the cleaners were kept in their houses and if dangerous cleaning chemicals were safely stored or not.

By the time they broke for lunch, the kids were buzzing with energy. Sydney had promised them CPR practice in the afternoon, which had sparked a mix of excitement and mock horror.

"Do we actually have to get the hearts started on those dummies?" Noah asked.

"We're more worried about the things little kids usually do. Like sticking things in their mouths," she replied. "But I will do a demo and let you try so when you take a full first aid course down the road, you'll be ahead of the game."

"Nice."

As the kids dashed off—bathroom breaks, lunch bags consumed, or just to burn off energy in the open gym—Sydney took the opportunity to slip into the washroom herself.

She hadn't lied about liking kids. If they could just pop into existence at ten years old, she could handle having a horde of them.

We'll figure it out together when the time is right.

The memory of Declan's firm commitment actually made her smile for a moment as she checked her watch. They'd been at it for three hours already. She'd give them twenty minutes to burn off steam and then corral them for the next unit.

The quiet *crackle* didn't register at first.

The sound came like a whisper—too soft at first to catalogue over the hum of air vents, the slap of sneakers on wood, the laughter.

When she stepped back into the hall, something caught her eye. Smoke. A thin ribbon of it, curling upward from the edge of the stage curtain.

Sydney froze for one heartbeat, then her training kicked in.

"Everyone out!" she yelled, her voice echoing like thunder off the walls. "Fire! Move! Outside now!"

She pointed toward the emergency exit door even as she scanned for the kids and the nearest fire extinguisher.

Noah and Lucas skidded to a halt mid-run, wide-eyed. Grace and Addie jumped at the sharpness in her tone but obeyed without argument. Sydney turned back to spot Hailey as she came tearing out of the bathroom, panic in her eyes.

They all moved toward the emergency exit like wind blowing over tall grass on the prairie.

The alarm triggered by opening the door rang loud and reassuring.

Sydney did a frantic headcount.

"One, two, three, four—where's Grace? Grace!" Sydney turned back to the hall, even though her gut told her the answer.

"She said something about her phone," Addie offered. "She left it with her notebook on the stage."

Dammit. Sydney stood in the open doorway and eyed the rising smoke. Rushing in when she didn't know which way to go made no sense even though her body screamed at her to get moving to find Grace.

The air smelled of burning plastic and something chemical. As her gaze reached the stage, her stomach dropped. The curtains were ablaze, flames licking up the fabric like hungry tongues. At the base the duffel bags were just visible, burning bright. The mannequins were melting, a pile of what looked like rags draped over them.

She couldn't see Grace.

"Doctor Sydney!" A shout rose behind her.

She turned for half a second to see Declan's truck skid into the parking lot. Jinx slipped from the passenger door as Declan jumped down, eyes scanning the scene as he took in the smoke, the children, the fire.

And her.

Their eyes locked.

The children would be safe with him. She turned and plunged back inside.

19

Smoke curled from the roofline of the community center—thick, black, rising fast.

A crowd of kids clustered near the fire lane. Noah, Hailey, Lucas, Addie—all there, wide-eyed, tears threatening.

"Doctor J went back inside!" Noah cried, pointing. "Grace is still in there."

Declan's gut turned to ice.

"*Jinx,*" he called, already heading for the door. Jinx skidded up beside him out of nowhere, as always, fast and full of attitude. "Stay with the kids. I'm going to help Syd."

"I'm coming too."

"No, you're not." His voice left no room for argument. "Make sure the fire department knows Sydney and Grace are still in there. The truck is close—I can hear them."

"But—"

"Jinx." He turned and hit her with the full weight of his big-brother stare. "That's an order. Watch them."

Her lips pressed into a thin line, but she nodded. "Go."

Declan took a deep breath, ducked low, then stormed

234

through the open door. Smoke rushed around him like a wave, heat roaring behind it. The building groaned above him as flames clawed their way across the ceiling. He pulled off his top shirt, pressed it to his mouth and nose, and pushed forward into the haze.

"Sydney!" he bellowed. She was here, somewhere, and she'd be fighting. He had to do the same.

Nothing but the sound of crackling wood and the distant whine of sirens.

He moved through the hall, squinting past the smoke. Heat built fast, turning the air sharp and punishing. Ahead of him the stage blazed like a bonfire, the curtains long gone, the frame glowing orange.

An explosion split the air—deafening, violent. Declan ducked, shielding his head as bits of ceiling hailed down.

A scream tore through the smoke.

"Help!"

Declan shoved forward, following the voice.

He found Grace halfway under a tangle of uneven mats and fallen gym gear near the stage stairs. A bent metal bar lay nearby. Her elbow was scraped and red, and she was coughing hard.

"Sydney—she pushed me out here when something exploded," Grace choked out. "She's still up there!"

Declan's chest twisted with fear. Of course she'd gotten the girl clear first. Time was flying, but he moved decisively, scanning the stage even as he struggled to shift the debris off the girl. He'd get Grace out as quickly as possible, but he could use her help at the same time.

The heat was worse now, and the fire danced as if it was hungry for more.

"Point to where you were," he commanded Grace as he lifted the final pieces of wood off her legs.

She lifted a hand, and for a moment, he couldn't see anything but flame—until he spotted movement through the smoke. A dark figure. Slumped.

"Sydney!"

She didn't answer. Just shifted a little, dragging herself to one knee. Her other leg was tucked strangely under her, and even from a distance, Declan could see she wasn't getting off that stage alone.

He hauled Grace into his arms and sprinted with her to the nearest wall, the area clear of all signs of the fire. "See the open door there? Run straight for it, got it? Help's coming. I'm going for Sydney."

She nodded, coughing again, tears streaking the soot on her face. She pumped her legs and sprinted.

In spite of every nerve screaming for him to move, Declan waited until she reached the door before he turned and ran.

The stairs to the stage groaned beneath his weight. The heat was a wall now, blistering his skin. Flames licked at the rafters. Somewhere overhead, beams snapped. He grabbed a fire extinguisher from the wall and sprayed a path ahead, just enough to get through.

"Sydney!"

She looked up this time. Her face was streaked with ash, hair damp and plastered to her cheeks. "Go back!" she rasped. "You can't—"

"Like hell," he growled, pushing toward her.

She tried to rise again and failed. Her ankle was already swelling—badly twisted or broken. Declan crouched, slung her arm over his shoulders, and half-carried, half-dragged her as he turned to retrace his path—

A section of ceiling groaned then crashed to the floor in front of them. Their way out vanished in a cloud of smoke and cinders.

Panic clawed at his chest. No time. No space. No way.

"Sydney—"

"Declan!"

He turned toward the voice.

Jinx.

She was crouched behind a gap in the back wall of the stage, eyes wide, one hand waving them forward.

"Crawlspace! This way! Move!"

Declan didn't hesitate. He tightened his grip on Sydney and all but dragged her toward the hole. The passage was barely high enough to crouch through—some kind of maintenance corridor under the stage, dry and dusty, but cool and sheltered compared to the inferno above them.

Jinx led the way with the flashlight on her phone, ducking and weaving.

"Almost there," she panted. "The path hooks behind the dressing rooms."

The narrow passage opened into a utility door, and sunlight poured in the open door that led onto the back side of the hall.

The fresh air hit him like a blessing, and he stumbled out, Sydney still held tightly in his arms.

Jinx bolted ahead, waving down the fire crew as they prepared to rush into the building.

"We've got her!" she shouted. "We're out!"

Firefighters surged forward, some dragging hoses, but one glance at the roof and their grim expressions said it all. They weren't going to fight the blaze. They were there to stop it from spreading.

Declan lowered Sydney to the grass. Grace rushed over and threw herself into Sydney's arms, crying again. Sydney hugged her tight despite the pain.

Jake arrived seconds later, driving one of the ranch trucks. He took one look at the smoke rising into the air, jaw tight.

"You okay?"

"I'll live," Sydney said, her voice raw. "My ankle's messed up, but I think it's a sprain, not a break. Grace has got some scrapes. Everyone else stay safe?"

"The kids are shaken but fine. Jinx kept them clear." Declan looked over at the girl in question. "Until you left them to come get us. I'm thankful...and pissed."

Jinx glared back. "I made sure the kids were all far from the doors. Then Grace mentioned Sydney was stuck on the stage, and I remembered about the crawlspace from when I did that school drama night. Some of the kids found it and figured it was a cool secret tunnel."

Sydney raised an eyebrow. "A secret tunnel?"

"Yeah," Jinx said, looking suddenly sheepish. "They were sneaking down it to go fool around in the utility room. I didn't. I swear."

Declan coughed—might've been smoke, might've been laughter. "Well, lucky for us you knew about it."

One of the firefighters came over, helmet off, face streaked with soot. "The building's done. We'll keep the flames from jumping to the adjacent lot, but the hall is a total loss."

Sydney nodded. Her hands trembled slightly, but her eyes were steady. "Thanks for being here."

Declan sank down beside her, the weight of it all crashing down now that they were safe. He could still feel the sting of smoke in his lungs—but it didn't matter. She was here. Alive.

He reached over and took her hand.

For one terrifying moment, he'd thought he would lose her.

"I saw you go in," he said quietly. "You knew I was coming, yet you went anyway."

"It was the right thing to do," she whispered.

She was brave—too damn brave. Yet it was part of why he loved her. Even if it broke him.

He didn't say another word. Just held her hand tighter, breathing in the clean air and listening to the sound of the fire hoses spraying and steam hissing as the voices of children—all safe—rose in the distance.

THERE WERE moments in life when the universe came right out and said what needed to be done. Sydney wasn't always happy to be taught her lessons so bluntly, but she was always grateful in the end.

She'd spoken with the fire marshal, and now fresh from a shower, her sprained ankle expertly wrapped by Lexie, Sydney sat on the porch swing at High Water, her foot propped in Declan's lap.

It was time.

Declan stared into the distance and she stared at him, taking in every line and every shadow. He had a small abrasion on his temple, and his knuckles were cut and bruised, and she didn't think he'd ever looked more handsome.

She hadn't ever needed anyone this much, and it was time to stop denying her heart.

"Declan?"

His blue eyes drifted to hers. "Yeah?"

"I love you."

His eyes widened. "Oh hell."

His grin was slow, wide, stunned.

Which made Sydney laugh out loud. "Right?"

He scooped her into his lap and cupped her face in his hands. "Excuse my language, but I figured it would take me until Christmas to get you to admit it."

"Time flies when you're having fun—you know, getting lit on fire, tangling with gangs, losing your funding." She pressed a finger to his lips. "And I mean those things in a totally *okay, now that I have my head on straight as to what the real issues in my life are* way. Telling you how I feel isn't nearly as scary by comparison."

"You might have to say it a time or two more for it to sink in," he warned.

"I love you, Declan Skye," she offered. "And we're alive after a fire that we have no idea how it started."

She kissed him, firm and direct, pulling back before he could take over.

"I love you, Declan Skye," she repeated, "Sometime in the next week or so, there will be a solution to the issue with Logan and his fucked-up brother's problems."

He clued into the routine impressively fast. He kissed her this time, hot and quick enough to leave her breathless.

Sydney went for the final round this time. "I love you, Declan Skye. And I refuse to stay silent anymore, which means I need to call my grandpa. Now."

Declan made a face. "Now?

"Now," she confirmed.

Declan didn't say anything else, just gave her a nod and squeezed her hand once before shifting to help her sit up straighter.

Sydney adjusted the porch swing cushion behind her, reached for her phone, and opened the video call app.

Her fingers were steady. That surprised her.

The phone rang once. Twice. Three times. Then Grandpa Nate's face filled the screen.

"Well," he said without preamble. "You look like hell."

"Hello to you, too." Sydney let her mouth fall into something resembling a smile. "It's been a week."

"I heard," he said, voice cool. "Your grandmother told me. A fire. Property loss. Minor injuries. What you were doing risking your skills teaching a *babysitting* class, I'll never understand. It's as if you go looking for chaos."

"I didn't find it," she replied evenly. "It found me."

"Still, I warned you when you moved to that place. Small towns are fine for children and the unmotivated, but they rarely contain anything a woman like you needs to thrive."

Sydney tipped her head. "You might want to hold your judgment until I finish what I called to say."

Grandpa Nate leaned back in his chair—leather, high-backed—the library behind him. She knew the whole aesthetic well. It was a room she'd studied in. Cried in. Learned Latin and anatomy and how to keep her face blank when it mattered.

"Well, go on then," he demanded.

"I'm in love," Sydney said plainly. "With Declan Skye. And I'm not willing to hide that anymore."

There was no change in her grandfather's expression. No intake of breath or furrowing of his brow.

"You're aware of the conditions under which I fund your clinic."

"I am."

"And you've chosen to ignore them."

"I'm choosing to reject them," she corrected. "You've spent my entire adult life telling me what I'm allowed to do in exchange for support. But that support has strings attached that are wrapped so tight they've cut off my circulation. You made it clear that love, especially for a woman, is a distraction from greatness. That men like Declan are fine companions but not fit to anchor ambition."

"He runs a ranch that rescues dogs," Grandpa Nate sneered. "Yes, I know who he is."

She ignored the fact that meant more interference and security than he'd ever admitted before. "Declan leads a community. He mentors men coming out of addiction, prison, and grief. He saved a twelve-year-old girl from a burning building yesterday. He's good and strong and kind, and I'm not giving him up to keep your name on the donor list."

Grandpa Nate's mouth thinned. "You'd choose love over medicine?"

"I'm choosing both," she said firmly. "I'm a doctor because I love people. And I love Declan because he reminds me why people are worth loving."

Silence.

It stretched long enough that she felt Declan shift beside her, a quiet breath moving through his chest.

"If your response is to cut funding and punish me for not being the kind of woman you think I should be—fine. I'll find another way." Sydney dug deep for courage. "I'm done pretending that the version of me you approve of is the real me."

He blinked once. "So that's it?"

"That's it."

"Three years of investment, and you're willing to throw it away for a man."

"No," she said, her voice still calm but her spine straight. "I'm throwing away the illusion that your support was ever about me succeeding. It was about you controlling the way I succeeded."

Grandpa Nate looked away for the first time, gaze flicking off-screen to his window, his bookshelves, maybe even his reflection.

Then he came back, voice colder than before.

"I'm proud of the doctor you've become," he said. "But I'm disappointed you think emotions are more valuable than excellence."

"I think love is more powerful than pride," Sydney said softly. "And for the record, I'm proud of me, too."

She didn't wait for him to reply. She ended the call.

Her hand dropped to her lap, the phone face-down. The air on the porch was still, and so was she.

Then Declan exhaled beside her. "That was intense."

"Yeah."

"Feel good?"

She nodded. "Better than I expected. Worse than I hoped."

He slid his hand into hers, his thumb rubbing slow circles across the back of her knuckles. "You did the right thing."

"I know."

"You're not alone."

"I know that, too."

She turned her face into his shoulder and rested there for a moment, letting the weight of the last fifteen years slowly burn away and drift like ash on the wind.

When she straightened, there were tears in her eyes, but her chin was high.

"I'll find a way to keep the clinic open. Even if it's small. Even if it means asking for help."

Declan grinned. "Well, it's a good thing you've got a community full of stubborn people who like you."

"I'll remind you of that when I'm elbow-deep in budget spreadsheets."

"I'll bring snacks."

Sydney let out a half laugh-half sob and leaned into him again.

She'd told her grandfather the truth.

And for the first time in her adult life, the woman who'd done the telling belonged to no one but herself.

20

———

*A*s the week stretched on, Declan felt like he was holding his breath, shoved beneath the surface and battered by too many currents.

Every morning started the same way. Sydney curled up next to him, her ankle slowly healing but her laptop never far from reach. Between breakfasts and clinic hours, she'd dig through spreadsheets and grant possibilities, chasing any thread that might keep her practice alive.

They brainstormed over coffee, mapped out backup plans that never quite felt solid enough.

No answers yet, but at least they were trying. Together. And somehow, that mattered more than the unknowns.

Declan balanced his time between the usual ranch duties and watching Logan out of the corner of his eye—giving the kid space but ready to step in if needed.

Nights meant quiet talks with Sydney on the porch swing, her hand warm in his, the weight of unspoken worries settling between them like dust. The kind of dust you couldn't sweep away, only wait to settle.

Through it all, the ache of waiting for Jake's contacts to confirm the next steps with Dean and the RCMP throbbed like a bruise just under the skin. His chest stayed tight, as if waiting to exhale.

Jake kept his phone close, stepping away from the dinner table more than once to take low-voiced calls. Petra spent the evenings at her laptop, eyes narrowed, muttering about timestamps and digital breadcrumbs.

He didn't press for details, but Declan caught enough to piece it together. Dean had agreed to talk to the authorities. Not on record yet, but enough to make the RCMP interested.

The deal was simple—if Dean followed through and verified the accounts Petra unlocked, they'd make sure the gang couldn't follow the trail back to Logan. All Logan had to do was keep his head down, and he'd stay safe.

Jake offered to do the drop. Declan had insisted Logan didn't need to be anywhere near it, and their contacts grudgingly agreed.

They hashed out the plan late one night around the battered kitchen table, maps spread out and Jake's phone on speaker, patched through to his RCMP contact who was acting as a liaison.

"West of Okotoks," Jake confirmed once they'd hung up. He tapped the spot with his finger. "Public enough to keep things aboveboard, isolated enough for a quiet conversation. We'll time it for dawn to cut down on surprises. We bring the package. They trigger the next steps."

"Who's 'we'?" Declan asked, although he already knew.

Jake leaned back, expression flat. "You and me."

"Figured," Declan said, dipping his head.

"Which means I'm coming too," Sydney said, crossing her arms. She'd sat beside him in silence for the entire evening, but Declan wasn't surprised she'd spoken up now.

Jake blinked. "Sydney, this is—"

"I know exactly what this is." She met his gaze firmly. "While we don't expect a double-cross, I'm a licensed professional, and if anything does go sideways, my word would mean a lot in a court of law. You're not leaving me behind when I might make a difference."

Jake and Declan exchanged a look, but Declan knew better than to argue. "Fine. But you stay close and don't play hero."

Sydney's mouth quirked. "Deal."

Oddly, it was the morning of Aiden's birthday when everything was finally arranged. They left High Water well before sunrise. They drove in silence, the grey morning a perfect foil for Declan's mood.

When Jake finally parked at the edge of the pull off, all three of them took deep breaths before tightening coats and stepping into the chilly morning air.

The meeting point was nothing—just a gravel space at the side of the road with a faded *no camping* sign and a trash bin with its lid busted off. The sky was low and grey, and silence pressed in around them like the pause before another storm.

Declan waited with his hands shoved deep into the pockets of his jacket, the wind cutting through the denim as if it had a personal grudge. He shifted his weight from one foot to the other beside the open tailgate of Jake's truck, boots grinding against the gravel.

Sydney stood a few feet away, arms crossed, her windbreaker zipped tight against the wind. Her presence steadied him as always—but even her calm couldn't untie the knot in his stomach. He couldn't stop picturing Logan pacing in his room that morning, pretending not to be afraid.

Declan's jaw clenched. The kid was trying so damn hard to build a future, and being implicated by his brother was the kind of mess that could tear it all apart.

The dark grey SUV pulled up without headlights, tires crunching on the gravel.

Jake stepped forward as it came to a stop, his posture relaxed but alert. Declan recognized the way he moved—back in police mode—deliberate, calm, like a man who'd dealt with enough dangerous people to know when to keep his hands visible and his voice level.

Two men stepped out of the SUV. One wore a sharp suit with the expression of someone who hadn't smiled in days. The other had on a plain RCMP windbreaker, the emblem barely visible in the dull light. Both of them scanned the turnout before coming to meet Jake.

"You brought it?" the officer asked.

Jake nodded and reached into his coat. "Everything we talked about. USB stick, hard copy of the file tree, the access notes our man pulled from the tech. We scrubbed it—clean copy only."

They all agree Petra's name would not be mentioned at any point, no matter how much she'd contributed.

Declan watched the officer take the envelope, slide it into a black evidence case, and hand it to the suit without a word. It was quick, efficient. Should've felt like relief.

Instead, Declan's jaw ached from clenching his teeth.

"Before we finish," the suit said, glancing at his notes, "We need to confirm the origin of the USB drive. The message came from a Logan Rutledge's account. We'll need him to verify—preferably in person."

"No." The word flew from Declan's mouth like a gunshot.

The man in the suit blinked as if suddenly realizing Declan wasn't just a random part of the landscape. "Excuse me?"

"You heard me," Declan said, stepping forward. "Logan isn't involved in this. Not beyond being the poor bastard his brother dumped this on. He's not a witness. He's not a player.

He's not even a damn courier, not really. He's a kid trying to survive something that's not his fault, and he gave us the USB because he trusted us to protect him. So no—he's not showing up, and he's not giving you anything else."

The man raised a brow, but it was the RCMP officer who answered. "We're not trying to put him at risk—"

"Then don't," Declan snapped. "You've got what you need. Our man pulled the info for the chain of access. Dean's already confirmed it was his. You want someone to stand in front of you and put their name on it? Put mine. But Logan's staying out of it."

Jake moved in beside him, arms folded. "He's right. We've covered it. We did the trace. Dean backed it up. You want to build your case? You've got enough. Push harder, and you'll lose your only clean handoff."

A moment of silence followed. The breeze caught the edge of the bag, rustling the envelope as if to highlight its presence.

Finally, the suit gave a slow nod. "We'll accept the chain of custody as presented. If Dean's preliminary statement aligns with what we find in the files, and if he follows through with his testimony, this will be enough to initiate charges."

Without further ceremony, the man turned on his heel and vanished back into the SUV.

The tension in Declan's shoulders eased slightly. Sydney moved to his side and slid her hand around his, warm and steady.

"You're sure Logan's out of this?" Declan asked quietly, needing to hear it one more time.

The officer who had remained motionless met his gaze. "We know who's involved. Logan's not one of them. This delivery covers what we needed. Your guy did the right thing by coming forward. You all did."

The officer nodded briefly at Jake then returned to his vehicle.

The SUV pulled away from the turnout, taillights vanishing into the dusky stretch of highway like ghosts retreating into the dark.

Declan let out a long breath he hadn't realized he'd been holding. His muscles felt like they'd been pulled too tight for too long, and now they were finally allowed to unravel.

Sydney squeezed Declan's hand. "This is what justice looks like," she said softly. "Slow, and sometimes messy. But it's a start."

Declan nodded, the tightness in his chest finally beginning to ease. "Just want to make sure it's enough."

Jake clapped a hand on his shoulder. "Come on," his brother said. "Let's head home."

Logan was waiting on the front porch when they pulled back into the driveway of High Water. He stood the moment the truck came to a stop, eyes searching for something in Declan's face—answers, maybe.

Or permission to breathe.

Declan got out slowly. The tension hadn't quite left his body, but he managed a nod. "It's done."

Logan's shoulders sagged. Not all at once, but like a man realizing he didn't have to hold himself together with duct tape anymore. "They take it?"

"They took everything. Petra's files, the stick, the notes. RCMP's moving forward with the case." Declan paused then stepped closer. "They asked for you."

Logan's face went pale.

Declan shook his head. "I told them no. You're not part of this, and you never were. You trusted us with the truth, and I'm not letting anyone twist it."

For a long moment, Logan didn't say anything. Then he

scrubbed a hand through his hair, and something like relief passed over his features. "I thought maybe I was dragging you all into something you couldn't fix."

Declan snorted softly. "You gave us the chance to fix it. There's a difference."

Logan nodded slowly then stepped off the porch. Without warning, he pulled Declan into a rough hug, the kind that said everything words couldn't.

"Thanks," he said, voice thick.

Declan clapped him on the back. "Anytime, kid. You're one of us now."

And for the first time in days, it felt like maybe the shadows were starting to lift.

Three days later, Jake got a message from his contact sharing that Dean had contacted the RCMP counsel and confirmed the full contents of the USB. The information Petra decrypted had been enough to trigger the first wave of investigations, and as promised, Logan's name never came up.

Logan said little when they told him, but he immediately headed out.

Four hours later Declan spotted him repainting the south fence line without being asked —

A quiet thank-you in the language of High Water ranch. Pay it forward.

THERE WERE EXACTLY six balloons taped to the corner of the porch, and someone—probably Tansy—had written *YOU ARE OFFICIALLY OLD* in glitter pen on a scrap of cardboard and hung it over the swing.

Sydney didn't feel old. She felt cracked.

Not in a bad way, just peeled back, armor stripped away,

and underneath was all the soft stuff she didn't usually let anyone see.

Love. Fear. Hope.

A woman who still wasn't quite sure what came next—but at least now she knew what she wanted.

The screen of her phone lit up with a call from *Mom*, and Sydney stared at it for three full rings before answering.

"Happy birthday, sweetheart!" Marie's voice was bright and warm. Behind her, a flash of Grandma Belinda's garden came into view before Marie turned the camera back toward herself.

Sydney propped her phone up on the porch railing then leaned back against the weatherworn wall, hands wrapped around a warm mug of tea. "Thanks, Mom."

"You look tired but better than the last time we chatted." Marie tilted her head. "Not working today, I hope?"

"Only accepting hugs and cupcakes from friends."

Marie grinned. "Good. Everyone should be spoiled a little on their birthday."

There was a pause. Not awkward, just weighted.

Sydney swallowed. "Thanks for calling."

"I always will." Her mother smiled again, but this time the expression was quieter, more careful. "You know, I've been thinking about our last call."

"I have too," Sydney admitted. "But I haven't really known what to say. Or how to say it."

"Start small, then."

Sydney decided to start big. She glanced toward the front door then back to the screen. "There's someone I'd like you to meet."

Her mother's eyebrows went up.

Sydney didn't hesitate. "Declan?" she called. "You're being summoned."

Declan stepped onto the porch with his usual solid presence, coffee mug in hand and a question on his face.

"Come here, please? I've got my mom on chat." When he stepped into the camera view, Sydney caught his hand with her free fingers and held on tight as she looked into his eyes. "Mom, this is Declan Skye," Sydney said, her voice gentle but sure, staring directly at him, speaking to him. "The man I love. The one who makes me feel safe and strong and like myself. And the one I absolutely plan to keep."

He smiled. The barest hint of a curl to his lips, but his entire face was filled with so much love she couldn't keep from smiling back. Offering up her own honest, heartfelt response.

A soft murmur finally registered, and Declan laughed, tilting his head toward her phone. "Audience."

Sydney refused to be embarrassed. She twisted to the phone even as she eased into Declan's side.

Marie blinked once, then twice, then her entire face softened like someone had flipped a switch.

"Oh my," she whispered. "Your expression matches the one Sydney's father wore when I introduced him to my mom."

Declan chuckled. "Hopefully that's a compliment."

Marie's eyes crinkled with warmth. "It is. Welcome to the family, Declan."

"Happy to be here."

They chatted lightly for another moment, Declan eventually stepping away to let Sydney and her mom continue.

"You love him," Marie said after a moment, no question in her tone.

Sydney nodded. "Yeah. I do."

"I'm proud of you." Marie's voice was soft but unshakeable. "You've built a life that's yours. And you finally let someone share it with you. That takes guts."

"Don't make me cry on my birthday."

"I won't. I'll just say this; if you ever need anything—anything at all—I want to help."

Sydney huffed a laugh, sipping her tea. "Sure. You want to invest in a medical clinic in Alberta?"

She said it flippantly, almost bitterly—because really, what were the chances?

But her mother lit up. "Well, now that's something to discuss. Yes. Tell me more."

Sydney choked. "Wait. *What?*"

Marie leaned closer to the screen. "Darling, your father and I have helped each of your siblings at some point in their lives. Sometimes with first mortgages, sometimes with business loans. Why would you think we wouldn't be here to help you when you asked?"

Sydney's heart slammed against her ribs. "You have those kind of discretionary funds?"

"Well, it depends. There is a limit, but if you're talking about the clinic you're currently running, we should be able to manage it."

"I can't believe this." Sydney shook her head, confused even as hope rose inside. "You never offered before."

"You never asked. You didn't share any financial details of the clinic or how you were establishing it until after your grandfather had already set you up. At that point, we didn't want to undermine your decisions," Marie said.

Tears sprang up, fast and sharp, catching Sydney off guard. "All this time, I thought I had to do everything alone. Which meant accepting Grandpa's help."

"Never." Marie paused. "I know we're different. You've always been fierce and independent and impossibly brilliant. And I've always been more comfortable making cookies and wrangling toddlers and making sure the house runs like a clock. But I've never regretted a minute of the life I chose. I want you to have that same confidence in your choices."

Sydney pressed her hands to her chest. "I do. Finally."

"Good." Marie's smile glowed through the screen. "Because it's not very correct to say this to you, but your grandpa Nate needs to butt out. He's shaped too much of your world."

"I hate that you're right."

"Hey, I love that you're starting to take your power back. We raised you hoping you'd be strong enough to know your own mind. Sometimes it takes a while to come into that power. Also, your grandfather is a bit of a jackass."

That made Sydney bark out a laugh.

Marie beamed. "There's my girl."

"I don't know what to say."

"Start with yes." Marie leaned back, her voice warm. "Let us help fund your clinic. Let us be a part of the legacy you're building—not for my sake, or your father's, or for Grandpa Nate, but for you. And if you'll let me... I'd like to come visit. Your dad too. We can be there for Thanksgiving. Help you with paperwork. Bring pie."

Sydney blinked. "You're serious."

"I've never been more serious. If I have one regret, it's not making it clearer to you that love and career can live side by side. I'm sorry you thought that your choices had to look like mine—or like your grandfather's—to be valuable. But the truth is, you've got your own map to draw now. I want to see what you make of it."

The screen blurred as tears ran freely now. Not from sadness, but relief. Something long buried finally loosened. Something that hadn't had a name before.

"I'd like for you to visit," Sydney whispered. "I'd like that very much."

"Then we'll be there," her mother promised. "We'll bring

things from the garden, and the wine, and we'll figure out the details for the clinic and celebrate the man who finally cracked open your heart."

"He didn't crack it," Sydney said. "He saw it and held it like it mattered."

Marie didn't say anything for a moment, just looked at her daughter with fierce, unwavering love.

"I always knew you'd find someone worthy of you."

When they hung up a few minutes later, Sydney sat in stunned silence on the porch.

Declan appeared with another mug of tea for her.

"How'd it go?" he asked, taking a seat beside her.

Sydney looked at him, at the mountain of quiet strength beside her, and shook her head with a smile.

"They're investing in the clinic."

Declan blinked. "The hell?"

"My parents. They've been waiting for years for me to admit that I wanted their help."

"Damn." He let out a low whistle. "You've got good people in your corner."

"I do."

"So, what now?"

"I guess now we talk to a lawyer. Then we plan for Thanksgiving." She leaned her head against his shoulder. "And I spend the rest of the night kicking myself for thinking I had to do this alone."

Declan kissed her temple. "You didn't know. You were doing the best you could with what you had."

"I gave up good things."

"Yeah," he agreed softly. "But sometimes the bumps and bruises along the way are what make the good things feel like miracles."

Sydney sighed. "You always say the right thing."

He kissed her again, this time slow and sure. "That's just because I've been practicing."

She let out a quiet laugh, threading her fingers through his. "We've got a future."

"We've got a whole damn life."

For the first time, she believed it down to her bones. The cracks inside her didn't feel like weaknesses anymore.

They felt like paths for the sunlight to trickle through.

21

The fire crackled low in the stone hearth, throwing a soft orange glow across the living room. Outside, October had taken a sudden turn into chillier nights, the kind that hinted at frost and early snow.

Inside, the warmth wasn't just from the fire.

Declan sat with an arm draped across the back of the couch, Sydney leaning into him. The rest of the people in the room were those he called his family. Tansy and Jake shared the oversized armchair opposite, her legs tossed over his lap like it was their standard position—probably because it was. Jeffrey was sound asleep on a blanket in front of the fire, head resting on Dixie's rump.

Aiden and Petra were tucked into the love seat, Jinx sprawled on the floor at their feet with a slightly lopsided scarf she was knitting covering her legs. Logan sat in the lone recliner, feet up as he thumbed through an old woodworking magazine.

The laughter between them all came easy. The comfort— they'd earned.

It had been a hell of a year since Declan and his brothers had made the move to Heart Falls.

They'd all been pushed to their limits. Threats from the outside, old fears, deep family wounds. And yet here they were, safe and together in the living room at High Water ranch.

"Oh, hey," Jake said, glancing around the room to make sure he had everyone's attention. "I've got an update."

That pulled everyone upright just a little. Jake never announced something unless it mattered.

"I got word back from my friends in the fire investigation team on the hall destruction."

A hush settled.

Beside Declan, Sydney stiffened slightly.

"Don't know if I mentioned this before, but for a while, I was worried the fire at the community center was somehow connected to the gang stuff we dealt with." Jake glanced around the room. "Seemed logical, considering the timing. But I was wrong."

Logan nodded slowly. "Good to know, but what was it?"

Jake tilted his chin in Sydney's direction. "Someone closer to home. Someone mad about a small situation that spun way out of control."

The room held still.

Jake continued, "Turns out, the source of the ignition was oily rags spontaneously combusting. A few larger fragments were recovered from the scene including a uniform shirt with a logo printed on one of the pockets. An auto shop in Hillcrest."

Declan tensed. That was a good forty minutes away from Heart Falls.

"My contact said they visited the shop to find out their protocol to deal with the flammable material. Once the shirts are trash, one of the staff packages them up carefully and then it's all sent to a hazardous waste centre. Only the usual staff didn't deal with them that week—Cindy did."

"Cindy who?" Tansy asked sharply.

"Nora Yemen's daughter."

Sydney shot upright. "Cindy?" Her voice cracked slightly. "But...*why?*"

Jake shrugged, but there was frustration behind it. "Best guess? She got embarrassed after you convinced Nora to move to the senior's residence. The video she posted online of the confrontation you guys had—the comments didn't go in her favor. Her pride got dented."

"I didn't even know she'd posted it," Sydney murmured.

"She said she thought shoving dirty rags into the bags in your shed would 'make your stuff stink'," Jake said, making air quotes. "She never meant to start a fire, but spontaneous combustion doesn't care about intentions."

"Unbelievable," Petra whispered.

Declan checked Sydney to see how this news was hitting. The fire wasn't her fault, but she was still learning to let go of trying to run the world.

Her eyes were wide, her jaw tight, but she exhaled slowly.

"These things happen," she said quietly. "People lash out for reasons that have nothing to do with reality."

Tansy wasn't so calm. "I want to drag her to the town square and make her watch that entire building go up again in slow motion."

"That's dramatic," Jake muttered.

She glared at him. "Cindy contributed to the destruction of a community landmark where dozens of bake sales, harvest dances, and memorable bachelor auctions have been held over the years." Tansy paused. "Oh. And also, Sydney almost died."

"Thanks for putting that priority list in order," Sydney deadpanned.

"Anytime."

Jake held up a hand. "The police have it handled. They confronted Cindy and she confessed. Which means community service and a serious dent to her reputation. Plus, a strict order to stay away from Sydney." Jake shrugged. "About as much as the law can do. Bottomline, there will be no more fire-starting rags in her future."

"That explains the terrible smell when I grabbed the gear," Sydney said thoughtfully. "I never did go back and recheck later because of my ankle."

"I'm shocked Cindy confessed," Declan admitted.

A rude noise escaped Tansy. "Probably realized it was that or wait until Petra tracked her down and kicked in her front door."

"I could still do that," Petra offered then winked. "But I'm trying to be the calm, mature version of myself now that I'm going to be a mother. Again."

Sydney blinked. "Wait, what?"

Petra grinned, her eyes sparkling. "Yeah. We've been waiting for the right moment to tell you guys. But yes—I'm pregnant."

The room exploded.

Tansy leapt to her feet, arms flopping in the air as if she was calling a touchdown. "Oh! Wait!"

She darted out of the room before anyone could say a word.

Aiden shook his head fondly then carried on. "And the *again* part of that announcement is because Jinx's adoption is now official. Paperwork's all signed. Just waiting for her new ID cards."

Jinx ducked her head, but the corner of her mouth lifted. "About time."

"About time...*Dad*," Aiden coaxed.

Jinx dove at him, knotting arms around his and Petra's

necks as laughter swelled. "You guys are the best," she repeated for the millionth time since the idea had been floated.

Petra kissed Jinx's cheek. "You're part of our family in every way now, forever."

Declan's heart filled. This—this was what High Water was meant to be. A place for people to land. To belong.

And sometimes to heal. Logan didn't say anything, but as usual, he watched the tangled hug with intense longing in his eyes.

Tansy came flying back into the room with two paper bags, thrusting one toward Petra and the other toward Aiden. "We planned ahead," she said proudly. "Well, I had the idea, and Jake made sure it happened. Teamwork!"

Inside were the obligatory candles.

Petra pulled hers out and burst into laughter. The label read, *Warning: Hormones May Combust. Light at Your Own Risk.*

Aiden's had a cartoon of a terrified man holding a baby, and it read, *You're Going to be a Dad. Panic Accordingly.* He lifted it in a toast to Tansy and Jake. "This I can do."

"And you'll do it brilliantly," Tansy offered as she dropped back into her seat. "I'm not pregnant, but in the vein of sharing TMI, we are trying."

"Ugh. I didn't need to know that," Jinx complained, squirming from the spot on the floor she'd returned to.

Tansy lifted a brow. "Just wait until your *mom* gives you the birds and the bees talk. I'm going to draw pictures."

"And on that note, I'm headed to bed." Logan rose and gathered his things, obviously looking to escape. But he was smiling, happy to have been included in the announcements. He paused, glancing at each of them. "Good night, everyone." He dipped his head when he met Declan's gaze. "I'll take care of the early chores."

It was Sydney who slipped to her feet and marched to his side, hooking her arms around him and squeezing him tightly. "Night, you. See you in the morning."

"I should go, too," Jinx said. She tilted her head toward the fire. "I'll get the Jeffster into bed if you guys want to stay out here for a while longer," she offered.

"You're an awesome big cousin," Tansy told her seriously. "Thanks."

Arms full of drooping five-year-old, Jeffrey's limbs dangling like a marionette, Jinx winked at Declan then paced toward the back of the house, Dixie strolling quietly at her side.

The six of them resettled.

Aiden spoke softly toward the fire. "Jinx is a great kid. And night and day different from a year ago."

"You guys are making that happen more and more," Declan affirmed.

Sydney nodded. "And Jeffrey's doing amazing as well. He seems so much more peaceful."

"Jake's the perfect daddy for him," Tansy affirmed. "A perfect dad, really. Thus the trying for more. And we're ready."

"I don't know about the perfect," Jake said. "But yeah, we're ready to see what happens."

Petra turned to Declan and Sydney. "Don't worry. We're fully aware babies aren't in your future."

Jake chimed in. "But fair warning, you will have full-time aunt and uncle duties."

"Bring it," Declan said with amusement.

Sydney smiled. Quiet. Content. "Oh, I didn't tell you guys yet," she said suddenly, "Lexie's staying on at the clinic."

Petra blinked. "Really?"

"Michael got his offer." Sydney said, eyes sparkling with mischief. "And it turns out he's allowed to work remotely. He's moving to Heart Falls. They're moving in together."

Tansy mock groaned. "Ugh. Happy endings everywhere."

"I know. It's so gross," Petra deadpanned.

Declan cleared his throat, nudging Sydney.

She gave him a sideways look. "What?" she said. "They already know."

"Not from you."

She sighed, and he grinned.

Declan raised his voice slightly. "Since we're spilling everything tonight—Sydney is in love with me. And I love her. Just so it's clear."

Laughter bounced back instantly, along with a throw pillow courtesy of Aiden.

"Oh, really?" Petra said, eyes gleaming. "When did you figure that out?"

"It was the moment you jumped into a burning building, wasn't it?" Tansy asked.

Declan nodded solemnly. "That definitely helped."

Sydney leaned into him and whispered, "You're such a drama queen."

"I learned from the best," he replied.

The fire crackled. The stories continued. Eventually, Aiden and Petra drifted to their suite, arms wrapped around each other. Jake and Tansy lingered a few minutes longer before they too retreated to the back of the house where Jeffrey already lay sleeping.

Leaving Declan and Sydney alone.

He stared at the glowing coals, her hand warm in his.

"I like this," he murmured.

"Which part?"

"All of it. The quiet. The fire. The knowledge that everyone's safe. That tomorrow your parents will show up, and there'll be chaos and turkey and paperwork."

Sydney grinned. "My mom has a spreadsheet."

"She and Jake are going to get along great."

She laughed then leaned her head on his shoulder. "It's not only that things finished well. It's that this feels like a real beginning."

"I've made my claim," he affirmed and kissed the top of her head. "Come hell or high water."

She looked up at him, stars in those silvery eyes and a whole lot of love. "Claim accepted. Hey, Deck?"

"Yeah?"

Sydney leaned forward and offered her brightest smile. "I do love you."

He dipped his head. "Good."

They were both laughing as they leaned into each other, the fire crackling low, the promise of tomorrow warm between them.

The Skyes of Heart Falls

A Cowboy's Bride

A Cowboy's Trust

A Cowboy's Claim

The Stones of Heart Falls

A Rancher's Heart

A Rancher's Song

A Rancher's Bride

A Rancher's Love

A Rancher's Vow

The Coleman's of Heart Falls

The Cowgirl's Forever Love

The Cowgirl's Secret Love

The Cowgirl's Chosen Love

ABOUT THE AUTHOR

New York Times and *USA Today* bestselling author Vivian Arend loves to share the products of her over-active imagination with her readers. She writes contemporary, western, and light-hearted paranormal romances. The stories are humorous yet emotional, usually with a large cast of family or friends, and a guaranteed happily-ever-after. Vivian lives in British Columbia, Canada, with her husband of many years—her inspiration for every hero and a willing companion for all sorts of adventures.

www.vivianarend.com